PRAISE FOR *STORM SIREN*

"There are few things more exciting to discover than a debut novel packed with powerful storytelling and beautiful language. *Storm Siren* is one of those rarities. I'll read anything Mary Weber writes. More, please!"

—JAY ASHER, *NEW YORK TIMES* BESTSELLING
AUTHOR OF *THIRTEEN REASONS WHY*

"*Storm Siren* is a riveting tale from start to finish. Between the simmering romance, the rich and inventive fantasy world, and one seriously jaw-dropping finale, readers will clamor for the next book—and I'll be at the front of the line!"

—MARISSA MEYER, *NEW YORK TIMES* BESTSELLING
AUTHOR OF *CINDER* THE LUNAR CHRONICLES

"One of my favorite things about this novel is how the pace unfolds just like a storm. . . . Don't miss this one!"

—SERENA CHASE, USATODAY.COM

Readers who enjoyed Marissa Meyer's Cinder series will enjoy this fast-paced fantasy which combines an intriguing storyline with as many twists and turns as a chapter of Game of Thrones!"

—*SCHOOL LIBRARY JOURNAL TEEN*

" . . . readers will easily find themselves captivated. The breathtaking surprise ending is nothing short of horrific, promising even more dark and bizarre adventures to come in the *Storm Siren* trilogy."

—*RT BOOK REVIEWS*, 4 STARS

"Intense and intriguing. Fans of high stakes fantasy won't be able to put it down."

—CJ REDWINE, AUTHOR OF *DEFIANCE*

"Weber builds a fascinating and believable fantasy world . . . Inventive and entertaining.

—*KIRKUS REVIEWS*

STORM SIREN

Book One in the Storm Siren Trilogy

MARY WEBER

Thomas Nelson
Since 1798

NASHVILLE   MEXICO CITY   RIO DE JANEIRO

Published in Nashville, Tennessee, by Thomas Nelson. Thomas Nelson is a registered trademark of HarperCollins Christian Publishing, Inc.

Author is represented by the literary agency of Alive Communications, Inc., 7680 Goddard Street, Suite 200, Colorado Springs, Colorado 80920, www.alivecommunications.com

Map by Tom Gaddis

Thomas Nelson, Inc., titles may be purchased in bulk for educational, business, fund-raising, or sales promotional use. For information, please e-mail SpecialMarkets@ThomasNelson.com.

Publisher's Note: This novel is a work of fiction. Names, characters, places, and incidents are either products of the author's imagination or used fictitiously. All characters are fictional, and any similarity to people living or dead is purely coincidental.

ISBN: 978-1-4016-9035-9 (TP)

Library of Congress Cataloging-in-Publication Data

Weber, Mary.
  Storm siren : book one in the Storm siren trilogy / Mary Weber.
    pages cm
    ISBN 978-1-4016-9034-2 (hardback)
  I. Title.
  PS3623.E3946S76 2014
  813'.6—dc23

2014006236

Printed in the United States of America
15 16 17 18 19 QG 7 6 5 4 3 2 1

QG 08-20-15

For Peter and my
one,
two,
three precious Muses.
For invading the world with your magic and bringing
my soul alive on this beautiful adventure.
You are the most daring dragon hunters I know.

And to Lee Hough, for the enormous honor of storming this
bookish castle with you as my agent. Save me a seat
in the Kingdom, my friend.

For my shield this day I call:
Heaven's might,
Sun's brightness,
Moon's whiteness,
Fire's glory,
Lightning's swiftness,
Wind's wildness,
Ocean's depth,
Earth's solidity,
Rock's immobility.

—FROM SAINT PATRICK'S BREASTPLATE

CHAPTER 1

F OURTEEN CIRCLES FOR FOURTEEN OWNERS."

I shade my eyes to block the sun's reflection off the distant mountains currently doused in snow and smoke and flesh-eating birds. The yellow flags above me snap sharp and loud in the breeze as if to emphasize my owner's words that yes, she's quite aware such a high count is utterly ridiculous.

Waiting for it . . .

"Fourteen?" the sweaty merchant says.

Ha! There it is. Eleven years of repeatedly being sold, and it's sad, really, how familiar I've become with this conversation. Today, if Brea has her way, I will meet my fifteenth, which I suppose should actually bother me. But it doesn't.

Brea nods. "Fourteen."

I smirk and turn to watch a gimpy minstrel roaming through the marketplace, which is the closest I've ever been to Faelen's High Court. The poor guy is singing so wretchedly off-key, I want to giggle, except he might be newly returned from the war front, so I don't. Besides, his odd version of the old ballad "The Monster and the Sea of Elisedd's Sadness" reminds me of my home up in the Fendres. *Have you been there?* I want to ask him.

Instead, I look over as the enormous merchant grunts his nervousness and retreats from me, giving the ground a superstitious spit. He eyes Brea. "Fourteen owners says either yer lyin' or she's got the dark-death disease. Whichever it is, you best get her out of my way. I got a money business to run." He makes to hurry off toward the selling stand, almost tripping in his fur-trimmed shoes.

I grin. *Yes, run away in your too-little boots.*

"Wait!" Brea grabs his arm. "Nym doesn't have the disease. She's just . . ."

The merchant scowls at her grip on his sleeve.

She releases it, but her roundish face turns stony with determination. "She's just too uppity for the poorer folk, that's all. There's only so much a master can take of a servant who thinks she's made of better than the rest."

What in hulls? Is she off her chump? My laugh bubbles up and I choke it back, waiting for *her* to choke on her lie. He creeps closer and slides a look of dislike down my partially hooded face, my chin, my half-cloaked body. "She don't look uppity. She don't even look decent enough for the favor houses."

Whoa. I bite back a prickly remark about his mum birthing him in one of those dung havens and look away. Neither of them deserves a reaction. Using my practiced haughty pose, I face the lively crowd gathered like giddy children in front of the selling platform. Five, ten, fifty people. They're all smiling as if the circus with its panther monkeys and manic dwarves were performing instead of a fat guy in little boots exploiting children. Seems even decent women are desperate for extra hands while the men are off fighting a war we've no hope of winning.

The merchant chews his puffy lip and studies me, like he expects me to help coerce him. *Is he jesting?* I raise an eyebrow and glare at him until, finally, he grunts again and pulls up the cuff on my right arm.

I stiffen.

His gloved fingers run over each thread tattooed around my wrist like tiny bracelets. "One. Two. Three . . ." He numbers the circles slowly, fourteen in a row inked into my skin with the juice of the black mugplant. I almost feel like I should clap for him.

Good job, I mouth. *You know how to count.*

The merchant's face twists into a snarl. He gives me a vicious pinch below my elbow and pushes my sleeve higher up my arm onto my shoulder. I shiver and, narrowing my eyes, start to pull away, but Brea leans into me.

"You hold yourself together," she sputters close to my ear. "And for fool's sake, keep your hair covered, or so help me, Nymia, I'll break your fingers again."

I bite my tongue but refuse her the satisfaction of dipping my gaze to my slightly misshapen left hand, which I'm now curling into a fist.

"How old are you?" the dealer growls in my face.

"Seventeen," I growl back.

"When was she first sold?" This question is for Brea, but I

feel his bristly glove squeeze my skin as if he expects me to alert him if she's dishonest.

"Age six. Her parents died when she was five and then she lived a short time with a midwife who had no use for her." She says this last part with a slice of disgust in her voice that's directed at me. And as much as I try to force it down, the hateful shame swells up to eat holes in my chest. She's got me on that one. Two parents, one midwife, and fourteen owners I've ruined, the latest being Brea's own husband. And it doesn't matter that I tried to warn every single one of them.

The merchant's eyes constrict. "There somethin' else wrong with her yer not tellin' me?"

"Nothing's wrong with her. She's perfectly fine. Just give me three draghts and she's yours."

"Three draghts?" I murmur. "How generous."

Either she doesn't hear or chooses to ignore me as the merchant rubs his huge, stubbled jowls and considers the offer. Although I can already sense he'll take it. Three is cheap. Beyond cheap. It's pathetic. I consider feeling insulted.

The minstrel limps by, practically giddy as he continues his fabulously bad recount of the Monster and the Sea. "'Twas the night compassion *forsooooook* us." He's singing, referring to the night an agreement was struck between Faelen's past king and the great, flesh-eating Draewulf. The price of which had been Faelen's children. "And the big sea, she roared and spit up her foam at the shape-shifter's trickery and our *foooooolish* king."

I swallow and feel my amusement over how much he's enjoying himself catch in my throat at what I know comes next.

"The ocean, she's begging for our salvation. Begging for blood that will set our children free."

And for a moment I swear I can feel the sea waves calling, begging *my* blood to set us all free.

Except just as with the Draewulf, my blood comes at a price.

"Blast the crippled croaker! Would someone put him out of his misery?" the merchant shouts.

A louder shout and then a cheer interrupt the inharmonious tune. Someone's just been bought for a higher amount than expected. The merchant looks at the stage behind us and smiles. Then, without glancing at me, he says, "Done," and fishes into his hip bag to drop three draughts into Brea's open palm.

Congratulations, Nym. You're officially the cheapest slave sold in Faelen history.

Brea hands the reins of my collar to the merchant and turns from him, but not so quickly as to confirm his suspicion that there's something else amiss with me. Just before she leaves, she leans into me again, and her black hair brushes against my cheek.

"Pity you weren't born a boy," she whispers. "They would've just killed you outright. Saved us all from what you are." And then she's gone.

And I won't even pretend I'm sorry.

The merchant yanks my leather straps like he's bridling a goat and leads me behind him to the side of the selling platform where twelve other slaves wait, tethered to a lengthy stretch of chain. Before he bends down to tie me in line, he pulls a thin knife from his right bootie and puts it against my chin. "Try to escape, little imp, and this blade'll find you faster than a bolcrane goin' for a baby." He breathes an extra puff of foul air up my nostrils and grins when I squirm in revulsion.

So, of course, I do what any self-respecting, uncooperative person would do. I spit into his annoying face.

"You little . . ." His knife is as fast as his fury, and before I can move he's cut into my skin just beneath my jaw.

I cry out, and then bite my tongue because he doesn't deserve to see my pain.

"I'll sell you off in pieces if I have to," he says, growling.

"Try," I mutter.

Obviously the heat's gotten to me because I'm smiling a bit crazy in spite of the sting—until his arm rises. I barely have time to brace before the back of his hand finds my mouth with a force that nearly knocks me over. Warm blood gushes from my lip to join the trickle on my neck, and suddenly I'm blinking to keep the whirling world in focus. Curse him.

He yells at someone I can't see, "Get her up front and be rid of her. Now!"

The assistant pushes me to the low base of the stand. Hands shove me onto the stage as a small girl with red hair, who can scarcely be older than five, is being led off the other side. My stomach twists at her frightened expression, at the terror-filled memory of my first selling—the brief image of coming home to the midwife after my curse had wiped out her entire herd of sheep. Within hours I was sold to a man who gave a whole new meaning to the word *monster*.

The merchant's assistant is standing beside me. He looms over the buyers and makes up attributes about me, of which he knows nothing and believes none of. *What a sideshow.*

The bidding starts low. Despite the aching slash in my neck, I stare into the faces of the individuals yelling out prices, evaluating them as they freely evaluate me. Their ballooning silk hats and ruffled shawls, I swear, look strikingly similar to a pair of lady's panties I saw in the sale booth last year. These people appear well-off compared to most I've known in our kingdom. Not as fancy as the politicians from the High Court, but clearly living above the poverty of the peasants. Panty shawls and all.

The bidding begins to climb with the same frenzy the onlookers have been possessed by for the past half hour. Suddenly, a male voice clamors above the rest, "Take off the hood and give us a better look at her. Let's see what she's made of."

I scowl and lean forward, jerking on my reins to yell back, "Why aren't you off helping win the war, you wastrel?"

"Right there, let's see her!"

"Yeah! Take off her cloak!"

The assistant grabs my shoulder. I bristle, but his hand is already reaching for my hood.

I shove an elbow into his skinny stomach, hard enough to knock the wind from him. "Don't touch me."

He yelps. Staggers back like the weakling he is.

Then the merchant swears, and before I can blink he climbs onto the stage and lunges for my wrists.

I kick him in his crotch.

He screams but doesn't crumble. A noise erupts behind me and just as I'm turning to check, two men grab my arms and the merchant is up and plows into my side, nearly knocking me over. He grips my cloak and yanks it off in one harsh sweep.

Before I can count to one, the three of them are stumbling back and tripping off the stage.

The crowd falls silent.

CHAPTER 2

MY HAIR SLIPS DOWN MY BACK AND shoulders and around my face like fresh snow falling on the forest floor. Pure white. I raise my chin as the onlookers stare. *Yes. Look.*

You don't want me.

Because, eventually, accidentally, I will destroy you.

It's what I do.

A child's gasp breaks the silence and out of the corner of my eye, I see the little redheaded girl at the outer edge of the crowd. The reins of her collar are in her master's hand. He's stalled in horror like the rest of them. But the little girl's features—they're painted in awe. Which, of course, makes a lump climb up my throat. The childlike mercy her innocence brings touches something within me. She's too young to recognize the perverse significance of my snowy-white hair and sea-blue eyes.

Apparently no one's told her about Elementals, or how they are not allowed to exist. No one's told her that a female version is not even possible. That I shouldn't be.

The hush has rippled out to the market stalls. Vendors and customers alike pause to find the source of the unnatural silence. I wonder if they're terrified as well. They should be.

Offstage, the merchant suddenly lets loose a string of curses, equally distributed between the long-gone Brea and me. I find his anger a bit funny, and it effectively shatters the spell of quiet and triggers an uproar in the crowd.

"What is she?"

"How can she be?"

"Is she dangerous?"

"Yes. Very," I whisper.

"What are all those tattoos on her arms? Are those owner circles?"

"What about the markings on the other arm?"

Memorials, is what I won't say.

The assistant I knocked the wind from recovers himself when he realizes the merchant standing just off the stand is now swearing at *him*. He scrambles back over and tries to start the bidding up again, but suddenly even those who've named prices are ducking their heads and backing away.

A gaudy laugh erupts from the sideline. It's so melodramatic and mocking that everyone pauses to look in its direction. It's the man holding the redheaded girl's reins. His face is as strikingly cruel as it is handsome. He waves a hand in the air toward me. "She doesn't look like much! How about loaning her out and letting me test her? Let's see what she's good for!" He jerks the small slave girl's collar and struts his way toward the stage, dragging her behind him.

Swine.

I force myself to look away from them both. *Hold it in, Nym.*

"C'mon! No one else is going to want her. Let me have her, and I'll pay you more if she ends up being worth it." The man uses his hands to boast, and the redhead's reins yank her little neck around as he swaggers through the captive audience who've parted to create a path for him. She begins to cry. He doesn't even notice.

My chest ignites. *Stop,* I warn my insides. *She's not you.*

In the back of the crowd, a noblewoman strolls over from one of the stalls. Her shimmery, gold-lined eyes match her brilliant hair and painted lips as she studies me. My shoulders smooth out. My eyes hope. "Please take me," I whisper. *Before I can't control it.*

Her gilded lips press together in a thoughtful line, then she turns away.

I drop my gaze on the man now standing directly below me in front of the stage.

"How about you show us a bit more skin and maybe I'll throw in an extra draght?" he hollers, brandishing a hand at the throng as if to earn their agreement.

A whimper beside him, followed by a squeak, and it's only then he seems to notice the little girl whose neck he's nearly cracked. She's sniffling and straining upward so she doesn't get hung by the collar.

I freeze.

He sneers at her. But she doesn't notice. Her gaze is glued on me. He looks back and forth between the two of us. Curiosity, then anger flickers across his face. I pretend to ignore it. Until he lifts the girl's reins and gives them a tug.

She winces and I grimace.

A sick grin twists his mouth. Slowly, deliberately, he raises her reins another inch so her toes are barely touching the ground. He watches for my reaction.

The girl's eyes go wild. She begins to writhe and spin, trying to hold her head high enough to keep breathing.

My fingers curl into fists.

Stay out of it, Nym. Close your eyes.

An awkward hush falls. The man's perverse pleasure is tangible as again he lifts the reins. But this time he doesn't stop until her feet are off the ground and the little girl's expression has exploded into full-blown terror. She is kicking, flailing, gasping. Choking at the end of her noose.

And he's enjoying every second of it.

I shut my eyes and feel the throbbing of my own neck. One . . . two . . . three heart pulses, and abruptly there's a pause in the air. As if the wind itself is holding her breath.

And then the sound of a choked spasm, so fragile in its hopelessness, signaling what I already knew.

He's going to let her die.

But I can't.

Thick clouds descend on the marketplace in a swirling rush and darken the sun. They sharpen the friction in the atmosphere, engaging with my infuriated blood, my skin. Sickened, I open my eyes in time to see faces draw upward. Their expressions slowly alter from humor to horror.

I'm so sorry, I want to say. *But all you fancy people in your pretty shawls? You should know better.*

Shouts pick up. "What's going on? Is *she* doing that?"

The cold sets in. My body shivers, followed by heat rippling along my skin's pale surface.

The little girl's owner lowers the reins and stares at me. As does the noblewoman in back with the gold-rimmed eyes. Is it in fear? Fascination? I don't know which and I don't care.

The sky rumbles and the wind quickens, wild so my hair is everywhere and the stand is creaking and a howl picks up through the market stalls. The shop vendors scramble to place their baskets and wares under cover and tamp down their tent stakes. The crowd scatters, diving for safety. Everyone but the half-choked little girl, her owner, and the noblewoman. Why aren't they running? *Go,* my eyes beg the child. Not that it would help the wretched man with her.

I tense.

Here it comes.

The familiar crackle rips along my veins, and then the pain pierces through as my muscles stiffen and coil inside me like the air above. Igniting. My body, both master and slave to the elements. And I don't know how to breathe, how to stop it, how to be anything but this thing fracturing the sky.

The first lightning strike lands in the middle of a meadow. Far enough away to avoid people but close enough to terrify.

People scream and stop running. Some look around. Some hunch over, as if making themselves smaller will save them. "It won't," I yell at them. They're about to die because of a curse I am powerless to control.

A raindrop splashes on my forehead. Then another. Then they're dripping everywhere. Pouring off their faces and dulling their cries, and in the middle of it all, the noblewoman is still watching, a growing look of hilarity on her face. She must be insane—standing in the storm looking like that.

Leave! I try to scream at her, but abruptly my voice is gone.

In front of me, the man has given up staring and is running now too—trying to escape with the redheaded girl. She's struggling so desperately that the reins slip free and she falls backward.

I sense it before I see it. The storm overhead snaps its fury.

My body jolts.

His violent death will be the only one that won't haunt my nightmares tonight.

A deafening crack and blinding flash. The marketplace goes white. Burning grass and flesh fill my nostrils as a repulsive thrill winds through my static-filled veins.

His body bursts into pure energy.

The crazy noblewoman laughs as the man crumbles to dust.

CHAPTER 3

It's snowing. Bits of ash and frost are biting at my fingers. I hold them out in front of me and watch, terrified, as the night's destruction swirls around my winter home in a smoky blizzard of hail and lightning. A dirty red trail leads all the way from the chateau to my little bloody feet, which are melting holes in the luminescent snow. The tracks look like a spattered path of scarlet bread crumbs.

It suddenly occurs to me that I don't know why I am outside.

I gag and cough in the thickening smoke. It's burning my throat in its spread toward the blurry tree line. I can't breathe. I'm frightened.

I want my mum.

Something moves on my right, but before I can look, there's a crash and one side of my home caves in and flames leap out. Followed by screams, first Mum's, then Dad's.

Scared. Then furious. Calling my name. My heart clenches and crumbles all in one breath. What have I done?

I scream and start running, tripping, clawing toward their voices, but hands pull me away and pick me up, and I'm tearing them off, trying to get back. I have to rescue my parents. But the grip is too strong. Tears freeze into rivers midflood down my face, and I can do nothing but watch it all fade as I'm dragged away. Knowing I have somehow destroyed the best part of my world.

"And thus the Sea of Elisedd churns noisy, and thus her sapphire waters turned salty . . ."

Oh good grief, is that minstrel still howling?

I open my eyes with a plan to inform him just how very bad my head hurts and how his serenade is not helping. But it occurs to me that his voice has altered to an octave higher and much prettier, and in fact has become very much like a girl's.

As has his face.

I blink.

Squint. Blink again.

What in hulls?

It is a girl, with auburn hair braided around a freckled countenance barely older than mine. She's singing and setting a tray of tea and bread by my bed. My insides dissolve at the smell. I can't remember the last time I ate. It would've been with Brea on the road yesterd—

I bolt straight up, scrambling my thoughts around the

canopy overhead and the soft substance beneath me. And then I'm out of the enormous berth faster than a whipping boy running for his mum—horrified at having been in it, let alone having been discovered there.

The room spins drunkenly for a second, swooning with my aching head as I grasp the nearest bedpost for support. *How did I get in here?* I can't remember anything beyond standing on the auction block.

The singing girl stops. "Ah, so you're awake."

"Who *are* you? And where am I?"

"It's 'bout time, cuz we gotta 'urry and get you ready, right?" She settles the tea tray and ignores my question. "Adora wants to talk to you before it starts." She tips her head my direction and clucks her tongue, as if chiding me to quit standing around.

Ready for what? "Where am I?" I repeat, taking in the room as quick as my eyes can absorb it. The huge, arched ceiling, the fireplace, the hideously expensive tapestries hanging on either side that are the color of my bloody feet from my nightmare. And the window—the giant window with its breathtaking view of the evening's purplish, smoke-strewn skies melting into a hillside that surrounds the High Court city. I peer closer at its white, pointy buildings and staggered streets leading up to . . . to . . . the Castle! And behind it the jagged Hythra Mountain peaks.

I turn back to the girl.

She's holding a steaming cup of tea. "You're in Adora's house," she says as if annoyed I've not caught on to this yet. She waves the cup precariously and frowns at the air next to my head. "You best be careful, cuz it's hot, right? And we 'aven't got a lot a time." She shoves the cup closer. Except she's not quite holding it toward me. More to the side of me.

My hungry stomach turns sour as awareness registers. "Are you *serving* me?" I back away, shaking my throbbing head. "Look, I don't know how I got in this room, but if they find me here, you and I are dead. I need to leave. *Now.*"

"Well, we'd do it a lot quicker if you'd just drink the tea already. Cuz it's Adora's orders you're in here, but now she's orderin' you downstairs, right? An' I wouldn't make her wait if I was you." She folds one arm across the cream-colored peasant frock draping her curved body like my mum's used to, and with the other hand continues to offer the cup at an awkward angle, her eyes still peering off somewhere behind me. "She *really* don't like to be kept waiting," she adds, voice lowered as if she's sharing a confidence. "Especially on party nights."

I rub my pounding temple. *Party nights?* I take the teacup with my good hand just so she'll stop standing there so uncomfortable, but she just keeps standing there anyway. I drink a hesitant sip. She stares without watching me and grins. "Good, i'nt it?"

It is good. And I'm famished. I gulp down half the cup before slowing under the gaze of her brown, unfocused eyes. They have a funny look to them. Suspicion surfaces. I tilt my head and shift my whole body to the right, to see if she'll follow my movements. She doesn't. Her stare is glued to the exact same spot. *Oh.*

She's blind.

Her smile becomes shy as if she's completely aware of what I was just testing. "Yep, I'm blind, and the name is Breck."

I return the cup to the nightstand, almost tipping it over in

17

my distraction. I'm embarrassed for being insensitive as much as for the inexcusable error she's made. It's a mistake no owner will forgive just because of blindness.

"Listen, Breck. I'm clearly not what you think I am, which is understandable seeing as you, well, you know . . ." *Great. Just insult the poor girl.* I clear my throat and look down at my clothes, which aren't mine but a thin gown of the softest silk clinging to my scrawny body. *Curses.* I lick my lips. "Okay look, if Adora bought me, then I'm supposed to be down in the slave quarters. I need you to take me there." I glance around. "But first I need to find my clothes."

Breck's mouth puckers. She nods. "I see. So you're a bit thick in the head, no?" She sighs and turns to walk off toward a large oak armoire near the window where she pulls open its doors. "Just don't let Adora know it, right? Try to act smart if you can. She'll have a lovely 'issyfit if she finds out she spent good money on an idiot."

I raise a brow. *An idiot?* I'm tempted to set her straight, except I don't actually care what she believes of me. I just need to get out of here.

She reaches into the armoire and takes out what appears to be the lone item inside—a dress of beautiful yellow, crisp material with simple lines that speaks of price and taste. "So here's the thing, right? Try to listen careful and follow what I'm saying." She speaks slow and precise like she's talking to a child. "Adora bought you from the merchant auction yesterday. You're in the right room, cuz I'm blind but not a fool. And you *are* a slave. Of some sort. You can talk to Adora 'bout that. As for your clothes . . ."

She carries the dress over with an expression of satisfaction. "She had me burn them when she brought you home last evening. And you're welcome. Now she's waiting for you downstairs, so we best get on it before she maims us." Breck holds the dress up to me as if she can visualize it. "Now be polite and give us your name."

I don't answer. I just stare at this person who is hands down the strangest servant I've ever encountered. In the most extravagant house. Under the most irrational circumstances.

My lack of speech only makes her nod all the more disappointedly. "So you really are an idiot, then." She bats her hand until it connects with my arm, then pushes me in front of her. "Well, let's at least get you dressed. Adora can't have you trompin' around here with yer looks matching yer dull-witted brains."

I'm a mute mixture of horror and confusion as she strips me down and goes to pull the fancy dress on over my head. I stiffen for the brief second my tattoos are exposed, just before the dress slides over them. Until I realize her blind eyes can't see the markings. And then the gown is on, snug and soft and wholly uncomfortable in its foreign luxuriousness. And I'm scared as litches because I know she's made a mistake and I'm going to get the insides gutted out of both of us for even touching this room and gown.

"Just one of Adora's old things. Nice, right?" Breck is muttering away. "Well, you won't think so once you see what she wears most of the time. That woman's like a High Court fashion stylist all in 'er own twisted self." She turns me around to face her and runs her hands down me to feel out the dress, as if picturing it through her fingers. "You gonna tell me your name now or just keep on bein' stupid and rude?"

"Nymia," I whisper cautiously. "But I go by Nym. From the Fendres Mountains."

"Nymia? Like the sea nymph? Never been to the Fendres, but I 'ear they got some fearsome animals. Now come 'ere and 'ave a quick look in the mirror afore we take you down to the ol' crazy." She steers me around the bed and shoves me in front of a tall looking glass on the other side.

I pause, then gasp and step backward, nearly tripping over Breck's foot. The person in the mirror is not me. She has my pale skin and blue eyes and everything about her heart-shaped face is mine, but . . . I lean in to peer closer.

The hair. Is not.

It's brown. A rich, burnished, not-anything-like-me brown. "What the bolcrane happened to my hair?"

"Ack! Should'a warned you. Adora had me put some walnut-root juice in it this mornin' while you was still passed out. That slave master must've hit you pretty 'ard at the market for as comatose as you been the last twenty-four hours. Almost thought you was dead. Anyway, she didn't want you walking around 'ere looking like . . . well, like what you are. Too many questions."

While she's talking she's rummaging through a small bag clipped to her apron. She pulls out three long hairpins and, quick as I've ever seen, twists my hair up into two messy knots and fastens them awkwardly to the base of my neck, then pets the top and sides of my head. She stands back. "There. How's it look?"

Ridiculous. Disgusting. Beautiful. Everything that is not me or anything I'm familiar with. A part of me wants to stare at this mirrored girl, knowing she'll never be real again. The rest of me wants to tear it all off because it's a gross fake. Like wearing someone else's skin that's better than anything I am—that I didn't ask to borrow. And I'm terrified for when the owner finds out.

"Now we gotta go, but you might wanna 'nother quick swig a tea. Adora—she can be a troll. You gonna need all the sustainin' you can get."

Wonderful.

I bite my lip and pull my gaze from the mirror before muttering, "Let's just go." *Time to get the lights beaten out of both of us.*

Breck clucks her tongue again and prods me toward the door. When she opens it, I swear a tornado has touched down inside the house. The hall is filled with voices and rich, tinkly music, the clatter of dishes, and servants running by us without a glance in our direction. The delicious scents of baked bread and roasted meats seep from the covered platters they're carrying, permeating the cherrywood walls and lush, silver floor carpets.

My stomach erupts in starvation as Breck forces me out into the wide walkway and, with a tight grip, proceeds to lead me down a maze of hallways and back stairwells. I try to keep up, impressed at how effortlessly she can wind through it in her blindness.

Two flights of steps we've tramped down before I ask, "How long have you lived here?"

"Me and Colin been here eight months." She turns a corner.

"Colin?"

Another corner and then she halts so suddenly in front of an enormous gilded door, I nearly plow into her. "My brother. You'll meet 'im eventually if you stay." Breck gives a rap on the gold with her fist, and the thudded sound it creates absorbs into the door and makes me wonder if it's solid or embossed. Either way, it's an obscenely ridiculous waste of money.

I hear a muffled, "Come in."

"Now, remember what I said," Breck whispers. "Try to look smart and sound like you got some brains in your head, or the ol' crow'll be done with you faster than her harem of menfolk."

"Harem of menfolk?"

Before I can press further, Breck pushes the door open.

CHAPTER 4

THE GOLD DOOR OPENS TO REVEAL A GIANT sitting room lined with richly draped windows and, beneath those, red velvet couches full of men chatting and sipping from colored goblets. Their perfume has practically condensed into clouds around them, and each one is dressed like a fairy-tale creature.

Bears. Centipedes. Rock-elves. Tiger-peacocks.

It's like a whole new circus of strange, and I'm suddenly trying not to react to the hilariousness of it or to say anything that will earn me a firm slap.

In the room's center, an enormous candelabrum hangs over a map-covered table where more gentlemen are leaning and whispering. Beside them, facing away from me, is a woman. Adora, I presume.

"Good luck," Breck mutters, and her voice sounds weak and nervous for me, which is not at all comforting.

"So here's the wretched girl I rescued. Glad you finally decided to get up and show some decent appreciation." Lady Adora turns her gold-lined eyes to me as she speaks—it's the woman from yesterday at the slave market. Messy images jostle my mind until one memory slams into focus: *I let loose a lightning storm on a despicable man there. And she stood watching.*

I inhale and nearly choke at the recollection before pulling it together.

Lifting my chin, I assess this insane noblewoman. And concentrate on the fact that, today, she is dressed like a frog. An exquisitely beautiful frog.

I cough to disguise my mockery. Clearly I'm in a loony house.

Her curly hair is dyed emerald green, and on top of her head is a tiny hat sewn to look like frog eyes. The glittery green scales that make up her clothes clutch her legs and arms like a man's hunting outfit, but with a bustle coming off the back to give the appearance of a dress. The recollection of her crazylike laughing in the lightning storm yesterday prickles my skin. She beckons me into the room with one hand while coldly flicking the other at the men to motion them out. I sneak a peek at Breck, but she's already slipping away down the dark passage.

"Don't make me wait, girl," Adora says in a crisp voice.

The last of the gentlemen slides past me as I enter, warily eyeing the frog-woman. She crosses the room to stand in front of a large and ornately carved wood desk beneath one of the windows. With one hand resting on it and the other cupping her hip, she looks as I imagine a gorgeous fairy-elf might, if a fairy-elf were wearing a frog suit that clung to every detail of her slim frame.

Drawing closer, I note that the makeup on her upper cheeks

is painted on to resemble butterfly wings with tiny jewels dotting the edges. It's the most incredible thing I've ever seen—and also the most disturbing. Partly because it makes her look like she ate the butterfly, and partly because something tells me those jewels are real. And just one of them would feed an entire peasant town for a year.

"Well? Do you speak? Or did I purchase a fool mute?"

I straighten my shoulders and level my gaze at her like I do with all new owners. It's better they know up front what I'm made of—mainly what I will and, more importantly, won't tolerate. "I speak. When I need to."

"Name?"

"Nym. And I'm not a fool."

"Properly raised slaves would've said thank you by now. So yes, you are a fool."

"Thank you," I say acidly and try not to choke as it comes out. *Charming.* I wonder if she wants me to curtsy too. Because I won't.

Adora waves her hand and walks around to stand behind her desk and glare out the giant window, which, like the rest, encompasses a breathtaking view of rock roses nestled among lynden shrubs on hills sloping into forest. All immersed in periwinkle light from the expansive evening sky.

I wait.

My new owner ignores me and taps her fingers on her hip in time to the waltz music filtering up from downstairs.

A minute goes by. The perfume saturating the air is sticky sweet. Gagging. I edge nearer the window for the fresh air and steal a look at what's below this side of the house. It's a garden lit by hanging candle lanterns suspended over ponds, and grass, and a colorful assortment of lemon trees and flower bushes. A quick flash of a ferret-cat running and then it's gone.

Two men stand talking, one well-muscled and missing his shirt, with his head shaved bald. The other, with black skin the color of richest onyx, scowls at him. He must sense Adora because he suddenly raises his eyes and stares right at her. She waves and smiles flirtatiously with her brightly painted crimson lips. He nods, then shifts his gaze to me, narrowing his eyes. Then he drops his head, and his jagged black bangs hide his dark expression as he goes back to speaking with the bald boy. And I am left with the uncomfortable awareness that even from this distance, he is one of the most attractive men I have ever seen.

Adora watches him for an elongated minute, almost to the point of her interest becoming awkward. I'm beginning to believe Breck about the harem. Except something tells me this dark-haired, dark-skinned man is someone Adora wants but hasn't managed to get yet. *Hmm. Good for him.*

"I assume you realize how serious your crime was yesterday." Adora turns away from the window. "You should be on trial for murder right now."

Part of me has spent my entire life wishing I was already dead. So what does she want me to do—thank her that I'm not? I cut to the ugly chase of it. "What do you want from me?"

She keeps talking as if I haven't said a thing. "I spoke with the few authorities who were there and convinced them how hard it would be to prove your responsibility for the lightning strikes. The weather can be so finicky. Isn't that right, Nym?"

She raises a curvy eyebrow high on a forehead surrounded by greenish tufts of hair. "Which I assume is why you've never been found guilty before. The authorities obviously can't vow you're an Elemental, since we all know female versions don't exist. Except . . ." She smiles coaxingly at me and spreads her hands out. "Here you are."

I look away. Something about her tone and expression makes my skin clammy. Like I'm waiting for the *but* in all of it. I've been through this enough times to know that the ax always falls, and a niggling tells me that her ax will cut sharper, deeper than that of the peasant owners who were more concerned with cheap labor than my dirty Elemental bloodline. The thought makes my stomach squirm. *What does she want with me?*

"So that leaves me to wonder, what exactly should we do with you, pretty Elemental girl?"

I narrow my eyes as I glance back at her. No comment.

She purses her red lips in an expression that demands an answer.

Fine. I shrug. "Put me to work in your kitchen. Your fields. Do whatever the litches you want." *Why is she asking? I'm a slave.* More than that, she knows I'm an Elemental, and she's rich enough not to have purchased me for the cheap price. Which means she's already got something in mind.

I hesitate. Then add, "Just don't put me with children."

That weird, insane smile hitches the sides of Adora's mouth. It sets off wrinkles along the painted butterfly lines of her face, and it suddenly occurs to me that she's much older than I thought. Her fourth decade maybe?

"Are you aware you killed that little redheaded girl yesterday?

Your lightning struck her right after you took out her new master." She looks closely at me and waits for my reaction.

It's swift in coming. Grief. Horror. Shock waves rock through me and knock the air from my chest so strong, I feel like I'm gasping and climbing and drowning all at once. My fists clench beside me. *No. It's not true. It can't be.*

But I know it is.

I've murdered a child.

Anger burns my throat. I swallow, striving for composure while hating the fact that even now, in the midst of ruining a little girl's life, I am selfish. I won't let the new master see my weakness. The little girl deserves my grief, my sorrow, my apology, but I'll do it alone. In private. Every day for the rest of my life.

From Adora's serious expression, she already knows it.

She turns back to the window.

"It must be painful living with a curse like that."

I can't see her face so I don't know if she's truly sorry or if the pity in her voice is invented. It doesn't matter. I want to get out of here. I want to run to my home that no longer exists among the snow. To say sorry to my dead mum and dad, and to find my way into Litchfell Forest where the bolcranes can have at me. "Here, monsters," I'd say. "I kill innocent kids outright. Eat me."

"The war is getting worse, Nym."

I look up. *What? What does that have to do with the little girl?*

"Bron's attacks are increasing, and we're losing men faster than we can handle. We keep up a good rally for our Faelen people, but our island kingdom's on the brink of destruction."

I stare at the back of her head. The kingdoms of Bron and Faelen have been at war for a hundred years, and it's well-known that Bron's attacks have recently become brutal. *But why is she talking to me about this?*

She spins around to face me. "Faelen has a matter of months before Bron takes over. Maybe less. Our king, Sedric, is coming to the party this evening to meet with those of us on his High Council, and when he gets here, by Faelen duty, I'm required to inform him of you. Of what you are. And of what you've done to one of his sweet child citizens. Which, as you're well aware, the law for both is death."

Her eyes suddenly soften and that hint of a mentally unstable smile comes through. "However, what if I told you there's a way you could atone for what you are?"

I narrow my gaze. "There's no such thing as atonement."

"Of course, you can never make up for the atrocities you've done. You'll have to live with the guilty horror for the rest of your life. But what if there was a way you could actually live with yourself, by spending your life making up for it?"

Right. "How?"

"As a fourth-generation High Council member, I'm King Sedric's most trusted advisor when it comes to war. I understand it, just as my father and his father did, and I understand what winning entails."

She pauses for dramatic effect before she steps toward me. "Your curse, Nym. If trained and controlled under the right conditions, you could become Faelen's greatest weapon in the war."

I cringe at her word *weapon*. It's synonymous with death. Perhaps she notices because she rephrases. "You'd be our greatest *defense*. Not a weapon used for harm, but for protecting your people, Nym. People whom, thus far, you've only managed to ruin and destroy." Her voice takes on a seductive tone. "What if you could help save those people?"

I don't know what to say. I don't believe her, nor do I believe that what she's saying is possible. But something inside of me cracks open without my permission. In that place covering the shameful hole where my soul exists.

I ignore it. "My curse can't be controlled."

"I have a trainer here. He's the best in the five kingdoms." Adora's eyelashes bat for the briefest second and I wonder if she's referring to the man still outside the window, who's now jousting with the bald guy. Her gaze follows my eyes and her expression turns stern. "You'd be surprised what he can do."

The tiniest ray of light slips through the internal fissure. A sputter of hope.

Hope I can't afford to bear. I shake my head. "I would kill him too."

Her tone turns impatient. "I'm willing to offer you a place to stay and learn, Nym. With a life far better than anything you've experienced in your pitiful excuse for one. In return, you'll trust that I know what I'm talking about. As the richest landholder in Faelen, I've a strong interest in protecting my holdings, which is why I've spent years finding and training Uathúils. So yes, I *do* know what I'm talking about. You have until tomorrow morning to decide. Otherwise, I will be forced to turn you over to the king's men first thing." She sits down and begins scribbling what appears to be the last part of a letter and waits for my response.

I'm stunned. This is so far beyond anything normal for a slave, let alone anything I've encountered, I don't even know how to absorb her words. It's as if I've just entered another kingdom where the rules have all changed, and instead of death or out-right slavery, she's offering me a form of redemption. It doesn't make sense.

Which means maybe there really *is* a way to control my curse. *But even then . . .* "Why?"

"Because we need you, Nym. Faelen needs you. The weapons Bron is bringing against us cannot be fought by peasants on the ground. They'll be annihilated before they know what hit them. We need power and nature on our side, and I believe you can give us that. You can bring the victory we need and protect what we hold dear."

"I doubt it."

"I've had my trainer, Eogan, work with other Uathúils before you, and they're the only reason Faelen hasn't fallen recently. But none of the ones he's worked with have had your particular gift-ing, nor the magnitude of your powers. He's currently training a boy, and when we think you're both ready, you'll step into the war. You will answer to me and only me, and you will do every-thing I ask, when I ask. And you won't tell anyone what you are or what you can do—you'll leave that to me as your owner." Her gold-lined eyes slide coldly over mine. "Even when it comes to the king. Is that understood?"

I bite my lip.

Adora folds the document she's been writing, then lifts it to her red lips and licks the edge. Her face suddenly flinches as if she's pricked her tongue and a second later a drop of blood drops onto the bottom of the sheet, spreading out in a pattern that looks like the shape of the poison-alder flower. I'd think she'd done it on accident except she doesn't look upset at all that it's stained the pretty linen paper. She folds it over again with one hand while reaching for melting wax with the other.

"As I said, you have until morning to make your decision. For tonight, you will stay with Breck and be allowed to observe the party from afar. You're not to speak to anyone. Nor are you to display yourself in such a way that people would notice you exist. Are we clear?"

"Fine."

"Breck!" she yells, her tone harsh and dismissive. I jump.

The auburn-haired girl appears immediately. *Was she listening at the door?* "Yes, mum?"

"Take Nym and see that she stays out of trouble. If she does anything . . . unfortunate, bring her to me." She motions for us to go.

I'm practically tripping over my own feet to get out of the perfume-infused, awkward room.

"And, Nym?"

I stop. Turn. "Yes?"

"Stay away from the barn."

CHAPTER 5

FANCY PEOPLE.

Tons of them.

Thick in embroidered costumes styled as everything from sin-eaters to exquisite fairy-animals topped with giant jewels and tiny hats that make their faces look even shinier. They arrive in a sea of glittery carriages, reflective of Faelen's commoners only in the variety of beautiful ethnicities represented as they spill out one by one like jellyfish onto Adora's estate steps. I've sat in an upstairs window for the last half hour describing each of them to Breck as they stand for exactly three minutes and visit with the frog-queen before entering the house.

"Their kiss-up moment," Breck calls it. "Where they get themselves in Adora's good graces so she'll invite 'em back again. Ridiculous if you ask me." She shoves another bite of greasy party food in her mouth.

"Nice to know groveling isn't a respecter of status," I mutter, and pass a rag over for her to wipe the butter and spices dripping off her chin.

"Nah, but money is."

Another oily glob dribbles from the quail leg she's chewing on and makes me cringe. The dinner upset my stomach after only a few bites—the rich flavors and fat so different from Faelen's peasant porridge. *No wonder half the guests are the size of whale cubs.*

Before tonight, the nicest food I ate was a slop of cheap wine and squirrel meat at a wedding for a village provost. At the time, Brea's attempt to get in the groom's good graces got me volunteered to clean the squatty pots after each use. The memory still makes me gag.

"C'mon!" Breck gives me an impatient nudge. "What else is happening?"

"The High Court and Castle are lit up." I stare out at the eerie glow created by the lanterns over the drive. The city hovers like a fairy goblin above the island kingdom's interior valley. More beautiful and strange and massive than I ever imagined—its white, pointy-roofed towers jutting up to touch the smoke blown in from the war front.

"Not that." Breck waves her hand and frowns. "I wanna know if King Sedric's here."

A scarlet carriage is pulling up. "Not sure. Hold on." I watch the coachmen climb down and wait for the occupant to emerge as I tug my dress sleeve back up onto my shoulder. The pettish thing keeps slipping off because my arms aren't as long as Adora's.

The man's stomach materializes ahead of his face. I crinkle my nose. "Is the king the size of a rhino-horse?"

Breck grunts and bats a hand toward the back of my head before I can dodge. "Idiot. Have you 'onestly never seen yer king?"

I shift in Adora's dress and scoot away from Breck. I don't like being struck, and her insults about my intelligence prick my nerves like the awful bone ribbing in this hand-me-down gown. "Have *you*?"

"I may not 'ave seen 'im with my eyes, but I've heard enough to know what the man looks like."

"Well, where I've lived, no one but the magistrate sees the king. And no one has time to care. They're too busy trying not to starve or freeze or lose their sons to war."

She should know this. She may live in a fancy house eating rich people's food, but she's been a peasant. And she's a slave. I turn to her. "Why? Where did *you* live before?"

"A bit here, a bit there. Colin an' I—we made a smart way for ourselves being useful and such. Which is how we ended up here, right?"

Colin again.

"Is he a house servant like you, or does he work in the fields?"

"He's like what you'll be." She rises to her feet. "If you decide you wants to stay and work with Eogan."

My dress almost rips as I scramble up beside her. "What's that mean? Is your brother the one being trained? Is he an Elemental?"

"You'll find out tomorrow, won't you?" Her tone makes it clear that's all I'll get from her. "An' never mind seeing the king, right? We can look at 'im later. Let's go get more food from the kitchen."

I don't want more food. I want to know more about Colin

and how he's like me. "Has he learned to control his curse?" I start to ask Breck, but she's already halfway down the hall. I shut my mouth and stack the plates with my good hand. Balancing them against my bowed one, I follow her, paying attention to where we're going this time.

When we reach the cookery door, Breck takes our dishes and tells me to wait in the hall. But as soon as she disappears, I turn about to investigate the wood-paneled corridor that continues on down this section. I need to know more about this house, about Adora and Colin and Eogan, if I'm going to stay here.

But all the doors I come to are locked.

I'm just about to pick my way up a thin flight of stairs I hope will lead to Adora's quarters when voices erupt behind the door closest to me.

Footsteps. Two sets of them coming toward me.

A lock clicks and the handle turns, and I lunge for the stairwell, practically tripping over my ridiculous dress in my haste. The satin rips beneath my foot. I tug my legs and the full skirt out of sight, disappearing into the shadows just as the door opens.

I hold my breath.

The male voices drop to angry whispers. "I'm telling you, Bron will win this war. And when they do, their King Odion will take over. You and I will be slaughtered with the rest of these pompous fool*sss*." The speaker draws out the ending, like a snake.

"You're insane," a gravelly voice says. "King Sedric won't allow it. He'll find a way for Faelen to win."

"Sedric can't stop it! He's in over his head, and the High Council's still stuck in the old way of acting as advisors when they should be forcing his hand. Mark my word*sss*, Odion will win. And when he doe*sss*, I intend to stand at his mercy, with a record of supportive initiatives."

"Listen to yourself. You're talking treason!"

"I'm talking survival. What benefit are we to Faelen if we're dead? You've heard the rumors. They're advancing weapon technology beyond imagining while we're here fighting with horse and sword. You've heard of the plague*sss*."

My chest is up in my throat, clamoring, clawing, cutting off my air. I make myself smaller against the stairwell and fight the desire to look at the speakers. *A real traitor? Here?*

"Even if Sedric can't stop it, the kingdom of Cashlin will step in. Their queen's already considering their involvement. Why do you think Princess Rasha is here?"

"Princess Rasha is less experienced than our king. Have you met the girl? She's a frothy bottle of drink, all giggles and no brain*sss*. Fates doom us all if that's where we're investing our hope."

"Maybe Drust will help, then. The Lady Isobel's set to arrive—"

A trumpet blast from nearby threatens to peel me from my skin. The voices halt.

I close my eyes and concentrate on breathing quietly in the echoing hall.

A floorboard creaks.

Another trumpet blast ricochets through. Coming from the direction of the dulled party music and laughter.

One of the speakers mutters something, followed by the sound of shuffling footsteps, and for a moment I think they're headed toward me. My heart pounds, and I'm about to make a dive up the stairs when another door opens almost opposite my position. Their steps hesitate. For the briefest second, I get a partial glimpse of two men's backs as the music swells through the open doorway. One tall and thin, the other shorter with a shock of orange hair topped by a dark-feathered cap. The men appear to match each other in silk doublets designed to look like birds. Ravens, I think.

"I'd like to show you something out*ssss*ide later to change your mind," the tall one whispers. Then the door shuts without the speakers looking back, and their steps fade.

I wait a few breaths before peeking from my hiding spot to examine the empty corridor. The hum of the festivities now lilts, faint in the distance.

One, ten, twenty . . . I count to a hundred before getting up. It's still quiet. I slip over to the door the men disappeared through, then press my ear against the wood to listen. The music is louder on the other side. Are those men really traitors? Another thirty counts and I open the door a crack and peek around it. Nothing but party noise fills the vacant hallway. I pause before sliding inside.

After sealing the passage behind me, I tiptoe in the direction of the merrymaking, which is growing louder by the second. The short hall passes by two doors, both locked, and then abruptly spits me out into a tiny alcove that is smack inside the house's tall, albeit not very big, ballroom. The excited buzz of voices hits a new high alongside the music and smell of strong perfume.

I'm in a serving alcove, but it's obviously not in use tonight. Drapes hang across the front so that while one could adjust them to peer out on the dancing couples, no one would see in unless on purpose. *Did the men come through here?* I scoot to the curtain's edge and peek out, but the amount of people jostling toward the ballroom's front entrance is overwhelming, and with so many wearing black it'd be impossible to identify the men, even with that orange hair.

Just as I stick my head farther through the curtain, a trumpet blasts next to my face. I jump and blink, then look to see if anyone has seen me.

Doubtful. They're all looking in the same direction, waiting for something. The sea of voices diminishes to a low, excited rumble, thick with anticipation.

Then a loud voice is announcing King Sedric and the Cashlin ambassador, Princess Rasha. I scramble for a better look but can't see either of them. Too many people are in the way. Charged whispers sweep through the crowd.

"They'd make a handsome couple."

Someone giggles. "I hear they already are."

"Not likely. He's only just met her. She'll have to be on good behavior for a bit."

"I hear she only got the ambassador position because of her queen mum. They want . . ."

I'm leaning out to hear more when Breck's angry whisper barks out behind me, "Nym! Where in hulls you at?"

Jumping back, I turn to find her standing with one hand on the hallway wall and the other laden with a plate piled high, a drinking jug in the crook of her arm. I purse my lips and move to help her. "Here, Breck."

"I been lookin' all over! Don't you ever do that again, right?

Or I swear I'll poke the eyes right out a yer head an' give 'em to Adora myself!" Shrugging my helping hand off, she feels along the wood paneling, then sets the tray down in a nook in the wall with an expression that reminds me of an owner who's been disrespected. She glares not quite at me and waits, as if expecting an apology.

I turn back to the curtain.

She's not going to get it. She's not my owner.

"The king's just arrived," I say instead.

The plate Breck sets down clatters as if she's almost tipped it over. Then she's cramming in next to me. "Is the Cashlin ambassador with 'im?"

"Yes, but I can't see either of them. Too many people. Everyone's saying she and the king might be lovers."

"I 'ope not. I hear she's a bit of a piece, if you know what I mean."

I have no idea what she means. "A piece?"

"She's a witch," she whispers. "The kind that can see into yer soul. At least that's what Adora says. And while Adora might be dense on men, the ol' crazy's spot on when it comes to the females."

"What do you mean 'see into your soul'? That's absurd."

"She's Luminescent. The Cashlin version of a Uathúil. Like you're Elemental? She can see past a person's facade to who, or what, he really is."

I'm instantly uncomfortable. *Into a person's soul?*

Maybe Breck senses my unease, or maybe she's uncomfortable too, because her voice lowers. "Eerie, right? I told ya. A witch."

I don't know whether I believe the witch part or not, but something tells me not to find out. I can only imagine what someone with that ability would see if she looked inside my soul.

40

Death? Hatred? Self-contempt?

Murderer.

Elemental.

I glance back out over Adora's ballroom and search through the unfamiliar faces for the king and the Cashlin princess, suddenly desperate to know what she looks like so I can avoid her.

Breck grunts. "You see her?"

"No."

"Well, this is only 'er second visit to Faelen, so not a lot 'ave. When you do, describe 'er to me. Gotta see what all the fuss is about. Cuz if you ask me—which no one is, mind you—she sounds like a floozy." Breck leaves the curtain and moves over to nibble on her food.

"Why did Adora invite her?"

She shrugs and takes a bite of oliphant meat. I force down a gag. "Adora has to," she says with her mouth full. "Princess Rasha is an ambassador. Meaning she might be useful, you know?"

Right.

"You want some?" Breck offers a slab of what she's inhaling.

"No thanks," I mutter, and try not to vomit. Is she aware it's oliphant meat? But then, the smell is unmistakable. I'm tempted to ask if she's ever truly eaten at peasant level, but maybe she has, and that's why she's so keen on the food here.

"Is there a way I can get closer to see the ambassador and the king?"

She smacks her lips and uses her dress to mop the horse grease from her face. "We can go around and haves a look out onto the banquet room. It's where they'll be headed." She takes a gulp from her water jug. "I'll take you in a minute."

The trumpet blares again, and it's just as disconcerting as

the other times. But Breck just goes on with her second dinner as if having your eardrums shattered by the sound of a honking monkey was the height in luxurious music for dining.

I sit. And glare. And tap my leg.

An eternity later, she wipes her fingers and stands. Burps. "You ready?"

I follow her back through the hall the men came down, past the doors in the first passage, and around the house kitchen, where Breck stops to drop off her plate and jug. She then leads me down another hallway, this one ending in a different kind of nook. It's shallow and walled in on all sides except the point where we entered. She pats her hand along the wall until she hits a square panel that's made to look like a miniature window. Sliding it open, she beckons me to peek out.

It opens straight into the main banquet room.

Party guests are already pouring in from one end, and the place is teeming with laughter and music.

Breck shifts aside to make more room for me and stands stock-still as if she's listening for bits of conversation floating about.

"How will I know which is the king?" I look around.

"He'll be seated next to Adora."

I search the room for the frog-queen amid a sea of gossamer gowns and brocaded vests. Guests in costumes ranging from rabid ladybugs to purple bears surround rows of food-laden banquet tables, while images of countless years of starving women and sick babies drift through my mind. I wonder if the king is as grandiose as his politically positioned subjects.

How can these people be so lard-headed?

Or worse, so unconcerned?

Someone in black steps right in front of my peephole and startles me. I begin to duck, afraid I've been spotted, but then realize he's not fully facing me.

I start to move my gaze on when the man moves his hand in a tipsy, familiar gesture. I squint and peer closer.

Breck is still chattering on about Adora and the king.

I stop listening.

The man. He's the pontiff from Poorland Arch, home of my seventh owner.

A sour bubble emerges in my stomach and pushes up my throat, making it hard to breathe. I pull my dress sleeves higher, tugging them close to my neck. The last time I saw him, he was flirting with a slave girl my age who kept trying to duck his advances. She disappeared that night, and no one saw her again.

He's babbling about the Bron king's missing twin brother, who'd been master general of their army, and how if he'd become ruler instead of Odion, Faelen wouldn't have lasted even this long. I can't see who he's talking to, but everything within me is recoiling. Without taking my gaze off of him, I interrupt Breck. "Do you know anything about the pontiff from Poorland Arch?"

"Describe 'im."

"Grayish-blond hair, drunker than a nursing—"

"I meant describe 'is voice. But yeah, I know who you's talking about." She hesitates. "Last week Colin 'ad a run-in with 'im over a servant girl they was both flirtin' with and almost got in trouble with Adora. I hear he's quite popular with the ladies. Why?"

I bet he is. My mouth turns tasteless.

"Why're you asking?" she asks again.

"Have you ever seen any of these people when they're not at Adora's parties? Like when they visit the villages they oversee?"

"Nah. But most of 'em don't seem so bad. Why? Have you?"

"It doesn't matter," I say. Because I don't want to explain something she obviously can't understand.

"You ever been to the High Court afore?"

Suddenly I don't know how to do this. I don't want to talk about any of it. I don't want to be here. The closest I ever got to the High Court was when the politicians came to collect taxes or announce a proclamation. A few officials were nice enough. But most? Most were known for eating all the food and then complaining it wasn't good enough while grabbing some poor slave girl's thigh beneath the table. Or worse. I glance back at the man standing close enough for me to slap. They have a smell you can never get rid of.

And now Adora's house is full of it.

"Let's go outside and find fresh air." I need to breathe. I need to be doing something, anything—cleaning, cooking, shoveling manure from the animals' stalls—other than just sitting here discussing an uppity world I can't relate to and recalling memories I can't bear.

Breck frowns. "Not allowed to. Adora's orders." She sits on the bench against the wall and leans her head back against the wood. "Methinks it's time for a nap, idiot girl. What say you?"

I don't say anything. I yank my wretched sleeve back up my shoulder and quietly slip away to find a corridor that'll lead me out of this blasted place.

CHAPTER 6

O UTSIDE, THE SALT-LACED BREEZES COOL MY face. My blood reacts to the briny air, pulsing in unison with the waves beyond the mountains.

I hurry along the cobbled path leading away from the servants' exit, staying in the shadows until the house is far enough behind. When I do pause to look around, it's amid the back area I'd seen from Adora's upper-story window. The loud music and laughter float away in the quiet expanse, as the candlelit lanterns swing in the breeze, illuminating the air above and the gardens around. The spacious lawn is edged on two sides by miniature ponds, and along the other sides are two structures. One, directly across from me, is a small cottage. The other, on my right, is a massive barn and stables. I can hear horses stamping and nickering within. *The barn Adora warned me to keep away from?*

I hike up my dress skirts and head for it.

The horses' musky scent envelops me before I reach the door.

Familiar. Earthy. Manure and sweat and peasant life. I close my eyes briefly and drink in a host of images—brushing down farm horses, fieldwork, housework, babies.

A noise behind me interrupts my thoughts, and I turn to snap at Breck for finding me.

But no one is there.

Tugging the barn door open, I step onto the slightly raised wood flooring and slip inside. A soft whinny greets me. Then others. Without the moon's enhancement, the space is murky, even with the lit lanterns hanging from the ceiling. When my eyes adjust, I'm staring at countless rows of stalls housing stately, midnight-colored, colossal-size horses.

The animals stamp their hooves and bob their heads. The one in the stall beside me huffs a greeting. I smile, and she gives me a responding click with her mouth. Then nudges her nose toward me.

"You're a friendly one, aren't you?" I murmur soothingly. "And pricey." I suspect much of Adora's money comes from inside this barn. I shuffle closer and almost slip in a puddle. A shock of cold oozes through my shoe as I catch my balance.

"What the—?" I pull my skirts up and look down to curse the dung I've stepped in—except it isn't dung. It's a pool of liquid slowly soaking into the floor and into my slipper, and it's surrounded by more dribbles leading farther into the barn. Each one an uncomfortable shade of red.

My mouth goes dry just as I note the clump of bright orange tufts stuck in the blood-colored fluid. It's the same fiery shade as the hair of one of the gentlemen in the hall earlier.

I straighten and shake my head.

It's just from an injured ferret-cat.

The horse nearest me whinnies again, as if calling for my attention and telling me to shake it off. I move to the beautiful mare and am just reaching my deformed hand up for her to smell me when I see specks of foam around her lips. Her neck has a slight glisten, too, like she just got back from a run.

"I wouldn't advise touching them."

I spin around to see a man standing at the door. His dark skin blends into the shadows, making his green eyes stand out like fireflies in the lantern light. They're shocking in their brightness.

"Who're you?"

He doesn't respond. Just tips his head toward the horse. As if I should pay attention.

I glance at the black beast distractedly just as the animal tips her nose down to meet my outstretched fingers. So beautiful. Then her mouth is opening wide, displaying razor-sharp teeth about to take my hand off.

What the—? I yank away right as the teeth snap closed. The beast gives a piercing whinny of anger and bites at the air where my arm just was.

"What the bolcrane? What's *wrong* with it?"

The man utters a low, rich chuckle that fills the space around us with charming ease. "Told you."

Then, as if not trusting me to refrain from attempting to touch the horse again, he steps closer. He's the man Adora was admiring through the window this afternoon. Eogan, if my suspicion's correct. Arms crossed, sporting a cocky smile.

And he's unreasonably attractive—curse him.

I scoot away, keeping the snapping horse in my perimeter. "So you did," I say, still catching my breath. But I see no reason to laugh about it.

His expression shifts to suspicious. "You're not going to faint, are you?" His tone makes it clear nothing would be more loathsome.

"You're not going to squeal like a little girl if I *do*, are you?"

"You should leave. You're upsetting the horses." He turns to go, and I'm abruptly aware that the horse who tried to eat me is in a rage, gnashing her teeth and knocking against the stall. The other horses are starting to join in.

But I won't leave based on some chump-man's orders. I strike my haughty pose. "What's wrong with them?"

"Nothing. They're meat eaters. You're meat."

"You *bred* them that way?"

"They're warhorses," he says. And saunters out the door.

The blood and hair on the floor . . . My stomach turns. I don't even want to know. The animals' chorus is growing. Becoming a call for flesh. Chills scramble up my back and hairline as I follow the gorgeous, irritating man outside, my sleeve half hanging off my arm. I yank it up higher, but something must have ripped when I pulled away from the horse because the right side won't stay up now. *Ridiculous dress.*

The man is striding away, across the lawn, beneath the moonlight and swaying lights. Toward the cottage.

I give one last tug on my sleeve and accidentally tear it off. Crumpling it in my fist, I trail after him.

My stomping is somewhat dulled by the grass and the slippers on my feet. But he hears me anyway because he tosses out, "Shouldn't you be at Adora's party?"

"I wasn't invited."

A pause. "Shouldn't you be *watching* the party, then? Ogling the pretty boys and dresses?"

"Shouldn't you be flirting with Adora?"

We've reached the cottage, and he spins to face me. He is tall and broad and has a snarl curving his lips that is begging to be slapped off. His glower lasts a few seconds longer, then relaxes. He straightens and smiles as if I'm a stupid little girl he finds bothersome for the moment. After opening the door, he enters. And casually swings it shut in my face.

I catch it with my foot before it latches and push the heavy wood open far enough for me to lean against the doorpost. He's stepped over to the fireplace where a pot full of silvery liquid is boiling and infusing the room with a scent of metal and pine. I wrinkle my nose.

The place isn't so much a cottage as a workshop filled with strange contraptions. They're made of tiny metal parts assembled into toys spanning from the length of my pinky finger to that of my entire arm. They look like boxy versions of animals and people. From the ceiling hang dainty ones with birdlike wings.

"What is all this?"

He doesn't look up, just carries the pot of boiling liquid from the fireplace to the worktable. "You shouldn't be in here."

"Really? *You're* in here."

"I live here."

I peer around. *Doubtful.* Then I notice the small door by the bookcase. There must be sleeping quarters in the back.

"Right. So why aren't *you* at the party?"

"I don't like people." He tips some of the smelly liquid into another pot.

"Clearly."

He glances up. In the cottage light, I realize he's younger than his confidence suggests. Four years older than me maybe. Five at the most. The firelight bounces off his dark skin, making it glimmer. It's beautiful.

He goes back to his pouring, growling, "You're not going to win, you know."

"Win?"

"Our little game here. Your little attitude."

I raise a brow. *My* attitude? I slide farther into the room, then plant my feet near the wall. If he wants me out, he'll have to kick me out. "I don't have an attitude. You have an attitude."

Flashing green eyes rise to settle on mine. "When I want you out, you'll leave."

I look away and fiddle with the torn sleeve wadded in my fingers. When I peek at him again, those brilliant eyes are peering between jagged black bangs, studying the owner circles tattooed on my arm.

"I hear you're a storm siren."

I frown. "What?"

"An Elemental." He moves to return the boiling liquid over the fire.

Oh. Right. I study the worktable and the contraptions near the steaming pots. A miniature metal wolf catches my eye. It's almost an exact replica of the real ones I recall from the snowy mountains I grew up in. Something inside of me wants to touch it, to soak up that reminder of home.

"Do you have fighting skills?"

"Is scratching and biting and kicking considered a skill?"

The briefest smile strains the corners of his lips and then it's gone. "The name's Eogan. Adora give you the whole lecture on what we do?"

"Save the world and that kind of thing?" My voice stumbles into a whisper. "Yeah."

He assesses me. "But you're still deciding."

I nod and go back to playing with the sleeve in my hand. "Pretty sure I'm not the save-the-world type."

"That's good, because I'm pretty sure the world's not worth being saved."

Is he jesting?

I don't think so. His face is dead serious as he lifts two molds onto the table and begins filling them with the hot, silvery substance from the little pots.

"But I love a good challenge." He answers my question before I can ask. "Why are *you* here?"

"My other option is the gallows."

His expression turns sour. "What makes you think you're worth avoiding the gallows?"

The way he says it feels like a smack in the face. An uninvited rush of warmth floods my cheeks and neck. "I'm not."

"Then why are you here?"

Why am I here? Is it as selfish as avoiding death?

"Because I want to learn to control my abilities."

He absorbs this, staring me square in the eyes. "A female Elemental is unique. That alone will make it difficult for you to learn control. But"—a challenge emerges in his gritty tone—"combine that with your attitude, and it'll feel near impossible."

I hate him.

I bite my lip and, ignoring him, walk over to look at the

metal wolf on the worktable. With my right hand, I poke a finger toward the animal, careful to keep my crooked hand out of sight, although most likely he's already seen it.

The contraption issues a metallic snarl and snaps at me.

I screech and jump toward the door. "What the kracken is that thing?"

The unreasonably attractive man doesn't answer. He's too busy filling the room with thunderous laughter.

I stomp out, eyes narrowed, cheeks flaming.

I'm halfway across the lawn before the strains of waltz music reach me from the house. They flit and dance through the air in an odd synchrony to Eogan's ongoing hilarity. *Blast them all.* I bite my lip. My soul twisting, throbbing, begging me to run.

Not that I'd get far.

I look back at the cottage. At my one chance of learning to control my curse.

So he likes a good challenge, does he?

Pulling the dress skirts higher, I grit my teeth. *Well, maybe I'll give him one.*

I turn and—

Booooom!!!

An explosion rocks the ground.

I hit the dirt just as there's another, and then I'm up on my hands and knees and scrambling toward the house. I listen for another strike, but even as the ground shakes, it suddenly occurs to me that the tremors are originating far away. *What in hulls?*

I glance up and see orange fire and unearthly-size embers shooting off one of the Hythra Mountains hovering over us. Like someone dropped a kettle of lava on the scene. The glow lights up the forests and snow like a sunrise. I'm just thinking I should tell someone when above the blaze I catch sight of the most impossible object I've ever seen.

An ocean ship made of metal.

Flying in the air beneath a giant balloon, the outline unreal against the lit-up sky as it heads away from the blast.

At the edge of my vision, I note Eogan staring at it too.

Then he's yelling at me to get inside, and everything moves so fast, my mind is a blur as Adora's guests spill out to point and scream that the capital is under attack.

CHAPTER 7

I'M GLAD TO HEAR YOU'VE SOME CAPACITY FOR wisdom, Nymia." Adora puts her pen down and beckons for a cup refill as the windows in the sitting room rattle behind her.

The vibration grows stronger, until I think the glass will burst.

Here it comes. I scan the sky and still-burning mountainside for another one of those Bron floating ships. The carpet beneath my feet starts rolling, then shaking. It's the fourth time in the past fifteen minutes the earth has quaked beneath the house, and Adora hasn't even flinched. After the first tremor, she made it clear it wasn't from an explosion like last night but didn't elucidate. I steady my gaze on her. If she's not nervous, I refuse to be either.

The rattling subsides.

"I'd hate to think of you hanging from the gallows," Adora

continues, as if nothing's happened. "It's such an unbecoming way to die—makes a woman's face look so puffy and unattractive. Something you deserve, but still . . . so hideous." She stirs the cup set in front of her by the nervous-looking maidservant, then takes a sip. The maid and I both crinkle our noses. Whatever the foul-smelling broth is, it's not working fast enough to cure the hangover effects of last night's party and late after-hours with the king and High Council spent assessing the "new development" in her chambers. The poor lady looks terrible.

Green tendrils of hair shoot every which way in puffs from their curly perch atop her head, as if running for their lives from the frog hat. And the butterfly paint on her face is smeared. Like she threw the bug back up after she ate it. Perhaps she should bathe her entire body in the stinky broth.

She takes another drink, and the smashed butterfly wrinkles. "I see Breck put you in the appropriate clothes."

I glance at the blue-dyed leathers Breck tossed me this morning—pants, shirt, and calf-high, lace-up boots. Even their casual wear here is glorified.

"You'll wear that outfit every day. When you need more, you'll request them from me. If I agree with your need and approve of the use you've made of your current leathers, I'll send Breck to purchase more. The only time you'll dress in something else is when I'm hosting a party, in which case you'll make a background appearance in a dress. Long-sleeved to hide your . . ."—she makes a distasteful face—"markings. Aside from the gown I generously gave you yesterday, I'll send Breck up with three more. Don't ruin them."

Apparently Breck didn't tell her about the torn destruction of last night's gown. I'll have to remember to thank her.

"You will take your meals with Colin. You'll not take advantage of my charity, nor will you waste my time or resources. Inside this house, you will display yourself as submissive. However, you'll also remember you are being trained as a . . ." I wait for her to say *weapon*, but she seems to catch herself. "As a defender of Faelen. And as such, I'll not have you moping like a pathetic servant. Outside of my presence, you'll display the attitude of one protecting my house and estate. You'll train fast and hard until bruised and exhausted because, as we saw last night, we haven't got time. Understood?"

"Yes, m'lady."

She looks closely at me. "Can you read?"

I nod. "My fifth owner, a schoolteacher, taught me." He believed teaching a slave to read was no different than teaching a child.

She seems surprised. But pleased. "Is that where you learned to speak properly rather than in the common peasant tongue?"

I nod.

"Well then, all free time will be spent reading the war strategy books you'll find in the library."

A slight tremor shakes the windows but doesn't continue on.

Another slurp of her stinky drink.

"You may go. You'll find Eogan and Colin out back. They've already begun for the day. Breck will show you out." She gestures me toward Breck, who's appeared against the back wall. Then Adora settles in with her drink and closes her eyes over a desk full of notes, which, from what I've deciphered, confirm the rumors that Bron airships do, in fact, exist—a feat of impossibility leading to questions of how far advanced they are beyond us. Although the council's not clear how many there are or how far they can reach. They think last night was a test run.

"You decided to stay," Breck says once the door is shut behind us. She directs us down the now-familiar passage, then toward the exit I used last night. She hesitates before opening the door. "An' I'm just goin' to warn you now that Colin says Eogan's a hard one. But 'e knows 'is stuff."

Hard? Hard doesn't even begin to describe that man's personality. But she's right about him knowing things if last night's "storm siren" comment was any indication.

Then, as if an afterthought, she adds, "An' the housemaids all say he's quite a looker, so I'll warn you now not to get all silly 'bout 'im. Adora'll 'ave none of it. She's got her own interest in 'im."

"Eogan? Isn't she a little old?"

"All's fair game when it comes to the ol' crazy. Rumor 'as it, last year she orchestrated a kitchen maid's death who was gettin' too invested in 'im. Doubt Eogan even knew the girl existed, poor thing. But he's in some league of 'is own in her mind. Not that *I* can see why. Obviously." She chuckles and shoves on the thick door, and we're abruptly immersed in a smoky morning breeze and toasty sunlight.

"Neither can I," I mutter. But for some reason I'm suddenly glad Breck can't see my warming cheeks.

She points in the general direction of Eogan's cottage. "Go behind there into the forest. Just make sure an' kick my brother's hindside for me, will ya?" Then she's gone and shuts the door behind her.

I tramp across the damp yard, coughing on the haze and gaping at the eerily burning mountainside, until I round the cottage and stumble into a clearing. It's surrounded by a giant, frothy-branched pine-tree forest, and the air is filled with their homey scent. Eogan's lithe, broad-shouldered frame is standing in the middle of the arena, wearing green leathers and scowling at the bald man I saw out the window yesterday. Except the man's not really a man. He's my age, maybe a year older, with the same freckled skin and brown eyes of his sister, Breck. He's got his shirt off, showing muscles hardened through what must've been months of training.

"Oh c'mon, you're hardly even trying," Eogan says in his low voice.

"What are you talking about? I'm better than *you*!" the boy yells. "You can't even—" His argument drops when he sees me. His gaze starts at my legs and moves all the way up to my hair, settling on the odd way Breck tied it up this morning. It looks ridiculous, but she was in a mood and insisted. I meant to take it down once I came outside but forgot. *Drat.*

The boy grins, and I'm pretty sure he flexes his stomach muscles for me as he strolls over. He sticks his hand up in a flat-palmed salute. "Hello, pretty lady. It appears you're a pet of my sister's."

He reminds me of the rascals in the marketplace who flirt with the servant girls, pretending each one is the love of his life. Until the next girl comes along. Usually it annoys me. But this one . . . something about his eyes is so sincere that I find myself approving. I like him.

"Nym." I give a half smile.

Eogan steps behind him and cuffs him on the back of the neck. "Quit flirting, mate, and show me."

I open my mouth, but Colin doesn't seem to mind. 'Quit flirting and show me,' he mimics as he skips to the far end of the clearing.

I smirk.

Eogan pays no attention to me, his gaze trained on Colin. "Your stance is still wrong," I hear him mutter.

Colin has his feet a pace apart, with one knee bent, his weight resting on it. The other is stretched taut to the side. He glances up and gives me a quick wink, then dips his body down and places both hands flat out in front of him, level with the ground, and shuts his eyes.

The earth beneath us begins to rumble.

Is that him?

The ground shakes.

He's causing this?

Then it's quaking so hard that the trees around us are swaying and tipping at dangerous angles. There's a great ripping sound, and a crack in the earth opens in the middle of the clearing. It begins to spread out, growing deeper, wider, until it's headed straight for Eogan, the earth crumbling away into a six-foot chasm.

Eogan doesn't move. He just stands there evaluating as the perfectly aimed fissure shoots for him.

I start to back up. Horrified. Fascinated. I glance at Colin. *Is this his way of getting even with Eogan?*

Seven feet to Eogan. Six feet. I scramble toward the cottage. If Eogan wants to die, that's his choice. But he doesn't even bat a black eyelash. If anything, he looks bored. I bite my lip.

Five feet in front of him, the crack slams into something and stops, sending dirt clods and pebbles up in the air, tossing sand all over me, Eogan, and the clearing.

Colin laughs. "That good enough for you, Master Bolcrane?"

Eogan runs a hand through his hair, ruffling out the dirt, which just ends up making his thick, ragged locks unruly and boyish looking. "Better. Now seal it back up."

I pause from wiping my face off with my sleeve to look back and forth between them. *Just like that? It's some kind of game for them?*

Colin stoops down and places his right hand on the earth. I tiptoe a few steps closer as his eyes close again. Then the rumbling starts back up, the groan of rocks and dirt moving, but this time it's deeper. The trees don't sway so much, and I'm able to stand without wobbling. The ground in front of Eogan creases together and seals shut, and then backtracks toward Colin, closing in on itself as it goes. Like someone is stitching it with a sewing needle. By the time it's shut completely all the way to Colin's hand, I can't even tell where exactly the crack had been. The needles and grass appear undisturbed. Colin straightens and gives a loud whoop.

"There you go. Now again," Eogan yells at him. "But this time wider."

"Wider?" I look to Colin, who immediately stoops to obey. I brace myself.

"So you decided to stay," Eogan says to me, without turning around.

"So you've decided to speak to me now that I've stood here for ten minutes."

"Colin's a Terrene," Eogan says. "Not as rare as Elementals, nor as dangerous, but still not one to take your attention from while he's in action."

Oh.

I squint at Colin. *A Terrene?* Other than his shaved head, I can't see anything different looking about him. He's a bit taller and thinner than Breck, but his face has the same personality. "He's a Terrene, but I'm assuming his sister isn't. How does that work?"

"Technically she is, but without any power. Terrenes are always born with a twin. One is gifted. One is cursed. From the country of Tulla originally."

I wrinkle my forehead. "So which of them is gifted and which is cursed?"

"Depends on who you ask," he says, not taking his eyes off Colin. "If you put it to him, he'll tell you his sister's the best person he's ever known. Now again!"

He has Colin repeat his earth-moving exercise another five times, and I watch in silent intrigue at what the boy can do. I've never seen anyone with such remarkable power, nor such ability to control it. *Could I reach this level of restraint?*

When Colin's finished, Eogan instructs him to head off for a jog through the woods to loosen his stressed muscles. Colin looks reluctantly at me, as if unwilling to miss out on seeing whatever Eogan's got planned for me, but one glance from Eogan and he acquiesces with a nod.

As soon as he's disappeared through the trees, Eogan strides over and holds out his hand. "Let's see what you've got."

I give him a wary glare and try not to notice how nicely his eyes match the emerald coloring of his clothes.

"I'm not going to hurt you. I just have to know what we're working with. Aside from the obvious shortcoming of your personality."

He may be unfairly attractive, but he's also unfairly awful. "What I've got kills people," I say dryly. However, I don't duck from his hand when he reaches for me.

His warm fingers touch my neck, right where my heart-pulse is. It pounds a little harder. Does he notice? Because his eyes flash before narrowing, and I swear his face pales the slightest bit. Then he brings his other hand up and places it beneath my chin where the cut from the selling merchant is still healing. He tilts my face so my eyes look straight into his.

"Don't," he says when I go to shift my gaze. So I stand there staring uncomfortably into his green eyes while he studies mine. What he's looking for, I can't imagine. But having him this close to me makes my stomach fluttery, and I'm acutely aware that his skin smells like pine and honey and sunbeams.

"What sets it off?" he finally asks without releasing me.

I shrug.

His gaze stays clamped on mine. Intent. Drilling. "If I'm going to help you, you need to answer the question."

"I don't know. Does it matter?"

"Can you set it off right now?"

"Do you want to die?"

He chuckles and slides his hand from my neck all the way down to my left wrist. Giving me goose bumps beneath my leather sleeve.

"Can I set it off?" He slips his fingers farther down to touch my deformed hand. Before I can jerk it away, he squeezes hard.

Heat surges within me. My blood responds with its wretched

craving for destruction. I yank away. "Stop!" But he grabs my hand again before I can retreat farther than two steps back to the house. I turn to slap him, but his expression makes me pause.

It's careful.

Bordering on comforting.

And I've no idea what to do with it because it's foreign and pathetic and it makes me feel visible. Like an actual person. I detest him for it.

Colin comes running up all out of breath from his jog just as Eogan places his hand back on my neck.

Aside from his panting and foot tapping, Colin stays quiet, seemingly content to pump his chest muscles and make faces behind Eogan's back. I crack a smile.

Eogan leans in until his face is all I see and his lips nearly touch my ear. I try not to inhale.

"Tell me about the little redheaded girl," he whispers.

CHAPTER 8

M Y MUSCLES TENSE AS MY HEAD JERKS BACK and my skin crawls with the stimulating air. How he knows about the little girl I don't know, but how dare he use it to summon my curse. He's not Adora. He has no right to use guilt against me.

A single cloud morphs out of nothing directly above us, and before Colin or Eogan has time to move, a bolt of lightning strikes the ground ten feet away, followed by a deafening explosion of thunder. The friction in the air crackles and another bolt detonates, and then Eogan's fingers are pressed into my neck again, on my heart-pulse, and suddenly the cloud and static dissipate.

And Colin is using some choice words owner number eight once taught me. "Teeth of a pig, what the litches was that?"

I don't answer him. I'm too busy sending my good hand flat across Eogan's face as hard as I can before I turn and stalk away toward Adora's house. He could've killed someone. He could've killed us *all*, idiotic fool.

Eogan waits until I'm all the way to the other side of his cottage before calling after me. "Going to give up that easy?"

"You're insane!" I holler back and keep walking.

A sharp laugh pierces my irritation. "Maybe so, but why did the storm stop so abruptly?"

"How should I know?"

"Why didn't the storm keep building?"

I halt in my tracks. *He's right. It cut short. The friction was still forming, I could feel it.*

So why did it stall?

I wait a full minute before giving him the pleasure of seeing me return. When I do, I have a scowl plastered on my face just for him. "What's your point?"

"Does it always stop that quickly?"

I purse my lips. *No. It never ends that way.* "It doesn't stop until someone or some animal is dead."

"Always?"

I nod. Unnerved. Confused. "What's your point? How'd you do it?"

"You've never been able to stop it at all?"

I shake my head and wait for him to answer my question.

He strides over and puts his hand out. "May I?"

I look at Colin, who's sitting with his legs crossed on the ground. Even though seated, his whole body can't seem to stop bouncing. He tips his head as if to say it'll be okay.

"Fine."

How I didn't notice it before, I'm not sure. But this time

when Eogan's fingers touch me, I feel it immediately. That sense of calm. It's like a smooth warmth, trickling through my insides. Dimming the thirst for violence in my blood. I look into his eyes and ask the only question I need an answer for. "How?"

Eogan removes his hand and shrugs. "No idea. It works differently on each Uathúil. Usually acts as a block, and usually I don't have to be touching them." He smirks. "As you saw when Colin so zealously tried to kill me. But with you . . ." That curious look emerges again. "With you it displays as a calming influence. Interesting."

"Does that mean you can control me?"

"No. I can just dim the reaction. And only for a matter of seconds, I suspect. If you create a hailstorm on us, it'll be the last piece of beauty we ever see. Elementals are on a level all their own."

Great.

He winks at Colin. "So try and avoid angering the storm siren, okay?" Then to me he says, "You ready to try again?"

Colin hops up. "Have her fight me! We can practice against each other."

"She'd kill you, mate. In fact, why don't you go stand at the tree line for a few minutes."

"What? She can't kill me!" Colin scoffs. He shoots a smile my way and kisses one of his biceps. "Can't kill magnificence."

Eogan sighs. "She'd disintegrate you faster than you could blink, Colin. Go stand at the tree line."

He doesn't move. Just eyes me as if I'm some strange animal he needs to figure out. "Well, how long's it goin' to take? When *can* we practice together? We gotta get on it—you saw what kind of weapons Bron's got. And what they did to that mountain! What if they come back to finish us off tonight?"

"Bron's not coming tonight; that ship was a practice run. It could be weeks before they launch full-scale, and either way, *we're* going to take as long as you two need. So go. Stand. By. The tree line."

Colin throws his hands up. "Of all the—"

"Colin." Eogan's deep tone takes on a warning. "I'm not jesting."

The boy's face falls. He lets out an "Argh" and stomps off with his head thrown back dramatically. As if the Hidden Lands creator has conspired against him to ruin his life.

Eogan looks at me. "Ready?"

I nod, then flinch as he squeezes my misshapen hand.

"Feel that? Tap into it."

For the next four hours Eogan prods and provokes me, trying to find what triggers will set off my curse. Sometimes his tactics work, sometimes they don't. Sometimes I just haul off and swear at him for being such a complete oaf and then clomp off the field. At those moments I hate the training. I hate *him*. I even hate Colin for perking up from his moody tossing of pinecones at squirrels to ask Eogan if I can fight yet. Each time, Eogan cautions the boy to "give her space before she returns from her tantrum." Which is wise since they'd both most likely be roasted meat if they moved even an inch toward me.

But I do return from my "tantrums." Again and again. Because something about Eogan's touch makes me want more. It's neither hungering for my body in the perverse way men crave, nor punishing. It's different. It's discovering that, for a few seconds, he can calm the storm within me before it destroys my world again.

It's safety.

At the end of the afternoon, I know next to nothing about

my curse, and I'm no further into learning how to control it, but that crevice of hope in my chest has grown a little wider. Along with an unbearable aching beneath. I find myself scraping for an internal lid to cover the black chasm of my soul as Eogan watches me—studying my Elemental eyes as if he can decipher whatever puzzle defines the curse I am. While Colin is clearly suffering from a level of boredom that's killing him.

"Colin, go on and head into the house for dinner," Eogan says finally without moving his gaze from my face. "Nym will join you shortly."

"Why? What are you two gonna do?"

"She'll be along shortly. Go eat. And put on a shirt before you stumble the ladies," he adds with a hint of sarcasm.

"Too late for that. But we're gonna practice on each other tomorrow, right?"

Eogan sighs and turns. "I don't know. But in the meantime, believe me when I say that if either of you act out away from me, you'll have my foot in your backside. So don't even consider it." He says this as if it's to both of us, but we all know he's directing it at Colin. "Neither of you are to display in public, or Adora will eat you alive once I've finished."

I expect Colin to argue, but he checks himself, obviously having heard this lecture before, and instead sends me a lopsided grin. "I'll save you some grub. Just don't let Master Bolcrane do anything new with you while I'm gone." He gives me one final chest flex and struts off to the house.

Eogan rolls his eyes. "He's a good kid, but . . ." He shakes his head. "His thirst for excitement will come with a price."

I can't be sure if he's telling me this as a caution or simply making an observation.

"Here. C'mon." He leads me around to the front of his cottage and, once inside, waves me over to the worktable. Near the wolf. This time I'm careful not to get too close.

"This'll only take a minute." He pulls a pot and woodstick from one of the many shelves lining the room and sets them between us. "Pull up your sleeve."

I bristle.

The circle. I'd forgotten. Of course Adora would have him do it. She'd never stoop to dirtying her hands herself.

And of course he'd obey her like a lapdog.

Any decent feelings I developed toward Eogan completely dissolve. I yank the leather up to my shoulder while my gut knots and turns numb.

He bends over my arm and pins my wrist to the table. I hold perfectly still and refuse to let my cheeks blush with my shame. Maybe my glare will burn a hole through the floor and drop us both into it.

Eogan's grip tightens. I stiffen. Then the soothing from his fingers sets in.

He doesn't look at me as he slices a thin cut around the circumference of my right arm just below the elbow. I flinch and bite my tongue to keep from swearing at him. The blood wells up and dribbles onto the worktable, staining it dark with my humiliation.

"What are the other markings for?" he asks softly.

I don't answer.

"The ones on the other arm."

How he saw the other tattoos, I'm not sure, but at this moment, he's no better than an owner. "Just do your job and get this over with," I whisper.

He nods and says nothing further. Just dips the thin wood-stick into the black mugplant juice and rubs its tip inside the cut in my skin.

It sizzles and smokes, eating away my flesh, and I can't help it. I cry out.

His handsome face grows darker and his hands work quicker.

After smearing the juice in, he wipes the excess off and spreads a thin layer of curing herb on my arm before binding it with a clean cloth. Finished, he stands and waits while I tug down my sleeve to hide all fifteen circles.

Straightening my shoulders, I force down the pain-induced nausea and rise from the table. With my head held high, I walk shakily to the door.

"You can do this, you know."

I close my fingers around the handle. I don't want to hear whatever it is he has to say.

"The gift you have. You can learn to use it."

I shake my head. I want to plug my ears. *Stop talking to me,* I want to tell him. *Stop pretending you have any idea what I'm capable of. You have no right.* But none of those words come.

Because it's the first time anyone's ever called my curse a gift.

I shoot him a look of disgust. "You're an idiot," I say, and stroll out the door.

CHAPTER 9

THE FRESH, STICKY BLOOD SWIRLS AROUND THE old memorial tattoos in my skin. The ones already stained into my flesh in suffocating threads entwined around my bones.

I lean against the stone of my room's fireplace and push the knife blade farther into my arm, just above my elbow, until the scorching pain sucks the air from my lungs. Then I grit my teeth and draw a thicker breath, arcing the tool around to complete the feathery bluebird that should be flying outside the window rather than grafted into my skin. For a shame-filled moment, I wish it would free itself and carry me from what I am.

But it doesn't.

It just bleeds.

Leaning back, I grab the drops of black mugplant mixed with ash. Even with my jaw clenched, the agony of spreading the mixture into the fresh cut drags a slew of curse words from between my teeth. It hisses and melts, and my already-shaky arm begins shuddering so hard that I'm going to either vomit or pass out.

I grab one end of the strip of torn undergarment and secure it in my mouth and wrap the other end around the new marking as many times as the length will allow before tying it off. I wipe down the blade I stole last night on the rest of the wadded cloth and slip it beneath the loose floorboard. Finally I reach over to toss the material into the smoldering fire.

I'm sorry.

I can't even whisper the words aloud. Grief—guilt—whatever it is, it keeps my lips shut for the redheaded girl whose summers I've replaced with forever-winters.

As if in response, the orange flames lick up around the cloth and then ignite in hunger. The warmth hits my face and dissipates just as fast as the fabric. It leaves me shivering and my stomach lurching. And before I can swallow it down, I'm throwing up into the fireplace, heaving what's left of last night's dinner onto the coals.

When the gagging stops, my face is hot and the fire is out, and I'm clinging to the cold stone mantel, my cheek pressing against it while I swear at the floor to quit dancing. Eventually, when it does, I ease back and glance around for something to clean up the mess. But there's nothing—not a mop, not a cloth. Unless I use one of Adora's dresses.

I consider it for two seconds, imagining her expression. Which brings a wry smile to my face. *Hmm. Probably not.*

I've only been here three days, but I already know enough to hope Breck's in a gracious mood today.

I leave the mess and walk to the mirror. Just as I'm about to pull my shirt on, I catch the reflection of my bandaged left arm. Thin. Trembling. The tattooed memorials like an unforgiving trellis of scars, travelling up my shoulder and dipping down beneath the side of my breastcloth all the way to my stomach. The hideous focal point was made in my awkward six-year-old hand. An inked-in cross for the two parents who'd died before realizing the extent of the curse they'd birthed.

I look away and yank the tunic on, hating the fact that no matter how much penance I create, I can never blot out the shame.

Breck's knock on the door comes just as I've finished plaiting my hair into its thick braid with pebbles and shells. She doesn't bother to wait for a response—just walks in with tea and porridge as I bend down to tie the straps on my soft boots.

She coughs. Then she sniffs and crinkles her round face. "Gimpy hulls! What in Faelen's name did you do in 'ere? You try startin' a fire again? How many times I gotta tell you not to mess with stuff you ain't good at? An' what the kracken is that smell?" She drops the breakfast tray onto the table and hustles to the hearth, where she pauses. And sniffs again. This time her expression goes cautious. "Did you . . . vomit?"

I cringe apologetically. "Last night's dinner didn't sit well. I swear I'll grab a bucket and clean it later."

"You ever 'ear of usin' a squatty pot, or are you too much an idiot for common sense?"

"I'm sorry. I promise I'll clean it later," I murmur loud enough so she'll hear me. And so she'll know I'm leaving.

Three days in Adora's house and I've got the hang of the

passageways. I'm outside within four minutes and gulping in the purple-dawn air, hoping it'll soothe the ache inside my chest. Clouds are curling in from the ocean as fast as the sun is cresting the snowcapped Hythra peaks. I slow my stroll to watch the glow materialize on the path and try to ignore the scavenger birds circling the charred, still-smoking mountainside. When the sunbeams hit the trees nearest me, it sends their quivering dew droplets into the pond below. I pause. Narrow my gaze. The ripples have disturbed a school of fish the size of my arm. *No.*

She doesn't . . .

But yes. She does. The illegal, silver-finned piranhas immediately bob to the surface in a lather—excited by my shadow and the scent of the wounds on my arms.

I look up at the frog-lady's window and wonder what in litches her obsession with flesh-eating animals is. *Is she really that disturbed?* A chill flits across my skin, and I'm suddenly grateful for the growing humidity. I'm also abruptly aware that the frog-queen is standing right where I'm staring, watching me beneath today's apparent choice of flaming-orange hair matched by a carrot-colored suit.

Her gaze meets mine and doesn't waver.

What do you do up there all day? If Breck's assertions are true, Adora doesn't even sleep—she just sits in her study eating glass, smooching men, and orchestrating war plans for the king.

"Adora holds a central role in the war," the blind servant informed me last night. "Some say she already knows which way it'll go, and which way Faelen'll fall, and that's how she's influencing it. Though I don't know as I believe that. The ol' crazy's no mind reader, if you get what I mean." Breck snickered to herself. "Otherwise she'd've figured out long afore now that Eogan's pro'ly ne'er gonna give in to her cravings for 'im."

I didn't respond. I'd no desire to discuss what that woman craved.

I drop my gaze from Adora's window and shake Breck's words away as the ocean clouds slide overhead and block the sun's glimmer.

I'm almost to the cottage when the dirt underfoot begins shaking and the sound of stamping greets me. I look up for new smoke—none—and then for a second I think Colin's beat me out here, except the vibrating earth is followed by a whinny. And I'm hoping Colin doesn't whinny.

Rounding the corner, I stop full in my tracks at the sight of the two oversized, man-eating horses standing in the middle of the arena, kicking the ground and huffing. Their eyes go wide the instant they see me, and their muscles strain at their leads.

"Easy now," a voice commands, and the beasts' bodies ripple and relax. Although the glint in their eyes says they're liable to change their minds any minute.

Eogan emerges from around their flanks, his black hair damp like the horses, and his shirt clinging to his chest like they've all been out for a run. "You're early," he grunts.

"So are you."

He shifts both horses and presses them toward the trees, using lead ropes that are unique compared to the plow ropes most people use. Made of tight metal chain, these are clearly stronger and thicker while maintaining their flexibility. I suspect he made them out of necessity to control the giant beasts.

"It takes them a good hour of warming up before they're disciplined enough to ride," Eogan says.

"And you're riding to . . . ?"

"Nowhere. You and Colin are."

I swear one of the monsters turns to bare his teeth at me. *Right.* "Um, I'm not riding that thing."

Colin's loud whoop fills the air. "About time he brought the horses out." He jogs up and bumps my shoulder in his remarkably shirtless state. His flirtatious smile melts my mood. "Lookin' nice, Nym. Do your hair yerself this morning?"

"Maybe. Forget to dress yourself this morning?"

"Only cuz I know you like it." He snickers and nods to the horses—one of which Eogan has managed to chain to a tree. "Can't wait for the rush, yeah?"

"Oh yes. The rush of being eaten by insane horses."

"Nah, they'll only eat you if you let 'em. You just gotta show 'em who's in charge. Isn't that right, Eogan?"

He doesn't answer. He's too busy adjusting the reins on the larger of the two beasts while keeping his hand and head a safe distance from its jaws. It snaps at him anyway, but he responds with a firm cooing noise that makes the horse back down. I lift an eyebrow. *Does his gift for calming me and others like me have the same effect on animals?*

When Eogan turns to face us, it's to bring the horse into the arena's center. And to focus a pair of emerald eyes on me from behind jagged, clammy bangs. "Nym, start walking toward me. Slowly."

"Oh good-mother-of-Faelen."

Colin chuckles. "I think Nym needs to see a *real* champion show how it's done!"

"Colin, stay. Nym, you'll either walk or Colin will carry you, but you're going to get over here *now* before Haven decides she doesn't want to play anymore."

"I didn't realize she *was* playing," I murmur. But I walk—well, more march with attitude—to where Eogan is holding the animal clearly begging to tear the flesh from my face. When I'm close enough, I recognize her as the one who almost bit my hand in the barn two nights ago.

"Go around behind me." Eogan tips his chin toward the horse's side, which is an enormous wall of compact muscle and fur I can't actually see over the top of. I pin the inside of my cheek between my teeth and obey while the beast watches me and chomps her bit.

"Now go ahead and pat her shoulder to say hello."

I pat.

"Like you mean it."

I pat like I mean to say, *Hi, horse, I hate this as much as you do. If you bite me, I'll sink my teeth into you faster than you can swallow.*

"Okay, good. See her jaw relax? She's tolerating you."

"How nice of her."

"Now grab the mane and pull yourself up."

I bite my cheek harder and look at the wall of horse. Then I look at Eogan and notice a sly quiver at the edge of his mouth, as if he finds my discomfort amusing. I glare.

The half smile disappears. "Do it, or I'll let Colin come show you."

Fine. I push the gimpy fingers of my left hand into the mane, wrapping it around my wrist before gripping it with my right hand as well. Then heave. Hot pain bursts from the new memorial tattoo, and before I realize it, I've cried out and fallen back flat on my hindside.

Eogan's mouth twitches as he goes back to cooing in his stupid horse language. The animal's whole body trembles, and suddenly her one crazy eye is trained right on me.

"Haven's a beautiful girl. Just focus on her strength. Convince her to work for you, and you'll become her master."

"Right. And then she won't eat me?"

"Oh, she'll try. She'll just know you won't let her."

I snort.

Colin gives a loud, impatient grumble from somewhere I can't see.

"Oh, nip it!" I holler.

He laughs.

I try again to climb onto Haven, but this time the tightness of the animal's mane wrapped around my wrist rips the memorial cut on my arm open, and the pain is so excruciating I don't even get halfway. As I fall back, the horse's nostrils flare wide and she jerks toward me, bucking and baring her teeth, and the only thing that keeps me from becoming her breakfast is Eogan's ironclad hold.

"Whoa, girl." he soothes. "What in hulls has gotten into you?" He tilts his head and assesses her, then drops his gaze and gives me an odd, confused sweep. And stops at my arm. I follow his frown and discover spots of brown on my sleeve.

"Colin." Eogan's tone goes tight. "Take a five-lap run, mate."

With minimal complaint the boy is gone, and Eogan holds the horse at arm's length while he grabs my sleeve with his free hand. His grip tenses as he visually inspects the bloody wrapping. The horse groans and whines. Then her moans turn to hissing, and suddenly Eogan is releasing my arm and jerking Haven away.

I look at the ground. At the trees. At anything but the piercing gaze of my trainer.

Waiting for it . . .

When his words erupt, they're controlled fury, like muted thunder across a meadow. "What in bolcranes were you thinking? Carving into your skin—*harming* yourself like that? Do you have a death wish?"

"*Me?* You're having us ride a man-eating animal!"

"These horses are controllable in the right environment. But you . . . you have fresh blood oozing from a wound that won't seal over for another few hours. And you, what—thought it none of my business? Between disease and these horses . . ." He snaps the chain to bring the animal's wandering mouth back in line. "You *do* realize Haven's smelling your blood right now, yes?"

I clench my teeth and watch his gaze flash down my neck, my collarbone, my arm. He narrows his expression. "You think cutting marks in your body will make a difference? Like it's some noble form of penance for the people you've hurt? Because it's not. It's foolish, and it'll just get you killed quicker."

I practically choke at his words. *How does he know what the markings are for? And who does he think he is? He's known me for two days and thinks he's already figured me out? Curse him.* "Who are *you* to pretend you understand me? You know nothing!"

"I understand you feel bad for those people and that you should show it in the way the rest of us do—with a totem or a nice shrine maybe. But instead you . . . you . . ."

"I what? Leave a mark? Like *you* did on my other arm? How dare *you* lecture *me* on what I do to my body!" I tug my sleeve up to reveal the stained bandage that still covers the owner circle.

He freezes.

My throat shakes; my arm trembles. I shut my eyes and pretend I can ignore him. *Focus on the smell of rain in the air.* I can practically feel its friction in the clouds above us. Waiting to descend.

"Look at me, Nym."

He has to say it twice before I give in and glare ice picks at his face.

When I do, he steps closer and, still using one hand to control the horse, pushes his other hand through his hair. Licks his lips. "It was either me or Adora's slave hands, and you don't even want to know what those men were plan—" He stops so suddenly I blink. The look on his face says he should've stopped sooner.

Except it's too late because I already caught it. The glint of something foreign in his tone. Of mercy. Of pity.

Of protection.

And judging from his expression, he's just as shocked by it as I am. Abruptly, his reaction lodges in the raw, aching space inside of me that's never known anyone who'd want to protect me, let alone why, and the impact is spinning me the same way his gaze does.

It shatters the air into a million jagged pieces that hurt to inhale but leave me begging for more. A growl erupts from the storm overhead, and suddenly the clouds burst and raindrops are sliding their fingers down my face and heart, and it's like fire along my bones. Soothing. Stimulating. Swirling my insides with a confusion I didn't even know I was capable of.

I look down at my boots as the horse gives an agitated snort at the storm. *I will not cry, I will not cry, I refuse to cry.*

Eogan shifts and clears his throat. "I was *protecting* your body," he murmurs, just as Colin emerges from the tree line. "And not so you could carve it up."

"What's Nym yelling about? What'd I miss?"

I blink a hundred blinks, and Eogan gestures Colin to stay back and me to move toward Haven again. "Keep your arms as far from her face as possible," is all he says.

It takes four times before I finally succeed in hoisting myself onto the animal, and by the time I do, I can feel the blood weeping freely through my bandage and a headache rising behind my eyes. I ignore both, as Eogan tries to control Haven with his cooing.

He waits for me to get settled while Haven shivers and shakes her mane.

"Good. Very good," Eogan says to her. He hands me her reins but keeps the lead chain entwined around his fingers. He clicks his tongue and lets her out ten feet, and before I can focus my breath, Haven is trotting in circles around Eogan, tugging away, then lunging in, as if performing a complicated winter-solstice dance.

For the first five minutes I'm gripping her reins and water-soaked mane for dear life, praying I don't die an awkward death in front of Colin and Eogan. But then the horse's huge muscles sync with mine and trigger a sort of sixth sense between the two of us. With my hands in her hair and my wrists against her skin, I feel her pulse align with the *thump, thump, thump* of mine as the wind whips the rain against my face.

One second I'm inhaling her wet, musky scent and the next my chest explodes with a rush, and I'm laughing. Because it's the most insane, exquisite thing I've ever done. And unlike the bird I carved into my arm this morning, I can actually experience the taste of flight.

CHAPTER 10

E OGAN LETS HAVEN PLAY AT THIS WEAVING BACK and forth for an hour before her personality suddenly shifts to more adventurous and irritable. Then he reins her in and has me slide off while keeping her face in front of his.

"Pat her side and tell her—" Eogan doesn't need to finish because I'm already petting and thanking her for the ride of freedom mixed with terror. And for allowing me to leave with all my limbs still attached.

While I stand under the shelter of the pine trees, grinning like an idiot in my stench of blood and horse sweat, Eogan takes her to the barn and returns to repeat the exercise with Colin on the other beast.

By lunchtime, the rain has turned to a thick downpour, with the threat of lightning pricking the hair along my neck. Colin and I hurry to the house kitchen for cold quail and potato pasties. We're just finishing when the door flaps open and Adora struts in, looking like a woman on fire in her orange ensemble. She crosses her arms as the kitchen staff cowers.

"Bron's taken the rest of our ships," she snips, "except for those holding the northwest waterway. We've a matter of weeks left, so I trust you're training hard."

Well, hello to you too.

"Absolutely." Colin jumps up and offers her his seat.

She ignores it and stares at me.

I nod.

She narrows her eyes. "Work harder." Turning, she glides from the room.

I don't look at Colin as we head back to the field to meet Eogan, who's standing looking up at the sky. The horses gone. The clouds no longer raining.

Colin snickers and jabs me with his elbow. "Watch this." Quick as a snake, he leans low and shoves one hand out. Instantly a growl erupts beneath our feet and one of Colin's fissures snaps across the meadow floor to where Eogan is. Our trainer glances over and raises an eyebrow at Colin just as the rushing dirt halts a few feet in front of him. He smirks.

Colin shakes his head. "I don't know how he does it. Stops it like that." He looks at me. "But I can't wait 'til you try to put one over on 'im. When you're . . . you know, safe and don't kill 'im."

Eogan's now studying me as if trying to figure out which broken part to poke next. "I'm pretty sure I'll always want to kill him," I mutter as he strides over.

"Colin, go ahead and give me ten paces and wait."

As the boy walks off, Eogan steps behind me to place his hands on my shoulders. I go rigid. He skims his fingers across my neck to move aside my long braid, and I try not to remember the protective look on his face from earlier or notice his earthy scent or the way my rib cage squirms as he leans in, like I've got a trapped butterfly in there.

"Today we're going to try a different approach. See Colin there?"

I tilt my head at the bald boy currently walking in circles on his hands.

"Good. Now imagine that he's in danger."

Colin pauses to do a one-handed push-up, while I try to picture him being harmed. He lifts an eyebrow at me.

"Now save him."

"What?" I turn to Eogan, but pain crushes my left hand as he presses into it, summoning the storm. When I start to resist, Eogan says, "It's what we want. Allow it."

But I can't. Especially not with his breath on my neck.

The static diminishes.

"Again," he says.

"I don't know—"

He releases my one hand and grabs for the other, then pinches into my brand-new owner circle. "But this time, imagine he's in danger from an owner."

The wave hurls back in. This time tenfold, and I'm terrified because I know at once it will engage and there will be no stopping it.

"Now acknowledge it without allowing it to take over."

What? How? I concentrate on "acknowledging it," but I have no idea what he means. Except the next instant the already-darkened day is dimming even further as the clouds above us swirl and dip lower again. I try to imagine the danger to Colin is coming from the tree line—away from any of us—but the storm keeps assembling and my sense of panic rises as it drones through my blood.

"Good. You've got it. Now close your eyes and aim for the trees," Eogan says, as if he can read my thoughts.

I beg the curse to aim for the forest, but the panic presses against my chest, overwhelming in its control, and I know I've already lost. As if I needed proof, my chin jerks up, and a thin strand of lightning sizzles the ground between Colin and me.

"Aim for the trees, Nym." Eogan's tone is firm. Focused.

I can't do this. Oh hulls—I can't do this! I shut my eyes and strain my mind for the trees.

Crack! The ground shakes and the scent of burning erupts as thunder rips through the clearing, and suddenly Eogan's hand is at my neck and his voice is a cool breeze in my ear. "Perfect!"

I open my eyes to see a tall pine tree still standing with a black slice right down the middle.

Colin shouts and runs to embrace me in a giant, awkward hug while I stand, mouth ajar, staring. Then I'm shaking and laughing and embracing him back because somehow we're all alive instead of miniature pyres of charred flesh.

We go through the exercise another four times until nothing is left of the tree and the poor thing finally tips over with a loud, crumbling thud. Colin jogs over to hug me again, and even though I pull away this time, it feels good to share this victory.

Even Eogan smiles and socks Colin in the arm in what almost looks like affection. "Now, see that fir over there?" he says when Colin socks him back. He points to the shortest one sticking out away from the rest. "She's going to aim for that, and you're going to stop her. I want you to shift the ground beneath the tree and move the entire thing out of danger. You'll have five minutes to see who wins."

Colin grins and moves eight paces from me. He hunches down. Then he stretches out his arm and beckons me with the tips of his fingers. "C'mon, storm girl. Do what you do."

"Just like before," Eogan says from behind me. He squeezes my hand.

I plant the tree in my mind and close my eyes. Scared. Thrilled. In the recesses of my chest, I command the storm above to obey.

A snap followed by a crack rips through the air, and my ears and whole body shudder at the effect. I open my eyes expectantly, only to discover that the tree's still standing.

It's just moved four feet closer.

My eyes go wide. The ground behind it is burned to a crisp.

"Blood of a bolcrane!" Colin shouts. "Did you see how I did that?"

"Yes, we're stunned at your magnificence," Eogan says. "Four minutes."

I give in to the crushing weight over my fingers again and the exercise repeats itself. Colin wins again.

"Three minutes."

And again.

"Is there a reason you're not trying?" Eogan's voice asks at the two-minute mark.

I squint. "I am."

"Liar."

I swallow. "I don't know. Maybe it's that you're having me strike a tree? Or maybe it's that I've spent my whole life destroying, and I want to learn to defend. Instead I'm standing here murdering helpless plant life."

"I can only help you if I show you exactly what you're capable of controlling on a small scale. Because at some point, when your attitude takes over and your emotions get in a huff, you'll need to be able to feel the difference between attack and defense."

When my emotions get in a huff?

"One min—" He doesn't finish before the tree is split into a perfectly neat, burnt lump of wood.

CHAPTER 11

Spattered tracks in the ashen snow. I count them—one, ten, twenty-two tiny, bloody footprints spreading out behind me. Like squashed fairy angels someone played hopfrog with.

What am I doing out here? I cough in the thickening smoke and begin to cry, but this time when I call for Mum, I already know she won't come. Because I've caused something dreadful.

There's a strange sound on my right—a male voice, I think—and then Mum's and Dad's screams start in as the fire hurls the chateau's roofing to the ground. I feel my heart hurl down with it.

Except the fire doesn't just consume my heart, but my fingers and bones and body. I start to scream, begging to make it stop, to get back to my parents, but the heat is tearing me up and eating me alive. I drop to the snow and watch the blood ooze from my fingers. At some point I become aware that they are no longer my fingers curling into fists.

They are the hands of a monster.

And the blood covering them is that of my parents.

"Pst!"

A thick finger stabs my cheek.

"*Pssssst!* C'mon, get up, lazy head!"

"Go away," I snarl to Breck.

Somebody pokes my side, his voice deeper. "Maybe she's a heavy sleeper."

I shove my head farther beneath the covers. "Leave me alone."

"Nah, not Nym," Breck says. "She 'ardly sleeps at all. Dumb thing jumps at the squeak of a rat."

"I swear I will maim you, Breck. Go away."

Another poke. "Well, maybe we shoulda brought a rat, then."

"What the bolcrane do you want?" I pull the blanket off my face to find Breck's round cheeks inches from mine.

She straightens. "Ah, there she is. See. Told ya."

"Go dump yourself in Litchfell Forest," I mutter, but I go ahead and sit up so I can glare at her from a better position.

Colin is squatting beside me on the bed.

What the—? I yank the covers back up to my neck. "What in hulls, Colin? Get out of my room!"

He laughs. "You're funny when you sleep. You don't look so crabby."

"Get. Out."

He jumps off the bed and keeps laughing as Breck leans down. "Colin and me is sneakin' up to one o' the High Court's common houses, yeah? An' we wants you to come."

"Go without me."

"We're goin' to hear what's being said 'bout the war."

Considering he and I have practiced every day in the sun and rain for the past eight days since my arrival—and most of my late evenings have been spent in the library or watching Adora's wretched parties—hiking anywhere in the middle of the night sounds akin to death. "Go without me." I start to lie back down.

"Ah c'mon, Nym." Breck pouts. "Adora's only gone for tonight. We won't get another chance for weeks! And then you'll be sorry for not takin' us up when we offered."

She has a good point. Rumor has it Adora is rarely gone.

And Adora would never allow us to go.

"Fine." I reach for my clothes at the end of the bed.

"Now there's a good, dull-headed girl, yeah?" Breck's round cheeks puff into a grin. "Colin, get outta here so she can dress."

As soon as he's gone, I change under the covers, which proves ridiculously difficult—thanks to my achy, crippled fingers— as I try to keep the freezing bedroom air off my bare skin. I'm shivering by the time I'm done because even though I've started to thicken a bit from the frequent meals, it's more muscle than insulation.

Breck fetches me a gray, hooded cloak I didn't even know was in the armoire while I tug my boots on. Then she's hustling us both out the door.

By the time we're downstairs and out into the moonlight,

Colin is standing next to two saddled horses that nicker as we approach.

I stall midstep.

"Are you *insane*, Colin?" I grab Breck's arm and put myself between her and the animals' mouths. So far we've ridden the beasts four times in the week I've been here, but always when Eogan was holding their harnesses so they couldn't twist around and bite our heads off. And here Colin is thinking we'll just take them out for a romp.

"They're the plow horses, Nym." He tosses me the reins to the closest animal and goes to help Breck onto it.

The mare nuzzles my arm, showing me he's right. These are smaller and friendlier. Although the warm, damp nose against my fingers makes my throat tingle for a second with the recollection of the warhorse's teeth.

I swag my cloak and get ready to climb onto the saddle in front of Breck when Colin is suddenly behind me, his hands on my waist.

I spin around and shove my elbow against his throat.

"Hey, whoa! Just tryin' to help you up."

I drop my arm. Something about the too-playful way he says it freezes in my chest. Or maybe it's the close distance between us. I step back. *Has his smile always been so flirtatious?* Abruptly I'm hot and uncomfortable.

"Hurry up, you two!"

I clamber onto the mare and Breck hooks her arms around my waist.

"Ready?" I say. With a low click of my tongue, the two of us are off in an awkward, arrogant gallop onto the main road before Colin's even mounted.

When he finally catches up to us, he's laughing and hooting, and Breck joins in with a merriment that invites me in. As does the balmy breeze, which is full of promise for a free night in the High Court after days spent trying not to take the world out in a hailstorm or punch the lights out of Eogan. What would he think if he knew we were breaking the "never leave the estate" rule? We'd be in trouble for weeks.

Which somehow makes the night trek more satisfying. I can picture the disapproving look in his green eyes. The clenching of his mouth. The surprise at thinking he knows me so well only to discover he hasn't a clue. Poor overly serious man. He could do with a little letting loose one of these days.

Maybe tomorrow when I'm angry at him, I'll tell him so.

For now, I settle into the ride and inhale the enormous night sky edged with smoke from the shoreline and fires from our own squadrons camped throughout the valley. The sound of clanking and the smell of war travel with us until we hit the main highway with its tall hedges that block out everything but the ricochet of our horses' hooves on white rock.

The road climbs a quick two terrameters before the hedge disappears and the High Court spreads out ahead of us with its giant stone buildings and beautiful archways covering steep streets leading up to the white Castle. It is a sanctuary kept safe for centuries by the Hythra Mountains' crescent range that extends from the waters up by Cashlin and curves around the base of Faelen. As we enter, Colin veers off one of the outermost lanes toward a low stone portico next to a row of stalls. "Let's tie them over here."

With the animals secured and chomping sugar cubes, Colin takes Breck's hand and winds us past stone houses and wood hovels, all well lit and noisy. My eyes are bugging out of my head, trying to soak it all in. The villagers I've known can't afford to burn candles late, but here, near the High Court, even the poorest area is alive.

The sounds are the same though. Snuffling comes from one home. Crying from another.

A lady's high-pitched laughter.

A man cursing.

I pull my cloak tighter and hurry past. Whoever it is, his anger is getting the better of him.

A small cry rings out from within his oversized hovel, and I suddenly realize it's not a hovel at all but a favor house, painted in the telltale crimson, and the shouting is directed at one of the girls. My gut turns.

I cover my ears and keep my gaze straight in front of me. *Let it go.*

Colin gives me a curious look, as if to say, "You okay?" Triggering the abrupt premonition in me that this may not have been the brightest plan. I still have no idea how to control my curse. If anything, Eogan's work has made me hypersensitive to it. As has his dumb prying into my personal issues.

We turn a corner and I keep with my fast pace until I'm certain the swearing and whimpering in the house have faded. I remove my hands and shove them back into my pockets.

Colin's still watching me. "You afraid of people fighting?"

He can't honestly be asking that. Unless he's unaware of what we just passed, or worse, doesn't care. "I don't like hearing people get hurt," I mumble, then quicken my stride.

He softens his gaze and continues his survey of my face. "Do you want me to go back an' check it out for a sec? Maybe I can do somethin'." And his eyes are so sincere I know he means it.

Even if his doing so would end up a complete disaster for all of us, of that I have no doubt. An image of the redheaded girl fills my head.

"I don't think that'd be a safe idea right now," I whisper, even as my curse twitches and my stomach coils. I glance away to Breck, who's got her head inclined to us, listening.

"Well, maybe we can at least lighten your heart with a feast." Colin bumps my shoulder and flashes an instant smile. He waves his free hand as if to bow at me, announcing, "Here we are," as he stops in front of the common-house doors looming in the dark. Glimmering lights and the sounds of hilarity ease out from a crack at the base, along with the smell of liquid forgetfulness.

Colin puts his hand on the door but doesn't open it. "Don't draw any notice to yerselves. Doubt anyone on this side of Court would recognize us, but still." He yanks open the squeaky door and we're flooded with light and raucous laughter.

"Hey-o! Looksy what the dark's dragged in!" a loud voice erupts. "More friendlies!"

CHAPTER 12

THE WHOLE ROOM TURNS TO FACE US, INCLUDING a group of men seated around the middle table, on top of which stands a taller-than-average dwarf.

"C'mon, c'mon! O'er here! Don't be shy!" the dwarf shouts. "We're all nice folk, right, chaps?"

A cheer breaks out along with a call for more drinks, but it's all a little too boisterous, too forceful, as if to conceal the strain of fear I sense in the air.

I look at Colin. So much for discreet.

He grins, then plunges toward the group of men and their dwarf, all of whom I'd guess to be mine workers, judging from the soot coating their bodies.

Breck nudges me. "Colin just went off an' sat with 'em, didn't he? Fool-head."

I shrug and, pulling her sleeve my direction, work us around the room's edges to sit at a side counter, opposite the room from a table full of court officials in shiny, embroidered breeches and gold-buttoned coats.

Breck pulls her hood back and settles in, then produces a small purse of draghts she uses to place our order.

"You recognize anyone 'ere?" Breck asks in a low voice.

"No." I glance at the officials, one of whom catches my eye. Probably because aside from me, he's the only other person who also has his hood up. A young, thin-faced man, he tips his head at me beneath the black folds of his cloak and shows his strong jaw and perfectly straight, shiny teeth in a smile I'm sure has dazzled a dozen barmaids. One of those teeth appears to be silver. I empty my eyes of emotion and look away.

"Who's Colin talking with?" Breck says in my ear.

"Half the room and a tall dwarf."

She grunts. "Figures." She lifts her nose and sniffs. "Reeks like frightened mine workers and a traveller."

I stare at her. *She can smell them?*

I'm about to ask what else she can smell, but our drinks arrive and Colin saunters over to join us, ignoring Breck's disapproving expression. "They're mine workers out for a bit o' fun afore they head to the war front." He points to the noisy group with the dwarf still standing on the table. "And that smaller guy hails from the traveller camps."

I look at Breck. *Impressive.*

"See that kid near 'em?" Colin directs my attention to an exhausted-looking boy our age who can barely hold his head up. "He just got back from the front. Not too willing to talk about it though."

Judging from the five empty pint glasses tipped over in front of him, I doubt he's able to talk at all. The look on his tortured face says he'd likely cry anyway.

"One of his mates said they never saw any airships. It was the plagues that did 'em in," Colin says. "Ravaging the coastal colonies below the western cliffs. They're cut off from the rest of us so we've not 'eard much of it. But they said by the time King Odion's generals and Bron showed up to wipe those colonies out, there was 'ardly nothin' there to take. After that, the disease started takin' out part o' Bron's army too."

I shift in my seat, facing away from the soldier. "What kind of plagues?"

"Wouldn't describe 'em. Just said they turned men 'unearthly.' Musta been pretty bad though, seeing as half his troop got wiped out."

"Did he say where they came from?"

"See that dwarf?" Colin tips his chin to the guy who's now reclined on the table with his head cocked, listening to his friends. "Goes by the name of Allen. Says the word among the travellers is that the plagues are the work of Draewulf."

Breck coughs and nearly spits out her drink on us.

Colin and I both look at her.

"Dumb commoners will blame any superstition on Draewulf," she says, as if sensing our questioning glances.

Colin smirks at me with a confiding air. "Breck's scared of 'im. She even sings that 'Sea of Elisedd' ballad just to assure 'erself it ain't real."

"Am not!" Breck growls.

"Are too. Always 'ave been. Squirrelin' around like—" He shifts to a mimicking, high-pitched voice. "'I'm a squeamish girl who can't handle talk 'bout Draewulf.' Same as you been actin' about that Luminescent Princess Rasha. Afraid one of 'em's gonna *steal yer soul*."

Breck hauls off with an awkwardly aimed hit that glances off Colin's shoulder. It sends him tipping back off his chair, but he bounces back laughing. I look around to see if anyone's noticed, but most are busy with their mutton and porridge.

Except for the strong-jawed, silver-toothed official across the room.

He's eyeing Breck and me up and down, not even having the grace to glance at our faces this time. I shift closer to Colin. Coming here wasn't a good idea.

Our food arrives. Warm plates of white-worm stew and crusty bread. Colin and Breck order more mead to go with it. I stick with my tankard of water.

"None for you?"

"Drink and I don't suit each other," I tell Breck.

"I'm bettin' she gets a little too friendly." Colin bats his eyelashes and makes kissy lips.

I snicker just as a shout erupts from the middle of the room, saving me from having to tell him to go to hulls.

"I'm tellin' you, she's Draewulf's daughter," one of the men from the rowdy group says. "Isobel, they call her."

Breck's head is up in an instant. She snaps at Colin to quit his slurping.

"Yes, except the Drust ambassador is real, and Draewulf's not!" a blond-haired man yells from the table of court officials. He breaks into a cackle, and his friends join him. But they're the only ones laughing. Everyone else just glares.

"Some say she's a Mortisfaire. Can change your heart to stone," the dwarf pipes up from his perch on the table. He leans over to a man beside him and pokes him in the chest three times, each with more emphasis. "With. One. Touch."

I look at Colin and mouth, *Stone?*

He just shrugs.

"Maybe it's not her touch, maybe it's her looks," someone yells. "I hear she's somethin' to behold, if ya know what I mean!"

"She can touch me if she wants!"

A fresh wave of hilarity sweeps through the room.

I move uncomfortably on my stool. *Blasted men.*

"Well, we'll find out when she arrives next week, won'ts we?" says the dwarf. "And maybe our king'll get some answers from 'er. Like what 'er Draewulf father is up to."

"It's a load of posh!" the blond-haired official pipes up again.

"No, it's true. Tell the story of the Draewulf, Dwarf!"

"Yeah," one of the ladies near us says. "Tell 'im the story!"

"You want me to tell it? You *sure* you want me to tell it?" the dwarf asks, hopping on one foot and then the other.

The audience erupts with shouts and the pounding of their metal mugs on the tables until he gives in and shushes them into delighted anticipation. The little man licks his lips and sweeps his hands in front of him like a magician.

"'Twas a hundred years ago and still known as the bloodiest night in Faelen history. Bron'd been hounding the coast for weeks on the one side and Drust attacking from the other. Three kingdoms at war, and Faelen in the middle set to fall." He pauses for breath. "Our little island's High Court streets was smothered in a fog-cloaked mood tha' evening. The trees, bare from winter frost, rocked back and forth, back and forth."

The dwarf rocks back and forth like the trees, in hypnotic timing, luring his listeners into a trance. "They say the bark was peelin' down the trees' white trunks like the ghost fingers of a dead man."

He lifts his fingers above his head and curls them into tree-like claws. A collective shiver ripples through the crowd. Even the politicians stop drinking.

"Twenty bodies they found," he growls. "Men, women, young-sters. Draewulf had slain them one by one tha' night, in his hunger to wear human flesh. Shape-shiftin' into a man to draw 'em in, then returnin' to his real form for the kill."

"And what *is* his real form?" a woman near us dares to whisper.

My dream flashes through my mind—of me lying in the snow with bloody hands. It makes my neck tickle and my hands clench.

The dwarf leaps around to face the speaker and slams his little foot down on the table, causing half the room to gasp. "Not sure really. Altho' some claim he's a great boar."

He straightens for a second and cocks his head funny, scratch-ing his chin. "Or was it a bear?"

"He's a wolf, you dolt!" someone yells.

The dwarf laughs. "Just testin' you. Course he's a wolf. But when the captain o' the guard and the king's men caught up with 'im that evenin', he was dressed up like one o' the men he'd just killed. Stole his very essence, he did. That's how he does it—climbs inside a body and slowly absorbs his soul 'til there's nothin' left except his wolf self hidin' inside the person's skin. A perfect imita-tion of 'em. An' a hideous and ghostly way to die, so I've 'eard."

The dwarf's hands dance, making monstrous shadows on the common-house walls. My breath dances along with them as the story reaches the breaking point.

"An' the only reason he was caught? He *allowed* it. Cuz you can't tell he's taken over someone unless he wants you to. Twenty months he'd been at it—the great wizard Draewulf, king of Drust—makin' a three-way war with Bron and Faelen. Now he'd found a way into Faelen to get an audience with King Willem, to make a deal he knew he'd get offered."

I look around. Not even a drip of drink or an inhale. Even Breck looks spellbound.

"The old king demanded Draewulf return to Drust an' never enter Faelen again. But that wizard-king, Draewulf, was a smart one. Swore he'd be an ally against Bron an' save Faelen from fallin'. For a price."

I swallow and tug my cloak closer around my head. Somehow when the minstrels used to sing the story, it didn't sound quite so authentic. I want to crawl under the table and plug my ears. Instead I set my jaw. *Act natural.*

"The price was the Elemental children."

Suddenly the room isn't holding enough air. My eyes feel too blue, my hair not colored dark enough. My Elemental curse thumps beneath my skin, threatening to give me away. I peek around, certain someone must have just now recognized me. But every eye is on the dwarf. Even the black-cloaked official.

"The Hundred-Year-Ol' Deal with the Devil, they calls it. The treaty between Draewulf and our former king that cursed every Elemental to be murdered at birth. An' the older ones to die in 'protection camps.' And just like that, compassion fled our land with the monster's bloody *X* marking the edge of a treaty note. And now . . ."

I shiver, and Colin slides his hand over mine. He squeezes.

I pull away.

"Now the Sea of Elisedd, she's been churnin' noisy ever since." The dwarf winds down. "Cryin' for those Elemental boys whose voices 'ave gone to the graves of their fathers. An' Draewulf? Well, he went back home to Drust and took his army full force against Bron. Leavin' Faelen weak, but intact."

My shallow inhale sounds brassy in the room's quiet.

One breath.

Two breaths.

"Seventy years later, Draewulf lost to Bron, and Drust became a wasteland in which he disappeared. Altho' on stormy nights, some say they can still 'ear the monster walkin' Faelen's High Court streets lookin' to feed. And makin' sure no Elementals is there to resist 'im."

The blond-headed heckler stands with a raucous, grating laugh and claps his thin hands. "Bravo, Dwarf! Bravo! That fairy tale of yours nearly put us all to sleep. Except that the treaty was between two sane kings and it saved our nation from being torn in two! They were smart in taking sides against Bron and smart in seeing the Elementals as dangerous!"

"It's no fairy tale—it's the truth!" a woman yells. "An' the Elementals weren't dangerous. They was our only defense!"

"The Elementals would've destroyed Faelen! They were too arrogant and capricious with their powers, and they were growing too numerous. Sacrificing them to gain Drust as an ally was strategy."

I slouch lower in my seat.

"Draewulf's no ally! Never was. He got rid of the Elementals so we'd be powerless against him. And now he's *helpin'* Bron!"

"He's not helpin' Bron," someone says. "He's helpin' himself."

"That's ridiculous!" the official yells. "First he helps us, then he's against us? You peasants are superstitious!"

"Exactly," Breck mutters a bit too loud.

"An' what do you know of war?" the woman sneers. "You ever been in it? Cuz my husband has. Lost his arm, he did. And now he's back there gettin' hisself killed so the rest of us can sit here and argue about it."

I watch the agitated crowd, all vying to add their pieces to the story. In my early years of being a slave, I assumed the story was a folktale, with Draewulf made up by my first owner to torment me. I can still recall him saying, *And that's what'll happen to you one o' these days. He'll come atcha in the night and eat your brains out while I watch.*

It took me years to sleep more than an hour at a time after that.

A trickle of sweat runs down my back. I suddenly want to get out of here. And yet, I want to hear more. About Draewulf. About Bron. About this war I'm supposed to help win.

"Tell us about Bron," Colin shouts. I shoot him a grateful glance. "How close are they? And why do they want Faelen so bad?"

"They don't just want us!" the drunk boy-soldier responds. "They wants all five kingdoms of the Hidden Lands! Faelen's just the blockade keepin' them from those other kingdoms. But what do our allies do? They wait and watch while we get slaughtered!"

"That's what's losin' us the war," the bartender says.

"No, it's not!" someone fires back. "It's the fact that Bron's got industry that we 'aven't. They've got armor for their soldiers and crossbows that shoot faster and farther, an' they've got more of 'em. Rumor has it they even got these self-moving carriages that don't need horses! While we've spent the past hundred years twiddlin' our thumbs, the Bron kings were developing weapons we can't even replicate! An' now King Odion's got these flying ships dropping boiling explosives. The only reason we lasted this long is because he killed his smarter brother. If the twin had won the throne instead of Odion, we'd already be dead!"

"How do you know that?" another voice yells. "Odion seems plenty smart to me. Why do you think he's never even met with King Sedric for negotiatin'? It's because Odion's too busy makin' those war machines to actually fight face-to-face."

"It's more than Odion's weapons that's losin' us the war." The drunk soldier gets louder. "It's the plagues an' Draewulf, I tell ya!"

Breck rises and places her hands on her hips.

Ah kracken. I eye her empty drink mugs. *I should've cut her off.*

"Well, maybe you all should be workin' on inventions rather than standin' here scarin' yerselves with talk of imaginary wizards when we gots an enemy that just bombed us!"

The soldier's chair flips out behind him as he jerks up and stands to wave his hand at Breck and the officials. "Shut up. You've no idea what you're talkin' of." He sways back and forth. Someone reaches out to help steady him, but he shrugs him off and wags a finger at the room. "You arrogant fools. The plagues aren't natural. They're a curse. Sent by Draewulf hisself. And there's a Dark Army of unnatural things followin' him. *Monstrous* things."

The blond from the officials' table guffaws. "Go home, drunk. No wonder they sent you back from the war. Can't even hold your liquid!"

I put one hand on Breck's elbow and prod Colin's shirt collar with the other. "C'mon, let's get out of here."

The tipsy soldier's expression dissolves into hatred. He lifts that finger he keeps pointing and thrusts it at the official and his companions. "You're only a doubter because you send the rest of us to do your dirty work. But when Draewulf's monsters come for *your* throat?" He moves his finger to his neck and with a slow gesture makes as if he's slicing it open.

I tug on Breck's and Colin's frozen forms, pressing them toward the door. "We have to leave *now*," I whisper with a mouth that tastes like fear and smoke and the bone dust they'll all become if my curse gets free. I catch the hooded official's gaze on me. He smirks as his companions rise, as if challenging me to stay for the entertainment about to erupt.

My stomach performs a somersault as his blond friend tosses a slur at the soldier.

"Oh hulls, not again," the bartender says.

CHAPTER 13

FIIIIIIGHT!" SHOUTS THE DWARF, AND I'M instantly shoving my friends in the direction of the door as the room explodes. Someone throws a pint glass at the dwarf, and it barely misses Colin's head as it sails for its target.

The dwarf catches the glass and throws it back so fast, the female recipient crashes into Breck, and the two of them end up taking us down with her. The lady sits up dazed while I scramble away amid a forest of legs all suddenly in motion, only to realize Breck's foot is trapped beneath the woman's wide girth.

I clamber back to her to push, then tug, while Colin regains his feet and just stands there glancing back and forth between us and everyone else in the chaotic place. His body bounces, caught up in the excitement of the brawl.

"Help us!" I snap at him.

He focuses on me and blinks with eyes as wide as hen's eggs, then bends over to assist. We extricate Breck just as the lady grunts and grows lucid. After a head shake and knuckle crack, the woman grabs the nearest man to use for hoisting herself up and tramples him as she charges back into the mix.

Colin ducks, then clamps his hands onto Breck's shoulders and drags her between the sweaty bodies and flying stools as I etch a clear path in front of them. I think Colin's yelling, but it's hard to tell above the clamor of breaking wood and bones.

Something smashes into my back and suddenly I'm pitching forward. My eyes blur as my knees slam onto the floor. But then I'm up and my aching body is crawling for the door as terror wraps its talons around my veins. If I don't get out soon, none of us will. I can feel the curse itching, like a crossbow trigger begging to be pulled. All it needs is the right fist hitting at the wrong moment.

Just as I reach the entrance, I look up to discover Colin and Breck have made it. He turns to search for me when an enormous object flails through the air and hits him flat across the chest. The impact sends him through the doorway and skidding along the outside stones for a good three yards.

I lunge the last few feet between the legs of two men. And then I'm outside and feebly stumbling to where Colin's sprawled out with what looks like a body on top of him. *Please be breathing, please be breathing.* I start to tug the thing off of him with my good hand when I realize it's wiggling and yelling things. I pull back and squint at it.

The dwarf?

The little man shakes free, stands, and dusts himself off over Colin's gaping mouth that's clearly seeking the air knocked from him.

The dwarf glares at me, straightens his shirt, then turns to the broken door and cups his hands around his mouth. "Hey, boys! The fight's out 'ere!"

Not that he needed to announce it. When I turn around they're already spilling out—with the common-house owner leading the charge. I don't see Breck, so I reach for Colin's hand and yank him to his feet. But as soon as he's standing, someone grabs my arm and flips me around.

My fist is in the guy's stomach before I even recognize his face. He folds over, then lifts his head, eyes flashing, and slowly rises to his full height. It's the blond-haired wretch of an official.

Colin shoves me so hard, the next thing I know I'm picking myself up and he's ten feet away, bent low to the ground. And the earth is starting to rumble.

"Colin, no!"

The blond man lunges for Colin, and it's as if the blur of bodies surrounding them speeds up, blocking my view. The stone street beneath us is groaning harder now, and as angry as I am that Colin's using his Terrene abilities, I'm also holding on to those growing vibrations as consolation that he's still okay.

Suddenly the crowd's yells change tune, from riotous to confused. The fighting slows. Or maybe it's just my imagination, as the whole common house and nearby buildings begin swaying.

With a tearing sound the ground shreds in a perfect circle around the pile of men still encompassing Colin. Like crumbling puzzle pieces the stones break apart in a thin swirl and sink down a half foot.

Shouts break out, scared rather than angry now, triggering a fresh tide of sweat sweeping over my skin. The cries sound similar to ones I've caused before. *Except unlike me, Colin is in control.*

Right?

The men scatter like ants, scrambling to hop over the shallow crater Colin's created. Although, from their bewildered expressions, most haven't figured out what, or who, the source of the disturbance is yet. But the blond official seems to have. As the crowd clears, I see him rise from his fallen position, and steadying his legs, he stalks back over to Colin.

I scream Colin's name, but the crowd's too noisy.

The official draws a knife from the sheath at his waist.

Blast you, Colin.

The thunder surges in so quick, my hood and hair whip back in a frenzy as a fracture tears through the sky. Loud. Immediate. The blond official glances up at the same time as Colin, and before the man can recover, Colin's rolled out of the way.

I shut my eyes—sick with what's to come as the energy snaps and sings along my nerves, charging the air with static. *No,* I beg it. *Please don't do this.*

I force my thoughts to focus, to imagine Eogan's fingers on my neck. Soothing my pulse. My fear. My anger. His breath a lazy breeze whispering words on my skin, telling me to aim for the trees. Except there aren't any trees, just hovels, and pointy towers, and staggered streets leading up to the white Castle, and stone.

Stone.

I aim for the wider stone street in between a host of the buildings.

Focus. On the stone.

On Eogan's voice.

On pine and honey and emerald-green eyes that slow my heartbeat.

The static crackles.

Focus on his words.

The friction dissolves as quick as it tensed, and my whole body lags.

And it's over.

I open my eyes to see raindrops beginning to fall from the unnatural storm clouds, subduing the mood of the disarrayed crowd. Prompting some into laughter even. The blond official drops the knife as Colin's foot finds his gut.

There's no lightning strike.

No thunder.

No deaths.

Colin rushes over and takes my hand. He pulls me as the shower turns heavy. "C'mon, Breck's waiting for us!" But I'm still looking around in thrilled wonder at what I've just done. *How was that possible?* I want to yank away from him and run and shout and twirl like a child in the thickening downpour.

I think better of it, however, when I notice the silver-toothed official with the black cloak standing on the porch of the common house. His hood is pulled back, probably from the scuffle, and his thin, handsome face is looking at me. All around, the people who'd just been fighting are now prancing in mud puddles or nursing broken bones. But he just stares. Curling his lips into a snarl.

As if he knows what I just did.

I shake off the feeling and follow Colin around the corner beneath an archway. And almost trip over Breck hiding in the shadows. She's got a bit of shirt in her fist from whomever she bested, and in my euphoria, I start to hug her and laugh. And then I can't stop even when I'm out of breath, and neither can Breck or Colin until we finally reach the horses.

The ride home is a flurry, partially due to the fact that we're galloping the entire way with the storm pressing behind us. And partially because while I may have caused the storm, I also controlled it.

My heart lunges within my chest, like a bluebird trapped behind a bone cage that's just discovered the hope of actual freedom.

And like those few times I've experienced it around Eogan . . . I want more.

Is this what I can do to turn the tide of the war?

Can I end the fighting? Even better—turn it into laughter? Perhaps both sides need to be reminded that they're at the same mercy as the rest of the world. At the mercy of elements that Colin and I control.

As we near Adora's estate, the rain slacks off, and I swear I can still hear Eogan's calming tone in my head, telling me to focus. Everything within me is bursting to tell him how incredible I did, but the knowledge that he'd feed my body to Adora's lethal fish will keep my lips sealed like a tomb.

At the house I climb down from my mare and hold the reins while waiting for Colin to help Breck. But for whatever reason Colin's suddenly next to me, and his hands reach for my waist.

Breck's still laughing at a level sure to wake the ghouls. "Did you 'ear that one man squeal? That official sounded so angry!"

But Colin's not listening to her. My breathing stalls. His head moves in. *What's he doing?*

"I think I should get Breck inside," I say, but the words are absorbed in Colin's cloak as he wraps his arms around my neck.

He chuckles. "You were amazing."

I try to jerk back, but his hands are strong as he leans in to kiss me. My insides reel and collide with my backbone, and I do what I've always done with men who get too near.

I clout him across the jaw. Hard.

Then turn and run.

CHAPTER 14

W HAT THE BOLCRANE WERE YOU *THINKING?*"
Eogan roars. His hair is standing straight up where
his hand plowed through it, making him look like
a rooster.

I smother a laugh as he stops in front of Colin and glares.
"Are you insane, mate?" He points at Colin's chest. "*You* I guess I
should expect it from. But her? She's not even close to ready. She
could've killed someone!"

I can't tell if Colin's silence is due to wisdom or the fact
that his bottom lip is the size of a plum. My face goes warm
at the memory of what, admittedly, might have been a slight
overreaction on my part last night, and the kissing event that
initiated it.

"And here you . . . you . . ." Eogan looks close to a connip-
tion attack. "You take her out and expose her like that? And then
you display your Terrene abilities? *In the High Court?* It doesn't

just matter that people *saw you*, Colin, but do you know how it would've ended if *she* had a flare-up? You would've been dead. *Everyone would've been dead.* Which is why you are *never allowed to leave* the estate without asking me."

He turns and stomps off across the grassy area. Colin smirks at me with his giant, fat lip while keeping his eyes on Eogan.

"And don't you dare smile about it," Eogan hollers.

Colin gives a loud, innocent cough that fools no one and whispers, "Did *you* tell 'im?"

"Nope."

"Obviously he doesn't know 'bout yer flare-up."

"And I plan to keep it that way," I say as Eogan flips around and comes striding back to stand in front of me. *My turn.* He glares at me up and down. "What about you? Did anyone recognize you?"

"I already said no one—"

"I'm not asking you, Colin."

I shake my head. "No one knew who we were, and no one followed us home."

Eogan tightens his jaw and runs a hand across the back of his neck. "Probably too scared of genius boy over here," he finally mutters. "Did anyone notice you? Was there any out-of-the-ordinary attention?"

An image of the shiny-toothed man in the black cloak sweeps through my thoughts. The expression on his face just before Colin pulled me from the scene.

"No," I say.

I flinch because my hesitation was too long. Eogan's eyes become slits, accusing me of lying, but he doesn't press it. Just asks irritably, "And are you hurt?"

"Fine."

"Are you certain?" His eyes won't release mine. Still with the grumpy, searching attitude.

"She was fine," Colin interjects. "I made sure. I swear I wouldn't 'ave let anything get outta hand. I knew she could 'andle it. And if she couldn't, then I would've put a full stop to it and gotten her outta there sooner."

Eogan's gaze blackens to the onyx color of his skin, and it's more frightening than any of his yelling. He turns to Colin. "Okay, *you* do not decide what she can or can't handle. Because what if she *had* gone off, mate? What if she couldn't control it? Not only did you risk the very lives of the Faelen people whom you're so anxious to save, you risked hers as—"

"She can't be killed by her own power."

"Maybe not! But do you think she could live with herself if she'd taken out that whole common house? Could you live with *yourself*? It would destroy her."

Colin's wriggling under Eogan's anger like I've never seen him. He glances at me and attempts a smile. Bumps my arm. "But she's fine. She was good. Right, Nym?"

I nod halfheartedly. I'm still stuck on the whole "I can't be killed by my own power" comment.

"This time maybe! But—"

"Wait. Why can't I?" I interrupt.

Eogan's forehead creases. "*What?*"

I look back and forth between them. "Why can't I kill myself with my power?"

"Because you'd pass out," Eogan says distractedly.

"I don't understand."

He sighs and shoves his hand through his hair again. "Look—have you ever fainted in the middle of an episode?"

I nod.

"So that's your internal mechanism. All Uathúils have one. But"—he leans over and directs an eyeful of daggers at me—"that's not really the point, is it?"

He straightens and looks at both of us. And waits for an answer.

"Right." I nod very seriously. "That's not the point."

I'm tempted to add that no matter what the point is, he looks like an old man when he gets mad and lectures. Like he should be some very important general telling some very important army what to do instead of two people who are supposed to save the entire blasted free world.

"Good. Because from now on, you're training three extra hours a day."

"*What?*" Colin and I erupt at the same time.

"You'll go in late for dinner, and you'll come back out when you're done. You'll work twice as hard. Because if you have the extra energy to get into trouble, then obviously you've got more energy to give me." Eogan crosses his arms. "And when we're done each day? I'll know exactly where you are and who you're with. Am I making myself clear?"

"What about Adora's parties?" Colin asks.

"Oh, you'll attend those. And you'll stay the entire way through."

"Are you jesting?" I blurt out. "Have you *been* to those parties? They're horrid! One week of haunting them every other night, and I'm ready to burn my eyes out."

"Pardon me, but those are the people you're trying to save! And most of them are involved in every detail of every plan of this war. So if *either* of you had half a brain in your skulls, you'd be haunting every member and *using your ears* to listen! Why else do you think I require you to be there? For entertainment?"

"I thought it was Adora's idea . . ." Colin's mouth closes as we both stare at Eogan.

It's his fault we attend those things. I shake my head.

"I requested Adora to require it. Because if you two actually paid attention instead of moping around like bolcrane babies, you'd pick up more information in one night than the highest generals of Faelen are privy to."

My whole body goes still. *Like that traitor in the back hall on the first night.*

"Honestly," Eogan mutters, "I doubt it matters *which* side wins the war, seeing as it's all hulls in the end anyway. But if you *want* to help Faelen, you'll need more than just your Uathúil abilities. You'll need to know who holds what positions on the council, how decisions are made, and whom you can trust. And more important, whom you *cannot* trust. Right now you have access without anyone noticing you, so for kracken's sake take advantage of it." Our trainer pauses and looks up at the sun, which is halfway to noon already. "Now, can we get on with today's knife-throwing lesson?"

I lift my brow. "Knife throwing?"

"As I said, you need skills, not just abilities. But first, why don't you both give me three laps?"

Colin raises his hand to salute Eogan, but before he struts off, our trainer stops him with a hand to the chest. "By the way, need I even ask where you got the fat lip?"

Colin's freckled skin floods pink from the top of his shaved head all the way to his bare stomach. He keeps his gaze clear of me while mumbling something about earning it in last night's fight, then takes off to the meadow outskirts. I start to follow just as Eogan turns and catches my sheepish expression. I scramble to wipe it clean, but not soon enough.

That unfair, annoying smile of his glimmers to the surface.

My own skin flushes, and cursing it, I clamp my mouth shut and take off after Colin before the butterflies in my stomach start getting edgy.

The routine Eogan inflicts on us for the rest of the afternoon is a cycle of twenty-minute workouts encompassing physical strength training, bow shooting, ability control—which his calming knack is proving helpful for—and knife throwing. To his credit, it appears he fashioned our blades himself. Never mind that mine are smaller than Colin's and we have to give them back when we finish. But by the time the dinner bell rings, my good hand is aching and my muscles and emotions are screaming from the strain of controlling my attitude and its effect on the weather. Especially since, upon returning home early, Adora gave explicit instructions that her last-minute party needed clear skies tonight. And nothing on Eogan's face hints he's about to release us.

"He's hopin' to starve me to death, I swear," Colin grumbles, sending an enormous dirt clod hurling toward a rock.

"What was that, Colin? You regret last night's decision to leave the estate?" Eogan yells across the field.

I take the rock out with a single lightning bolt before losing control and dumping a flood of water on the three of us.

"Oops," I say in response to their glares.

Eogan sighs and asks me to clear the skies.

I'm almost finished after a half hour of him telling me to steady my breathing and center the storm inside of me in order to calm the one above. I want to tell him that it's harder than it looks when you've got an infuriating man touching your skin who ignites your senses in their own little messed-up storm.

The clouds have finally thinned enough when Eogan's hand drops from my neck, and I feel him take a giant step back. Turning to see what I've done wrong now, I spot Adora across the meadow, watching the two of us. Her mouth is pressed into a tight, not-happy line. *Ah litches.*

She beckons Eogan with those long, beautiful arms that are stark white against a gown of purple gossamer and feathers. Lots of feathers. Layered in exquisite twirls and spirals with five giant plumes coming up off the back. They rise and frame her head and purple hair like a male peacock in hunting season.

Colin lets loose a low whistle. "You gotta admit she's a sight for us men to admire." He strolls up beside me.

I frown and consider telling him to keep his drool to himself, but instead I curl my deformed hand into a fist and cause the sky above us to growl.

He snickers. "Ooh, jealous. I like it."

"Don't flatter yourself."

"Too bad 'er personality is as shallow as 'er looks." He turns to me with that sudden sincerity. "Unlike you, Nym. You got the good heart *and* nice looks."

I bite down my bitter laugh that says I don't know how to reply and instead watch Eogan and the frog-queen-turned-male-peacock exchange words back and forth. She's grinning and twittering her hands to and from her mouth, as if she's blowing him kisses while at the same time deadly serious about whatever she's saying. Her eyes flash to me once, but after a quick sweep over my appearance, they're back to her heart's one pant-worthy desire.

When Eogan strides back to us, the peacock-frog-queen stands a moment longer, watching him with raw, unabashed hunger before turning a smug gaze onto Colin and me. She flips her fluffy gown and struts off to the house. Her tail feathers waggle behind her.

Eogan crosses his arms over his chest, his expression pinched. "You two are to go inside now and change for the party. Clothes will be set out for you. Breck will see to your hair, Nym."

My hand flies up to my messy braid. I try not to blush.

If Eogan notices, he doesn't care. Just says in a distasteful tone, "Apparently His Majesty will be in attendance tonight, and Adora plans to present you both to him as members of her extended family. With absolutely no mention of your Uathúil abilities."

Colin breaks into a grin, and from the corner of my eye I see his stomach muscles flex. "So the ol' girl wants to show us off."

"Yes." Eogan chews on the word like he's considering the ramifications. "You've seen how these parties go. Adora expects you to be near her when the king enters, and you will wait for an introduction. You're going to need to smile and bow until he nods. After that, go ahead and go straight to the banquet room where you'll eat together seated out of the way. If anyone talks to you, simply ask questions to get them chatting about themselves. That's all they'll want anyway, and it'll keep you from getting into trouble. Hopefully." He eyes Colin with a begrudging smirk. "Any showing off as a Terrene, and I will personally put your head on a pike and haul the rest of you to Litchfell Forest. Understood?"

"Will Princess Rasha be there?" I ask cautiously.

"No, just—" He stops and frowns. "Why would that matter?"

I shrug. "Breck said she can see a person's soul. I figure if you want us to keep a low profile, being around her might not be the wisest idea."

His expression says *Nice try*. "She's touring Faelen at the moment. But even if she were here, she'd know what you are and wouldn't care. And as far as your soul—her abilities don't work quite like that. Now are you both clear on what you're to do? Good. Then go on and get out of here. And for crane's sake don't make me regret this."

An audience with the king? I head off to the house with Colin following. *What if I have to talk? Worse—what if I have to dance with anyone? Oh hulls, I've never even seen the king, and I'm supposed to act proper around him?* I consider tossing myself in Adora's piranha pond as we pass by.

CHAPTER 15

BRECK'S CLEARLY NERVOUS FOR ME ABOUT THE party, too, because she does my curls in four different styles before settling on a thick pile of ringlets swished high on my head. How she can tell the difference is beyond me, but when she's finished, it's stately enough. Even if it's so heavy it makes my neck ache. I shift beneath my own scrutiny in the mirror as the fake me with brown hair pretends to curtsy and do the tinkly laugh all the ladies do.

The laugh turns caustic.

It's not me. It never will be. All the fancy. All the overindulgence of these parties in the face of Faelen's people going hungry. All the war plans being talked over while real soldiers are out there getting slaughtered.

"I can't do this. They're going to know I'm a fraud."

"Everyone's a fraud, you idiot. You'll be same as the rest of 'em. You just put one foot in front of the other and 'opefully not in yer mouth. Now 'urry up cuz I'm missin' my dinner."

But when Breck pulls out the dress I'm to wear, I know I won't be the same as the rest of them. Not even close. It's soft and filmy with odd-angled layers sweeping one beneath the other like the morning ocean tides. And blue. Like my eyes. *What was Adora thinking putting me in this?* Breck helps slide it on and pins it so tight I can hardly breathe. It pushes my chest up so it's near hanging out and barely cuts in high enough along the collar to hide the tattoos swirling round my shoulders. "I'm going to suffocate," I gasp.

Breck just yanks the buttons tighter and tells me to "stop talkin'." She fastens up the sleeves like she's tying me into a cloth coffin. But surprisingly, when she's done, the soft material melds into my skin and I don't rip the thing when I bend down to slip on its matching blue slippers. I turn to the mirror and the full skirt swishes around me, light and foamy, like the sound of the ocean. My breath catches because I look almost beautiful, but it's followed by a groan of guilt because I shouldn't look anything other than a slave.

Then I see my eyes. Standing out like sea sirens—clear, salty, ice blue. I don't even look good enough to be a slave. I look like a curse.

"You 'ave fun tonight and tell my brother to keep his 'ands off you."

"Breck, I can't wear this," I whisper. My eyes are too much. Too blue. They'll know. I don't care that Adora picked this out. Eogan will be furious.

But she's already left, shutting the door behind her.

I'm tempted to lock myself in the room, but Adora would be up in flames.

I tug a swag of bangs in front of my eyes. *A little better.*

But not much.

Before ducking out, I pull my knife from its hiding spot beneath the floorboards and, with a slash to the inside lining of the sea-foam dress, take a thin strip of its material and tie the blade to the outside of my thigh. Just in case.

The vedic harpies are singing so loud when I reach Adora's ballroom side door that I almost miss Colin's whistle behind me. "Hello, sea nymph." His eyes shimmer, as if assessing me. He brushes my bangs from my face.

I shove them right back, and then the trumpets are blasting and the king's being announced, and I'm simultaneously stressed to go in and grateful because I can't have Colin looking at me the way he is. It makes my stomach hurt. He takes my arm and pushes me through the door, and suddenly I'm terrified and wishing I had a squatty pot to throw up in.

The room is crowded. Beyond crowded. The place is unbearable. Everyone is squishing together like sea walruses, all facing the same direction in expectation that the king might glance his or her way. I try to strain a peek over their heads, but most of the men are taller and keep blocking us as Colin shoves me through, telling me to aim for the front.

I turn to argue, but then the music stops and we're standing near the entry, smack across from Adora in her peacock plumes. She's fawning in front of a young man with sandy-brown hair and broad shoulders whom I can only presume is the king based upon the facts that his attire is very kingish and he's not old enough to have accumulated the layers of arrogance the rest of his entourage has.

I tuck my misshapen hand into a fist and slide it among my dress folds. Colin yanks me down on my knees before Adora drags her eyes our direction. Her jovial gaze turns to hoarfrost when she sees me, but before I can wonder what error I've made, she's plastered on a smile and extended a long hand indicating us to the king.

My mouth falls open. He's not just young—he's *very* young. Maybe the age of Colin, maybe a year older, with a brave face and kind eyes that should be laughing. Except he looks too tired, like he's got the weight of the three kingdoms resting in his hands. Which, I suppose, he does. His crown and velvet red clothes fit his stately frame exactly as people would want for their king, but there's a shocking lack of glitter and jewels. Compared to him, Adora and half the guests look downright garish in their indulgence. I find myself approving of this boy-king.

He beckons us to rise as Adora says, "Your Highness, I don't believe you've officially met my nephew, Colin. And allow me to introduce my niece, Nymia. Twice removed."

Right. Because we look so much alike.

"The poor things were orphaned by the war with Bron," Adora's saying in a bleating voice. "So of course, what could I do but offer them my home?"

I expect Colin to snicker at this as we stand, but he's trembling just as hard as me.

"Your Ladyship is too kind, I'm sure," the young king says with a bit more interest. His brown eyes light on mine and I catch the measure of scrutiny as his gaze drifts down my face. I smile, and he responds with one of his own before I notice my knees seem to have melted to mush. I'm trying to get them to work when a handsome man in black, with his cape pulled back, steps next to the king. I gasp.

It's the man from the common house.

Firm jaw. Silver tooth. He's wearing the same look as last night as he stares at me from beside the king. I dip my head. Maybe the crowd will swallow me into their gluttonous stomachs.

"Ah, Lord Protectorate Myles!" Adora's voice rings out. Too loud. Too cheerful. "I was just introducing my impoverished extended family to your cousin."

Cousin?

The young man in black nods, his eyes never leaving my face. "Charmed, I'm sure."

I curtsy as best I know how before Adora waves Colin and me off. "But not too far, lovelies."

I retreat into the crowd, pulling Colin with me, as dinner's announced and the music soars. Weaving through the maze of guests, I lead Colin to the banquet room still feeling the man in black's gaze haunting me.

"Did you recognize him?" I ask Colin when we stop in front of the enormous spread of fruit and pasties and cakes and disgusting amount of meats on Adora's dinner tables. Bodies squeeze around us like jelly, already shoveling food onto their plates.

Colin follows suit. "Recognize who?"

"The king's cousin. Lord Protectorate Myles."

"Sure, I've seen him afore. Why?"

"He was at the common house up by the Castle last night. He saw us."

"The common house? Doubt it."

"He was there, Colin. I swear."

He shoots me a dubious look. "There's no way Lord Myles was at that place. But even if 'e was, 'e wouldn't recognize us now. Look at us." Colin sets his plate on top of mine for me to balance so he can slide a cup from a maid's tray. He slips his hand around

127

her waist and winks at her. She giggles and comments on his slightly swollen lip. I bite my cheek to keep from telling her how he got that slightly swollen lip.

"A girlfriend of yours?" I ask irritably once he's done flirting.

"Nah. Just reminds me of one of the girls from back home. Just as nice too."

"I bet," I mutter, leading us toward a bench against the wall from which I can watch most of the room—especially the guest-of-honor table, which I expect the king will soon be filling. I hand Colin back his plate and immediately feel guilty for being crabby with him. It's not his fault the king's cousin was at the common house, or that I nearly annihilated the man's blond friend. And if I had anyone around to connect me with home, I'd be sidling up to him too—just for the moment of warmth.

My throat tightens. "Tell me about your home."

"Not much to tell really. Except that Tulla's beautiful this time o' year. Warmer and not so many *storms*." He makes a meaningful face until I can't help but smile.

"I apologize for those storms."

"Nah, I'm just teasin'. Mainly that maid reminds me o' my mum though. Always laughing and makin' Breck an' me laugh too." He pauses. "Nowadays, Breck's different. She doesn't laugh so much anymore."

He pushes a lump of cabbage around on his plate, and I wish I knew what to say. Wish I could recall my own mum's laugh. "How did you come from Tulla to Faelen?" I finally ask.

"Our mum died. The febris plague took 'er one night. The next morning I came completely unhinged, an' that's when my powers erupted. Ne'er knew I 'ad 'em 'til that day. Dad was a drunk so he was always gone or in a rage. By the time I calmed down, I'd nearly leveled our village and the people were so afraid o' me, Breck an' I knew we 'ad to move on.

"Our people are proud of their Terrenes. Our King Mael is one. But they train 'em starting young. One in my condition—whose powers displayed so late—would be considered a threat wherever we went. So we bought a passage over to Faelen and kept my power a secret while we worked to keep food in our mouths. Training on my own until I could control my abilities enough to go back home. As luck would 'ave it, I was practicing one day, an' Adora found me and brought me to Eogan. Breck and me been livin' here since."

He ducks his head and goes back to his pheasant, and for a moment I catch the pain in his eyes as they crease. "Up there," he adds after a minute, "my mum was a lady with an inheritance. Respected even."

My eyes warm, and suddenly they're filled with wet pity. I blink. He smirks, but it doesn't reach beyond his lips. "I'd ask you about yer home, but something tells me you'd just sock me again."

Right. I bite my cheek. "I'm sorry about that."

Sorry for everything is what I want to say. But I don't.

Instead I stare off across the room and sift through the bright clothes and smiling faces. A man in black is laughing, but when he turns, it's not the king's cousin. He's amused at someone who's entertaining quite a crowd, and when he moves a little more, I see the source is none other than Eogan. Here. At Adora's party. Dressed in a gray suit made to resemble the beauty of an arctic wolf. Fluid and fanciful. Dangerous. He's stunning. My chest clenches awkwardly. His eyes move and latch onto mine and a sparkle emerges, but he keeps talking to the huddle surrounding him, although everything about his posture tells me he's bored.

Suddenly he smiles in his dazzling way, and something says the smile is for me. To remind me to relax.

"You two look like you're having more fun than should be allowed in a place like this," a slurring voice says, and instant chills slip like spiderwebs around my legs.

I glance up into the red, perfume-drenched face of the pontiff from Poorland Arch. The one who made the maidservant disappear. I feel my face drain of warmth to match the icy shade of my dress.

I look back at Eogan, but he's gone.

The drunk man chuckles and places a hand on my shoulder, his sweaty fingers rubbing the skin between my collarbone and chest. "You look like you could do with some wine, young lady. Oh, don't pull away. The party's just getting started. Young man, fetch us some drink!"

The dagger pokes my thigh beneath my dress. I reach for it and nervously look at Colin, who catches my movement and shakes his head. It's only then I recall Breck's comment about Colin and the pontiff's recent run-in. Colin hesitates, then stands and switches into an instant smile and shifts the man's hand onto his own shoulder. "Actually, I was just off for more food. How 'bout you and I both find somethin' the lady 'ere might enjoy?"

I love that boy. Clearly, I should be nicer to him. He winks as if to say I owe him one.

The man glances back and forth between the two of us—at first resistant, but I throw him my hugest, most flagrant grin and he acquiesces. "Don't go anywhere," he whispers behind Colin's back. And it's all I can do not to spit on him.

As they walk away, I take off in the opposite direction to hunt down Eogan. *What's he doing here?*

Besides watching us squirm.

I pass three generals discussing the war and Bron's airships and pause to listen. From what their spies have deciphered, the ships can only carry one or two explosives each, and each boat can only carry one extra bomb along with the necessary fuel and man power. After that, the airships have to return to Bron, while the boats can stay to launch limited attacks of their own or unload soldiers. "It's only a matter of weeks," one says before their talk switches to the subject of iron deliveries from Tulla and more crossbows for arming our ranks.

"If it isn't the girl with special power*sss*," a snakelike voice says in my ear. A cold hand grips my elbow, and King Sedric's cousin is in my face, leaning his mouth against my hair while his fingers tighten into my skin. I go to pull away. His hand bruises me.

"Such beautiful abilitie*sss*," he whispers, and a mental image forms of him standing with the orange-haired man in Adora's hall, not five steps from the staircase I'd been hiding in on my first day in this wretched house. He was talking of treason and of Faelen falling, and now my mind is spinning at the implications of who he is. And what he's done.

My skin crawls. Rigid fingers grip harder into my elbow, so cold they're spreading frostbite through my dress.

Run.

I look frantically around the room of people. *Where's Eogan? Where's Adora?* But all I see is a mass of bodies, eating and swaying to sickening, harpy voices.

His other hand slides around my waist, and his breath catches against my neck. He begins to sway to the music with me. "Hmm. I wonder what other powers you might have."

I bristle and jerk back, shaking. "I don't know what you're talking about. I believe you've mistaken me for someone else, Lord Protectorate."

His hand is ice, unrelenting, even as his lips pucker around that one silver tooth in amusement. He drifts dark eyes over me. "Hmm. Don't think so."

"Release me." My voice, my breath are searching for firm ground. "I live under the protection of Adora, and you'd be wise to remember it."

"Yes, well, considering that one aspect of my job is keeping Faelen purged of Elementals, her protection may be useless. I'm certain His Majesty will be most interested to hear that his brilliant strategist Adora is harboring a girl with the powers of a storm. How doe*sss* it work for you? Do they still call you an Elemental even if you're female?"

My free hand slides toward the knife beneath my dress. "Just as I'm sure His Majesty will be interested to hear his faithful cousin is a traitor against the crown."

Fear slips through his face so fast, I almost don't catch it. Then he cocks a handsome smile and leans closer. "Look*sss* like we each have our little secrets. But if you tell mine, it's not yourself you'll have to worry about. I'll cut Eogan's throat and watch him beg as he bleeds out. Oh, don't look so surprised. I know all about your trainer." He squeezes down on my memorial scars, and it triggers an image of blood on the barn floor with that patch of orange hair stuck to it.

I let out a cry. And feel the surge within.

"You know I've always found the weaker sex to be flaring with insecurities," a different low voice says.

Lord Myles turns, exposing Eogan to my view. Up close the gray suit brings out a feral warning in his green eyes, and his hair's as messy as ever.

Myles hesitates, then straightens and laughs, keeping his hand on my arm. "That they are. Which makes them so unstable, eh, Eogan? This*sss* one and I were just having a little chat about that."

The rhythm in my veins is starting to build. Strumming with the music. Louder.

Eogan steps closer and places his hand on my neck and my pulse instantly calms. "I wasn't speaking of her, Myles." He blinks politely. Charming.

The man's gaze narrows. "How rare to see you at these parties, Eogan. One can't help but wonder what brings*sss* you?"

"Nothing more intriguing than seeing you squirm, I assure you."

The lord protectorate's face goes black. He grazes my ear with cool lips. "Remember what I said or he'll be dead before you can conjure a raindrop. And believe me, I'll enjoy watching him finally bleed. Excuse me," he says louder, and, releasing me, pretends to flick a fly from his black suit. Then without glancing back, he walks away at a brisk pace to blend in with the party guests.

"An unfortunate person. I take it you've met before?"

"Last night at the common house," I whisper.

"Hmm."

And it's all he has to say. I scan the room to avoid his eyes. The nobles are drinking. The couples are dancing. The frog-lady-dressed-as-a-male-peacock is flirting with the king.

"He saw me almost lose control last night," I finally admit.

"I'll bet he did."

Surprisingly, he doesn't sound angry.

"Did Colin tell you?"

"The look on your face this morning did. Why do you think I yelled so much? I figured something happened."

"You're not furious?"

"I'm debating it."

The way he says it almost makes me smile.

"He said he kills Elementals for the king."

"It's one facet of his position, although I doubt he's done so more than once. His predecessors saw fit to purge Faelen to the point of extinction. But trust me"—his voice hurries on—"Myles is more interested in seeing what you can do rather than getting rid of you. Especially if you controlled your power last night."

Something in his tone draws me back to his gaze, which is studying mine. "How'd you manage to stop it?" His voice is a spark of starlight. Curious.

Umm.

Well . . . I thought of you.

And your eyes. And your warmth. And your fingers on my skin.

"I . . . I just did," I say as stupid heat hurls itself at my face. I clear my throat and wonder why the air in the room suddenly feels so thin. "What are you doing here anyway? You hate people."

"True. But clearly someone has to keep an eye on you. Because, if I'm not mistaken, I've witnessed two male toads get under your skin within five minutes. But you didn't answer my question as to how you did it."

I open my mouth and the stupid heat hurls itself even hotter, like summer petals bursting over my cheeks, my neck, my barely covered chest. I swallow and move my gaze down his perfectly cut, gray-vested suit that smells of honey and pine and effortlessness.

I need to get out of here.

He steps closer and chuckles. "That bad, eh? Must've been quite something to make you blush like a berry."

I shake my head. "You're *such a blasted bolcrane*," I sputter.

"That I am," he whispers. And his eyes are no longer just on me but on *all* of me. Taking in my height, my low-cut gown, my nervous fingers that don't know what to do with themselves so they keep feeling the dagger beneath my dress. Something shifts in his expression. He takes my hand and subdues my flitting fingers—his laugh almost inaudible. "Did you seriously bring a knife under there?"

"Maybe. No. Yes. If I say yes, are you going to take it away?"

"Depends who you plan to use it on. That pontiff guy, for instance, please tell me you'll aim straight for his, uh . . ."

My breath lets out in a whoosh of chuckles, and it hits me how much I crave him near me, setting me at ease. Just like I crave the way my hand feels in his, my skin with his, even if it's just his job of calming me.

His fingers keep mine as he watches me laugh, until his lips part and his expression opens, as if he's allowing me a glimpse into his soul. To show me something beautiful. Merciful. Incomprehensible.

Because it's the recognition that he craves being near *me*.

My internal lid begins sliding so quickly, I'm grasping

for something, anything—anger, annoyance, frustration—everything I make a habit of feeling toward him—to spout out and use to cover the chasm so he won't know the depth of my brokenness.

But my heart expands inside its cage anyway.

His breathing shallows.

I swallow.

"Nym, I need to speak to you." Adora's voice makes me jump.

Abruptly, Eogan drops my hand. I watch his openness collapse into a wall and a frown slip over his face. I search for one of Colin's fissures to crawl into.

I clear my expression as Adora's peacock fronds waggle into view behind my trainer's gray-suited shoulder. She slides a hand beneath one of Eogan's arms and across his chest. His pupils tighten.

"Eogan, how rare to see you at one of my galas." Her gaze consumes him like a slab of venison. "And so dressed the part."

His jaw shifts. "Thank you, m'lady."

"Perhaps we could get you to come more often."

"Your Ladyship honors me with the invitation." He slides from the woman's hungry grasp. He tips his head to her and snaps his eyes my direction, but they're dim. Cold. "If you ladies will excuse me, I'll check on Colin."

Then he's gone. And I'm left standing, wondering who keeps emptying this blasted room of air.

My owner stares after him until he's drifted into the crowd, then turns to raise a perfect, purple eyebrow at me. "I assume Breck chose your dress?"

"I thought you had."

"Me? Absolutely not. I've given her a selection to go from,

but in the future I expect you to speak up regarding colors. That thing practically trumpets what you are."

"Yes, m'lady."

She slides a hand along my low collar and eases her tone. "Poor thing. You all but scream 'woman with loose morals.' No wonder the men have been chatting you up."

If she'd slapped me across the face, it would've stung less. The shock reverberates all the way down to my stomach. *Is that why Eogan wanted to be near me? And Colin? And the man from Poorland Arch . . . ?*

She scans the dining room. Sniffs. "Not that any of the men here would be seriously interested, but it's best not to give the impression you're desperate. Or available. In the future, you'll remember your place when allowing a *blind* servant to dress you."

I imagine the floor swallowing both of us.

"As far as Eogan goes . . ." Her purple-lined eyes narrow on mine. "I'm wondering if I should be concerned at your growing level of attachment to him. You've hardly been here nine days and yet already seem too familiar with him. Therefore, outside of training hours, you're not to go near him. During training, you'll limit yourself to as little contact as necessary and only so far as it furthers your usefulness. I will not have a slave humiliating herself by imagining she can seduce my trainer. Am I clear?"

Breck's warning on my second day here flits through my mind. The one about the death of the kitchen maid who'd had a thing for Eogan. I nod even as my gaze grows stiff, unyielding. I can feel the siren in me rising.

She drops her voice and leans in, that insane smile emerging. "Good. Now let me be even *clearer.* If you so much as bat an eyelash at that man, I will carve your face up, one pretty cheekbone at a time, and then cut your tongue out. You don't need either of those to win a war. But first? I'll carve out Colin's tongue as well."

And I have no doubt whatsoever that she means it.

CHAPTER 16

A lightning strike, and the terrible heat is burning my insides. I scramble through the fire and snow, whimpering, panting, flailing like a dancer following a bloody trail of terror.

I can't remember why I'm here. I can't remember anything but the unquenchable fear as Mum and Dad scream and the house explodes.

My dream morphs and suddenly it's not them screaming anymore. It's Colin and Eogan. Holding up swords and fire sticks, warning off their attackers. I refuse to look back as I rush to join them. "Don't let it get me," I try to yell. But my throat doesn't work.

Not until I reach for them does it occur to me that they're not looking behind me. They're staring in horror at my hair, my Elemental eyes, my face where my grief-filled tears have frozen to fury. They're staring at my fists as my explosions pelt around us and a thousand voices cry out—my curse tearing the kingdom apart in the midst of my guilt. My hatred. Because deep down, I am the real monster. I murder the innocent.

I murdered my parents.

And I could murder these—my friends.

"You in here, Nym? They's tryin' to leave!" Breck's round cheeks blur through my vision as I'm jolted awake on my library window perch.

"I'm here, Breck." I rub my eyes and stoop to pick up the Hidden Lands history book and return it to its shelf before blowing out the lantern. "About time. I swear Colin and Eogan take longer than Adora to get ready." I grab my bag from the hall and pat Breck's arm. "Thanks," I say, and head off to find Colin and Eogan through the predawn dark.

I can already taste the friction in the weather mimicking my strained emotions today. It's been nineteen days since Adora purchased me, and over a week since Eogan's and my tension-filled moment at the party. And just as long since he's made any eye contact or conversation with me other than his reserved, you-can-do-better-than-this training speak. The recent days have begun morphing together in one long, gruelingly awkward training session in which he's utilized his calming ability to focus me on separating and using individual storm elements.

So far I've succeeded at wind manipulation and pulling

lightning from the sky with my hands without killing Colin. Unfortunately, the more control I manage means the less I need Eogan's soothing touches, making them as brief and infrequent as possible. Which maybe I should be grateful for, seeing as it's exactly what Adora wants. Obviously she needn't have even threatened.

But the pressure keeps building. In me. In the smoky air. In the Faelen people. And in between Eogan and me, and Colin and me, and in Adora's house every third night as bald boy and I now smile for Adora's festivities at which she has us appear, elaborately dressed, refined, reserved, in her banquet room. And Eogan has us always listening for the key to turning the war that's about to destroy us. But he never asks what we hear, which just makes it easier to keep silent that Lord Myles is a spy—as does the mental image of him slicing Eogan's throat open—until I can figure out what to do about it.

I shiver and walk faster through the gray mist.

Haven bucks to say hello when she sees me. She's annoyed at the saddle Eogan's making her wear and pushes her beautiful black head my direction, hoping for a mouse or mole to snack on for comfort.

"Whoa," Eogan soothes. He tightens her reins. "The sleeping dead arises."

I nod toward Colin. "I know. I thought he'd never get up."

"I've been 'ere for a half hour!" Colin leans down from his horse to pat its neck. "Isn't that right, boy?" The beast issues a quick warning snip, and Colin jerks back. Working with the horses has made us familiar, but overconfidence won't be tolerated on their part, nor on Eogan's.

I hide my laugh and hook my bag to Haven's saddle while Eogan holds her steady. I whisper in Haven's ear that I'll find her a morsel soon enough, and by the time I'm mounted and ready, Eogan's on his horse, with a broadsword on his back, steering us south toward the mountains at the base of our Faelen island.

"A break from the familiar for a few days," Eogan informed us last night. "You'll practice your abilities in other types of terrain, specifically the southern altitude and snow."

I feel Adora's gaze on me as we ride out, searing her warning about Eogan into my skin as he directs us away from the High Court and Castle and down toward the Hythra Crescent's southern peaks. The same mountains that, along with our now nearly-wiped-out armada, have kept us safe from Bron for years. But not anymore. I look up through the dim to where the airship bombed.

"Why so far?" Colin asks once the horses are trotting at a good clip. "Why not any of the northern ridges?"

"Because I want to show you something."

And with that, the ride settles into uncomfortable silence.

The road isn't one I've travelled, but it's familiar enough terrain once we get galloping. By the time the sun hits the first immediate town and its outlying villages, women are already up and working with their bedraggled children and half-clothed slaves, farming their barren earth patches or setting out feeble wares to sell even though few people are out on the road this early. And even fewer seem interested. We give a wide pass to a unit of soldiers probably heading to the northern front. When Eogan hails them, they offer nothing more than a nod. One's missing a leg, the other an eye. A third looks like he won't survive the day.

Next comes a merchant pulling a chain of cows with a goat and an old woman in shackles. She has four owner circles on her wrinkly arm. My throat sticks together, and I want to say something. To ask her name, at least. But one look at her face is enough to tell me that, whoever she used to be, she probably doesn't remember.

Eogan falls back beside me. I look at him to see what he wants, but he stays quiet. His gaze is on the old slave woman too.

Just keep riding.

We pass more soldiers and edge around the outskirts of a larger town. And while the people in it are poorer, it reminds me a bit of my fourth home with its corroding stone archways and moss-covered sheep sheds. A young mother yells out a doorway for her slave to keep an eye on the kids, then retreats and slams the door. The poor, bedraggled servant looks about the same age as the unruly brats she's supposed to be watching. Also reminiscent of home number four.

Is Eogan trying to make me erupt through memories? Or just torture me?

By lunchtime, Eogan is riding beside Colin again, and his mood has eased to such that the two of them are exchanging jokes like old schoolmates. The sun is hot and reflecting off the cracked clay road, in a section where the clouds don't overflow as often. They drift above us, high on their sun-speckled wind currents, while we stop long enough to eat oranges and pasties and water the horses at a stream by a crop of trees.

I catch a field mouse and feed it to Haven. Then we're moving again. Hour upon hour. Soldier after weary soldier. Village after village. They all blend together with flashes of most every home I've ever known. My stomach squirms at the premonition of seeing someone I recognize—one of my former owners perhaps, or their surviving kin. The thought makes me huddle in my seat and keeps me tugging my dyed hair forward to remind myself it's brown. I look different now.

I am different now.

After five hours of riding, Eogan appears in no hurry to stop, and I can't stand the discomfort any longer. I nudge Haven forward between the two men. "What do you know of Drust?"

"Why?" Eogan responds without looking over.

I shrug. "Everyone is always talking about the war with Bron, but no one says much about Drust."

"So are you asking what I know of her history or what I know of the kingdom now?"

"Her history. How did Drust come to be?"

"Same way all kingdoms come into existence. People fight. Alliances form. The strongest survive. Drust has had six hundred years of kings, and I suspect they'll have six hundred more."

"But Bron conquered Drust. So technically shouldn't their king be Drust's king?"

"Bron beat Drust, which took a toll on both and made them allies of a sort. That doesn't mean Bron had the man power thirty years ago to rule it, or even until recently for that matter."

"When King Odion took over," I say, recalling the library book I'd been reading.

Eogan nods.

"Took over?" Colin asks. "I thought he inherited it."

I adjust to look at him. "When the old Bron king died, he left the kingdom to his twin sons. It didn't go well, and Odion got the kingdom, and the other disappeared—supposedly offed by his brother." I pause before glancing to Eogan. "Is that why our king's never faced King Odion in person—because he's too dangerous?"

Eogan's jaw flexes slightly. "Doubtful. The way I hear it, Odion prefers the tactical side of things rather than dirtying himself in battle."

"But have they never tried to negotiate?"

"King Sedric has. Odion just doesn't respond."

Colin furrows his brow. "Well, why'd Bron start fighting Drust in the first place?"

"To eliminate them as a threat," our trainer says. "If Drust got Faelen, it would've taken Cashlin and Tulla as well, and those are the kingdoms Bron's been fighting to get all these years. Faelen's just an obstruction."

"Why Cashlin and Tulla?"

"Their resources. Wood. Metal mines. Bron's severely depleted their natural resources, and Drust is basically a wasteland."

Clouds drift overhead as the sun starts its fiery plunge toward the Sea of Elisedd beyond the southern mountains, bringing a chill into the valley. I glance at Eogan. "But *did* they eliminate Drust as a threat?"

He laughs, and it's a hard, callous sound. "Not by any means. If anything, Bron's arrogance has blinded them to the real danger in recent years. Their focus on Faelen will be their undoing. Whether Faelen's around to see it or not."

"How?" Colin tugs his horse as close to Haven as he dares.

"Yer not . . . yer not sayin' Draewulf an' his Dark Army's real, are you?"

"He's a wizard. Why wouldn't he be?"

"I thought he was a wolf," I correct.

"A shape-shifter, actually." Eogan turns to look at me for the first time in over a week. Really look at me.

I stare back, as if to defy him and whatever his problem has been. Except something hungry stirs behind his gaze, and the next thing I know he's taking my heart for a thirsty leap into green depths, and I'm drinking him in as fast as I can, excruciatingly aware of how parched I am.

He blinks, then tears his eyes away to refocus on the road, which is quickly heading into shadows. *Why does he do that?* I curse him under my breath as the sky overhead mimics my grumble. *What does he want from me?*

"You're lyin', Eogan," Colin says. "He can't be real. He'd be a hundred years old."

"One hundred and thirty, or so I'm told."

Colin's eyes widen.

"As I said, he's a wizard."

"He can't die?"

"Of course he can. Why do you think he eliminated the Elementals?"

What? I jerk my gaze around. "What does that mean?"

"Let's just say he has a particular aversion to their power."

"Can he shape-shift into anything he wants?" Colin asks.

"Only the person he's taking over. And even then it's not so much shape-shifting as possessing. He climbs into their skin and absorbs their essence until there's nothing left but him."

A gag squeezes my throat and I try not to think about what that would be like.

"What about his Dark Army?" Colin presses. "Are they actual monsters?"

I detect the waver in his tone. I feel it in my own breath.

"As I said, mate, he's a wizard."

My legs must've clenched too tightly into Haven's sides at this because she gives a light buck and snaps her teeth back at me. I loosen my grip and swallow. "But how can he have an army? Bron wouldn't allow it."

"As I said, their arrogance is blind. And Drust has no love for Bron in recent years, meaning they'll ultimately do what benefits Drust." Eogan looks over at Haven. "We'll break and let the horses hunt, then keep going."

"Keep going?" Colin says.

"We're riding through the night."

Pink-ribboned cloud streams melt into the landscape as the sun exhales and the shadows set in. Deep. Dank. Twisting into strange shapes around the nearby forest, which is far from any hovels or townsfolk. The only hints of civilization come from a plume of dust in the far distance ahead of us and the sound of bells and hooves carried to us on the breeze. It's an entourage of horses and yellow carriages from what I can tell.

"Princess Rasha's retinue," Eogan says. "Probably done travelling Faelen and on her way back to the Castle."

"Why *was* she touring Faelen?"

"Assessing. Extending courtesies. As a Cashlin ambassador, the princess is expected to show good faith not just toward the king and High Court, but to commoners as well."

My hands tighten on the reins. I wonder if *assessing* means rooting out our weaknesses. "You said her Luminescent ability doesn't mean she can see everything. So how does it work?"

"Luminescents see on a spectrum. The more decided a person's intentions, the clearer they become. And the stronger that person's motivation is, supposedly the easier they are to predict."

"You think she's ever met Draewulf?" Colin asks with a snicker. "Wonder what she'd see of 'is intentions."

"Not likely. Cashlin's avoided Drust just as much as they've avoided the war," Eogan says, directing us to a copse of trees.

Something howls just as we dismount. I shrug off the chills it brings and set to work brushing Haven. When I've finished, Eogan whispers to each of the horses and sends them off while Colin starts on a fire and I pull out a meal of apples, cheese, and bread.

Colin and Eogan talk over the information Colin's managed to pick up from Adora's parties, mainly the concern over Bron's airships. I try to imagine what the metallic ships must look like up close. What it would be like to fly in one, sailing on wind currents, uninhibited by the restraints of earth and expectation. I trace over the bird tattooed beneath my sleeve and study the moon lifting his head over the horizon.

Colin pulls a wineskin from his satchel and pours drinks for Eogan and him. I shake my head when he offers it to me.

"What, scared you'll start throwin' yerself at me?" He winks and kisses one of his biceps. "Understandable."

I smile. "Yes. That's it. Hold me back."

"Well, maybe just for experiment's sake, let's say you try it. An' if you can't keep yer hands off me, I promise I'll help you resist."

"You don't drink?" Eogan looks surprised. "It's practically water."

"I don't like the taste. It doesn't sit well."

"Oh c'mon." Colin pokes me. "Go ahead an' tell 'im the truth. It makes her crazy 'bout me. Girl can't keep her paws off. You shoulda seen 'er at the common house. I was like, 'Nym, please! Come on!' It was embarrassing, I tell ya."

Eogan raises a brow at me, as if he's assuming Colin's joking, but he'll wait for me to deny it.

"Practically begged me to marry 'er! Talk about movin' fast. It was awkward."

Eogan narrows his eyes and then they're boring deeper as if suddenly analyzing my feelings for Colin, although I don't see why he'd care. But he keeps prying with that emerald gaze until I want to tell him to direct it elsewhere so I can stay above water and remember how to breathe.

Tell him why you don't drink.

Colin keeps talking big. Eogan keeps liquefying my insides with his questioning eyes until I'm nothing more than a pool for drowning in.

Tell him why.

Fine. "I killed the sons of owner nine."

Colin stops midsentence.

I can't look at either of them.

Just hurry through. "The two of them thought it'd be fun to get me drunk one night. They were laughing and getting chummy with their hands, and when I tried to scream, they discovered the drink had incapacitated my voice. And then not just my voice, but my body. Apparently, drink saps what little control I have and

149

paralyzes me. I couldn't breathe and I couldn't fight." I stand, trembling at the memory as much as my blatant confession. "Before they could do anything . . ."

I pick up my satchel. "My hailstorm tore them limb from limb." I walk away without giving either of them a chance to respond.

CHAPTER 17

I'M JUST REPACKING MY THINGS WHEN THE HORSES slip back to us like ghosts from the dark. Haven's chewing on what appears to be a deer bone. I demand she drop it before Eogan saddles her up. She whimpers and tries to wipe her blood-stained mouth on me. I sigh and push her off, muttering, "You and I are a perfect pair."

We ride along the side paths rather than the main road, keeping to the moonlit trails as we begin climbing the cascading southern foothills covered in firefly trees. The trees are starting in with their evening glimmer. I slow Haven, waiting to take in the brilliance. The only place in the five kingdoms they exist, and I've never gotten used to their magnificence.

The firefly lights flicker. Then flash brighter.

I hold my breath as the moon slips behind a cloud.

"What the—?" Colin whispers, and the forest surrounding us erupts in pure, color-lit splendor.

"Teeth of a naked ferret-cat," he mutters. And even Haven seems impressed. She prances, head high, through terrameter after terrameter of trees filled with fireflies blinking their tiny lights of purple, orange, pink, blue. It's the bugs' mating season, and they're bragging their most exquisite displays, fluttering among the overhead branches and breezes. We pass beneath in silence, soaking it in without disturbing their dance.

It's an hour later when the performance is finished and we emerge from the trees. The foothill path we're on becomes steeper and cloaked in night's dark shroud. Twice I catch Colin dozing off. I prod his arm to keep him from falling forward and garnering his horse's meat-loving interest.

He mumbles and says something about tying himself to the beast, then begins to snore. Eogan falls back to tie Colin down, keeping one hand on Colin's reins as the animals work to keep their nimble feet steady.

The dark deepens until it's hard to see farther than Haven's head. When my own eyes lull, I stretch my neck and let the cold air seep through my cloak collar. I need something to keep me conscious.

I glance in Eogan's direction. "Where are you from?"

I can't see his face, but I hear his breathing change as if he's surprised I'm awake. "Faelen."

"Before Faelen."

Silence.

"Who said I've lived anywhere else?" he says after a minute.

"You speak like the upper class and work with them, despite the fact you hate them."

His reply is a soft chuckle through the dark. "Perceptive."

"So?"

"Does it matter? I came as a wanderer like the rest."

"But you're not the rest. You block powers. You know how to train Uathúils. You understand war."

"Things easily learned in life when one pays attention."

"Liar." In fact, something tells me that whoever he was in his former life, he's now either desperately hated or dearly missed for those talents. "Have you ever been to Drust?"

"You're full of questions tonight." His tone drops. "Why are you asking?"

"Call it curiosity. I'm trying to stay awake."

"There are more interesting ways to stay awake, believe me. Perhaps Colin and his irresistibility could teach you a few," he mutters. Then, after a pause, he says, "But yes, I've been to Drust."

"Have you ever met Draewulf?"

"Have you ever considered you're not the only one who doesn't enjoy discussing the past?"

"So that's a yes on Draewulf?"

"That's a what in hulls are you getting at, Nymia?"

My mouth falls open. I've never heard him use my full name like that. And even though he's saying it in annoyance, for some reason it makes my stomach flutter. I peer through the blackness, wishing I could see his expression. "I'm not sure. I just want to know who you are."

"You know who I am," he murmurs. "At least, anything worth knowing."

My breathing skips. *Do I?* "How long have you been with Adora?"

"Three years."

"How'd you start?"

"She was looking for a new trainer. I saw the objective she was trying to accomplish and the usefulness of a position there."

"And do you like it? Working for her?"

He hesitates. "Let's say it's a relationship of efficacy. She gets what she wants. I get what I want."

The horses' hooves clip through the darkness. One of the beasts snorts.

She gets what she wants . . .

Wait—oh no. Oh, disgusting. "What do you mean 'she gets what she wants'? Like you two . . . you both . . . are together? Like . . . *romantically*?"

"What do you mean 'romantically'? Are you asking if we're *lovers*?" From the sound of it, he nearly falls off his saddle. "Curses, Nym, have you ever considered minding your own business?"

I gulp and the world starts sliding. "Is that a yes?"

Inhale. Just inhale.

"No, it's a definite no! But do you really need to ask? Is that what you think?"

Exhale. The world tilts back. "Well, you said she gets what she wants."

"I guarantee there are things she wants more than me."

"But Breck said Adora killed a kitchen maid because of you."

"Trust me, she's killed for a lot less," he mutters.

A chill envelops me, reaching through my skin to rattle my bones. Horror blooming, I look through the dark toward Eogan. "Then why haven't you stopped her? How could you just stand by?"

"Do *you* always stop the people you know harm others?"

"No. But only because when I try, I hurt *everyone*. But with you, you're in control. You can—"

"It's not as simple as that."

"Seems pretty simple to me, I say."

"It's not," he snaps. "Are we done here?"

"No. Maybe. Yes."

"Good."

Unless you want to tell me why you've been cold to me for the past week.

After a quiet minute, he sighs. "So what about you? What's this thing between you and Colin? Are you in love with him?"

"What? No." It's so loud, Haven jumps and I think Colin stirs awake. I pause and gulp and pray to Faelen he didn't hear us.

His snoring resumes.

"Such passion," Eogan muses. "They say the louder you deny something, the more you desire it."

I'm thankful the blushing flames licking my face aren't illuminating the dark. "You're such a bolcrane," I mutter, and nudge Haven to pick up her pace as Eogan's soft laughter ricochets through the night. The rest of which passes in silence.

By the time dawn hits, the forest is smothered in smoke carried in from the war front. My hands and thighs are glued to Haven, and my lungs are on fire. It takes a minute for my fuzzy mind to decipher the smell mixed in with the haze, but when I do, I nearly throw up in my seat.

It's the distinct scent of death.

The clatter of horses and clanging metal greets us before the forest spits us out into a village whose main path is lined with soldiers preparing to depart. They ignore us as we hedge through, while the few townspeople eye us with open suspicion. I can practically taste their fear.

We dismount in front of a market of three stalls and an inn

smaller than Adora's barn. Yellow and red flowers, the colors of Faelen's flag, wave from one of the windows. A man who's clearly the squadron's commander yells at his men to saddle up, then clips his horse over to Eogan. Our trainer sends Colin and me into the market for bread and fruit. As I walk away I see Eogan shaking the man's hand.

"Where you off to?" the inn's matronly owner asks me.

A little boy peers out from behind her legs. I wink at him. "Higher up the mountain."

"Gonna see what all the smoke and smells are about, eh?" Her tone is flat but her quick look at the little boy strikes of terror. Like she knows the war is right next door.

"Their ships have hit the water passage above the Fendres Mountains, you know," she says, as if reading my mind. As if the Bron army attacking 275 terrameters north of here makes her feel safer because their entire force isn't focused on the Crescent's open cliffs three foothills away.

"I wish strength for our soldiers," I say.

A slip of a smile breaks apart the weary lines of her face. "Me too. Go with the creator."

I nod and thank her for the food. Outside, I'm walking toward Haven and the noisily departing soldiers when the woman's little boy runs up and tugs on my shirt. He reaches his chubby little hands out, a flower in each. "For you."

And if it wasn't dissolved before, my heart is instantly a puddle. For him. For his mum. For the people of Faelen who have no idea what discussions take place and plans are being made behind the king's and Adora's war-chamber doors. They just know how to hope. And fear.

I tuck the blossoms in my shirt, next to my chest, and slide one of Breck's simple ribbons out of the braid in my hair and press it into his palm. His eyes enlarge to the size of bumblebee eggs. He laughs and hugs it to his chest, then runs off.

"Go with the creator," I whisper.

When I look up, Eogan is watching me with one of his heart-clenching almost-smiles.

We remount and continue to climb at an even steeper incline, and immediately the air is colder. I shiver and clasp my cloak tighter, thankful for Haven's body heat. Snow appears in patches, then thicker banks, until we've gone far enough that our surroundings are covered and starting to look like my first home in the Fendres. *My real home.*

My chest aches with the familiarity of the trees and winter-white. Except this area has something wrong with it. Something off. When I ask Eogan, he simply points to a flat spot higher up and reminds us to drink more water.

It's another two hours before we reach the place he pointed out, and by then I'm gasping from the smoke and thin air, and practically falling off Haven in exhaustion. But when we amble to the center of the plateau, everything—tiredness, burning lungs, weary legs—fades.

Because it's my first view of the Sea of Elisedd in months.

My body reacts to the taste of salt in the air, some of which is frozen into the snow around our feet, and my blood is puls-ing hot and alive like it's homesick for something bigger, wilder, more powerful than me. Something dangerous and beautiful and terrifying.

And then Eogan's pointing at the base of the cliffs below us.

At first I can't understand because a dense fog is in the way. I create a low breeze to push it apart, except it's not fog at all. It's smoke. Drifting up from the charred remains of towns and people burned along the entire coastline.

And then I see the boats. Hundreds of metal-plated Bron warboats with black stripes painted down their sides, surrounding the waters off the southernmost point of Faelen.

CHAPTER 18

WE RELEASE THE HORSES TO REST AND FEED while we make camp beneath the cold afternoon sky. Colin clears snow from the ground and I tug a breeze up to evict smoke from the air so we can sleep a few hours.

When we wake, the warboats are still in line of sight, ignited in burnished reds and oranges from the day's dying sun.

What are they holding back for? Why haven't they finished the assault with their airships?

It's a strange feeling—seeing them and their smoldering horrors on one side, while the land I've slaved in for my whole life is on the other. And as much as I hate my former masters, I know it's their servants and peasants who will suffer most when the bare cliffs two mountains away are breached. Looking out at the vessels, I give us a week, maybe less. And according to Adora, we have nothing to stop them except for Colin and me.

I wrap my cloak closer against the frigid air and look at Eogan.

Or maybe not.

"What about the other assassins?"

He glances up from the fire he's building. "Who?"

"The other assassins you trained for Adora. What happened? Where are they?"

His eyes tighten as he bends to blow on the sparks, and Colin jogs up, arms full of branches. Warm breath puffs from his mouth.

"They've served their purpose," Eogan says without looking up. "Some are dead. Some still around."

"What do you mean 'served their purpose'? Like they're just done and wandering around now, and you have no interest in them anymore?" *Is that what Colin and I will become to him? He'll train us and then move us on?*

"Don't, Nym. You don't know what you're talking about."

Colin drops the wood. "What *are* we talkin' about?"

"The other Uathúils he's trained," I say, watching Eogan. "Where are they, then?"

"Around. They don't announce themselves, as you both should know."

Colin plants himself near Eogan. "Wait a second. Yer answerin' *her*? Do you know 'ow many times I've asked and you said nothin'?"

I ignore him. "Were any female?"

Eogan frowns and tips his head as if wondering why I'm asking. "One," he answers slowly.

"Where is she?"

"She grew too cocky and got herself killed. She was a Terrene as well."

Got herself killed by Adora? I almost ask.

Colin nods as if he, in fact, was aware of this. "So 'ow many other Uathúils are there?"

"In all five kingdoms? I've no idea. Your people revere Terrenes but rarely associate beyond Tulla's borders, so it's hard to say how many there are. Cashlin's Luminescents rule their country, but their genetic line is sparse. The visiting Princess Rasha is one of only a few. However, they have other Uathúils, and they welcome all peace-seeking ones—as long as doing so doesn't put them at odds with anyone. There are also hereditary anomalies every so often, and those are mostly the ones Adora finds. And Elementals, well . . ."

"Being Uathúil is hereditary?"

"Usually." He glances at me, and I'm pretty certain we're all thinking: *Except for Nym, who's a cursed fluke.*

"So 'ow many are still alive?" Colin says. "Of the ones you've trained?"

"For Adora? Four. But there were more before I got involved."

"Why do they stay hidden?"

"Not all do. But it's definitely to their advantage to maintain the element of subtlety, especially in our current war climate where a sense of threat is already high."

"Well, 'ow come they 'aven't done more to stop the war?"

"They have. How do you think Faelen's survived this long? But unfortunately, some haven't been as strong. Others switched sides."

"Switched sides?"

He blows on the coals and lets that uncomfortable thought sink in.

Colin looks at me, steam from his half-clothed body rising in the cool air. His face is suddenly very serious, and I think I know why. Because it's rippling through my head too.

"So . . . if they couldn't win the war after all these years," he says cautiously, "what makes you think Nym and I have any chance in hulls?"

Eogan pushes a hand through his bangs and stares at the fire licking the kindling near his feet. His dark skin is beautiful against the snowy background. He glances at Colin.

Not at me though. He won't look at me.

Another swipe through his bangs.

"Because Nym's the most powerful Uathúil anyone's ever seen," he finally mutters, and turns to stride off.

It takes a few heartbeats for his words to sink in, but when they do, I don't know whether to laugh at their absurdity or cry at the horror. Either way, I can't handle thinking about it. So I busy myself with boiling potatoes for dinner.

We wait for him to return before eating in a silence broken only by the periodic sound of distant wolf howls. I stoke the fire higher while Colin cleans up from the meal and Eogan ties our food bags between three trees on the edge of the clearing. We layer our clothing to keep out the ice and snow, then drift off to sleep beneath a smoke-shattered moon.

Screaming.

I'm awakened by a child screaming.

Bloodcurdling and familiar. Memories of rot, and flesh, and limbs being torn from their sockets. I grab my knife and sit up as the sound tears across the mountain range.

It's not a child. *It's a bolcrane.*

The blood drains from my chest.

What is it doing this far from Litchfell?

The gutting cry erupts again—so eerie and disgusting in its perfect mimic of a child's tortured screech. I pull my blankets around me and look for the nearest tree to climb. *From the resounding echoes, the animal's still a long way off, but how fast is it moving? And what in hulls is it doing? Bolcranes don't travel out of Litchfell. Ever.*

A wolf howl reverberates across the range, followed by three others. *Is the bolcrane hunting the wolves?* I roll over to shove more wood on the fire and meet Eogan doing the same. His eyes connect with mine. He leans in and his fingers are cupping my face and slipping down, down, down my skin until I gasp at the craving welling up within me. *What's he doing?* Adora's warning flares in my head, but I don't give a blast because his touch is lightning, burning me alive and breaking me down.

My lips part.

His eyes flash and widen, and his breath catches when mine escapes.

Then he's sliding his fingers farther, to my neck, on my pulse, and telling me to sleep. He'll stand guard. I mumble that I don't want to sleep because the bolcranes are coming, but suddenly I can't remember what I'm saying or why I'm awake because I don't remember his calming influence ever being so strong.

When my eyes open the next morning, my head feels foggy, but I have the distinct sensation I've slept deeply. Colin's still snoring, but he's squirmed over with his sleeping blankets and has his head resting against my arm. He moans and shifts his freckly face onto my elbow. I sit up and jerk away. Mortified.

A low chuckle draws my attention to Eogan. He's sitting next to the fire, sharpening a pile of his handmade blades.

"I don't see what's so funny," I mutter, and scramble out of my blankets to scoot as far from Colin as possible.

"What? He likes you."

"He likes anything female."

"Maybe, but he also respects you. And that's harder to earn."

The casual way he says it, as if it's true, punctures holes in my attitude. I tug my fingers through my hair and unwind it from its waist-length braid. I frown at the fire. *Do you respect me?* I want to ask him.

"How about you? Do *you* have any love interests?" I say instead.

"You mean aside from Adora?"

He waits for me to look up before breaking into a laugh. "Only once. A long time ago."

"What happened? She break your heart?"

He's slow to answer. When he does, his voice is decidedly quiet. As if remembering. "You could say that."

Oh.

"How about you? Anyone ever swept you away?"

"Nope."

"Ever? I don't believe you. You're telling me there's no one you've ever had an interest in? Even now?"

One of these days I swear my face will stop exploding in flames, but clearly today is not that day. I glance at my hands as my skin ripens to the color of a sunburn and try to focus on releasing the final strands of my hair to ripple in the icy breeze. All the while I'm praying he doesn't notice that my heartbeat just turned into a blacksmith's hammer.

"Sure it's not him?" He tips his head toward the still-sleeping Colin.

"What? No." Fresh heaps of coals pour from head to toe.

"And yet she blushes," Eogan murmurs.

"I don't. I'm serious. I swear . . ."

"Or someone from the past still haunting the present perhaps? Young love cut short?"

I open my mouth. But nothing comes out. Except possibly steam from the heat I'm exuding. I cringe. I've never been in love. Ever. The only crush I had at the age of eleven *was*, in fact, cut short. By the boy's father. Most owners don't want their sons or servants distracted by a slave girl. Especially when they have their own lustful interests in mind.

I clear my throat and straighten my shoulders as the chasm of shame in me shudders and enlarges the crevice in my heart.

I stand.

"Nymia—"

I hear him behind me. But I pick up my pace because I don't want to break open in front of him. Maybe he knows this because he doesn't follow. Or maybe he just doesn't care.

When I return, half frozen with an armful of firewood, the sun is above the trees. Colin has returned from a quick run and Eogan is serving up breakfast. In my spot is a tiny leather belt with two simple metallic knife sheaths attached, from which two handles protrude. The blades Eogan had been sharpening.

I pick up the belt to discover it's the size of my lower calf and the flat sheaths have some kind of lock to keep the blades secure. When I push the lock, it acts as a spring, pushing the knife handles up the tiniest bit for a quick grip.

"For inside your boot," he says when I look up. He smirks. "Thought it better than that knife you've been tying beneath those dresses."

I nod and notice Colin holding a set too.

"Thank you," I whisper, before taking my food to sit alone. I don't speak further to either of them. Because I can feel myself losing. The more time I spend with them, the more exposed and tender I feel. As if I'm under the blade of one of those knives, my skin's becoming thinner, and I can't keep it covered enough to avoid seeing how bare I am. I find myself admitting to things, experiencing things, *feeling* things I cannot allow. But I don't know how to make it stop.

Mercifully, the rest of the day takes place in a hazy blur so I don't have to admit to anything more than being nauseous. Eogan says it's our bodies still adjusting to the high altitude. He has us drink ridiculous amounts of water before our first lesson, which is similar to the ones we've been practicing for the past week. Colin shifts rocks while I try to steal them with the wind, except I accidentally keep dusting us in snow every few minutes.

After lunch, Colin begs Eogan for us to start attacking the Bron ships, to which our trainer scoffs and just alters the lesson—having Colin fling the rocks at him while I try to whip them away before they connect. Not that Eogan's block would allow the boulders to hit him anyway, but it still feels good to shield something rather than attack.

An hour into the routine, a wolf howls, and it's definitely louder. Closer. My skin bristles the length of my back, and I brace for the bolcrane's scream to follow. But it doesn't. I turn to ask Eogan, but he cuts me off with a brisk, "Don't worry about it. And don't mention it to Colin. Poor guy has enough on his mind with having his skills foiled by a girl."

I give him an arrogant smirk and go back to foiling.

Late afternoon is spent with Colin griping about us "seein' the Bron ships but not doing anything," while we work on perfecting the new defensive technique, and Eogan teaches me to create icicles out of frozen air. I notice that more and more, his touch isn't just capable of calming my blood, but with it he's been honing my abilities enough that I can specify between wind and rain and lightning. But even though I'm halfway decent at icicle-making, by the time night falls, I'm also uncomfortably aware of how small scale it is compared to what Colin and I are looking at on the southern horizon. I'm defending one person. But those ships will take out an entire civilization. I eat and fall into bed beneath a smoky moon. *If I can't get this down faster, Faelen is going to fall.*

In the morning, after we've rinsed our plates and greasy fingers and I've washed my hair and shaken it out to dry with the sun, Eogan straps his broadsword on his back and takes us to another clearing four terrameters away.

It's slightly lower on the glittering mountain range and facing a sheer stretch of ice and snow on the adjoining peak above. It also has a clearer view of the villages dotted down the craggy, forested sides. I can see the yellow rooftops of the little town we visited on our way up, where the small boy with the chubby hands lives. His flowers are still in my pocket back at camp.

"Please tell me yer havin' us go after those Bron ships now?" Colin says with jittery excitement.

"Not exactly, mate." Eogan tosses a water skin at me. "Ready?"

I catch it just as a wolf howl pierces the air in front of us. *What the—?* It's followed by more howls all around as other wolves join in.

Colin recoils next to me. I shiver. "What in litches?" he mutters.

"They've been tracking us," Eogan says.

The howling spreads out, and from the sound of it, the pack is surrounding the entire west end of the clearing with its snow-covered pine trees and rocky ledges. An enormous wolf emerges on one of the ridges in front of us and bares his teeth. Two more slink out behind him, like giants, easily as tall as Eogan, and shaggy. The leader's long, gray coat is hanging off his bones, exaggerated by hunger-crazed eyes bulging above a thin, foamy snout.

Snow begins to fall, and the wind lashes my hair back as the thrum tweaks my blood. I sneak a glance at Eogan to ask what we're to do, but the words dissolve with the swirling snowflakes flecking his black skin as he stares calmly at the animals. *He knew they'd be here.*

A deep growl, and the alpha on the ridge centers his attention. Colin retreats three slow steps and leans to the ground.

"Colin, don't," Eogan says. "Let Nym take care of them."

Me? "What?"

"You need to know how to take down live, moving targets."

This is a test? I back away and toss the water jug down, keeping my eyes on the leader as he tests the snowy gravel flanking the ridge. The two wolves with him whine and circle. *How many more wait hidden?* I shake my head, nausea rising in my stomach. I can't. "I don't want to kill anything."

"I'm not asking what you want, Nym. Do it."

The alpha slides down the gravel fifteen feet to land in the clearing. The animal's growls become louder, vicious.

Colin bends low again. "It's fine, Eogan. I'll handle it."

"I said this is Nym's, mate."

Why? To prove I can be the bigger monster? My insides are buckling. The other two wolves scamper down the slope, and suddenly more emerge all over the clearing. Five, ten, twenty. They're growling and taking cues from their leader. They make their way toward us as the sky rumbles overhead. The falling snow feels like an inferno on my skin as the scent of smoke and salt in the air demands forth my curse. Eogan's already beside me, ready to clench my arm if I don't erupt, but it doesn't matter. Because the lead wolf charges.

Colin's gaze connects with mine.

The wolf jumps.

CHAPTER 19

MY MUSCLES SEIZE AND MY ARM JERKS BACK. A bolt of lightning hits the ground directly between Colin and the alpha. The beast yelps and flips back five steps. Shakes his head. He leaps again, and the next bolt nearly takes off his head. His yowl is consumed in the other wolves' snarls as they release and plow toward us, frothing, churning, angry.

My ears nearly explode from the fracturing sky as my hand pulls jagged streak after streak of lightning and slams them into the ground, cutting off the lunging beasts. Hailstones begin to fall. Then shards of ice. The wolves keep rushing, and I keep blocking their surge. There's an explosion of smoke followed by the smell of burnt flesh, and suddenly, all twenty of the pack members back away with their tails between their legs. In a chorus of weak howls, they turn and slink into the forest.

"Ease it off," Eogan says, his fingers on my wrist, and immediately the squall dims until there's only crackling in the air from the ebbing friction and depleting wind. "Perfect."

The area falls calm, except for the drifting ice flakes and the smoking, scarred ground. And the broken body.

"Hulls!" Colin yells. "You're incredible, Nym! How the . . . ?"

He keeps talking, but the words blend together until the only sound I hear is my own heartbeat pulsing in time with the labored breathing of the alpha lying on the ground. I walk over. The entire back half of his emaciated body is blackened with exposed pieces of smoking bone and muscle. He looks at me with pained, clear, beautiful eyes and whimpers. Broken. Wheezing. Thinner than any animal should be—a pitiful, starving creature who'd simply been looking for food.

And I've burned him alive like Bron did to those towns.

My mouth turns bitter.

A *weapon*. That's what Adora called me.

The most powerful Uathúil is what Eogan said. And now he's tested me out on something alive and breathing. Nausea churns up my neck. I've been shoving it down for weeks—for my whole life for that matter—hoping that with Eogan it'd be different, that I'd be capable of becoming something different.

But I'm not. I'm a monster.

I turn to Eogan. "You set me up."

"Pardon?"

My legs are shaking. "You set me up to kill him."

"No, I tested to see what you'd do, and you performed exactly as you should've."

"As I should've? I did the same thing to that wolf that Bron is doing to us! You're not teaching me to defend—you're training me as your weapon."

"That's an absurd comparison. You're not Bron."

"It's a perfect comparison, and you had me do it!"

171

"Look, I needed to see how far you'd go. Now we know."

"How far I'd *go*? For what—some sick practice game?"

His voice drops in irritation. "I tested you because this *isn't* a game. And like it or not, killing *is* one aspect of war. If you can't kill an animal, Nym, how do you expect to defend Faelen when lives are at stake? Because you *will* be killing people."

I don't know. I don't want to think about it. The nausea roils in my stomach. "So you're preparing me to decide between people's lives—to choose who lives and who dies?" I shake my head and start to walk away. "In that case, I don't want anything to do with this war—because unlike the rest of you, I can't justify it."

"Then those people will die and Faelen will fall."

I stop. Turn. "Excuse me?"

He stares straight at my face. Unwavering.

The sky growls and anger sparks along my skin, so intense I hear it sizzle. "Faelen will *fall*? Who are *you* to put that on me? To put that on *Colin*?" Blood pounds in my ears as energy snaps. I point at his chest. "When Adora says it, that's one thing—because she actually *believes* it. But *you*? You're not even sure the world's worth saving!"

"Nym," Colin says, and his tone sounds nervous.

"Or does it just make you feel good to have control? To boss us around because all your other Uathúils left you?"

"Nym," Colin says louder.

Eogan's gaze flashes above me and his expression is instant caution. His voice softens. "Nym. I understand you're upset—"

"You *think*?"

"But right now I need you to calm down."

"Calm down?" My chest burns, and my vision darkens, and my hands are shaking, and I'm not going to calm down because I

hate him. I hate them all. Adora. Myles. I shift my finger to point in his face. "You're all so disillusioned you'll have us fight for the sake of killing. And for what? To protect an upper class who kills Elemental babies and enslaves children and sells out their king to the highest bidder! You want me to protect people who cut each other's throats!"

"Nym!"

"Shut it, Colin!"

"Nym, you—"

"I said *shut up, Colin*!" But instead of my voice, it's an explosion. As if the storm leaned down and stole my words and ripped them like thunder across the sky. I look up in shock.

Black clouds rage, tossing static back and forth. *What the—?*

Abruptly come the echoes—mini thunderous eruptions of my voice across the entire range. So loud the ground shakes. And I know immediately it'll unsettle that glacier of snow on the mountain next to us.

Eogan must know it, too, because he grabs me and yanks me backward, but I can already hear the sound of the ice breaking.

It matches the sound of my heart, as the snow begins slipping, then sliding down from the neighboring slope above us, moving faster than an ocean wave. It's headed straight for the town of the little boy whose flowers sit wilted in my pocket. My eyes start to heat and blur. *Oh please no.*

"Colin, stop it!" he yells.

My body wrenches from Eogan's grasp, as if energy's being pulled from my bones, igniting my hands, my chest. I have to stop this.

"Nym, don't!" Eogan jerks me back. "You'll only make it worse." He presses both hands into my skin, willing me his calm.

"Let me go!" I scream, and I'm beating his chest and fighting to push him away even though I know he's right—no amount of lightning or wind will help. It'll only build the avalanche faster and destroy the boy and his mum sooner, and I am the cause.

I am useless.

Helpless.

No better than the Bron army.

Oh hulls, what have I done?

The little boy's face wavers in my gaze.

Suddenly, it's not only him but every face I've ruined, every person I've killed, and that lid I've been trying to seal over my broken soul for so long comes flinging off, and there's nothing underneath but death and grief and horror.

And tears.

They rip through me like a hurricane, tearing out my lungs and replacing them with a heaving flood. Eleven years I've kept them in, and now they erupt, wave after wave.

Over the mess I hear Eogan's voice right next to me, but the wind is picking up too loud. I can't understand him. The storm is too fierce . . .

The storm.

I open my eyes as Eogan's words click through my head. "Nym, you have to stop."

Around us roars a blizzard of my creation. Lightning bolts splice the ground beside our bodies. Pine needles and branches whip above our heads. I try to stop. To tell my curse to listen to his fingertips and calm down. But I don't know how to stop anymore. I can't. I only know how to weep and crumble and break as the fissure in my chest opens wide to swallow us.

And then Eogan's lips are on mine. Pressing. Calming. One hand slides to my waist while his other tangles its way through my hair, pulling me in, forcing his heated mouth harder to mine. The shock wave ripples down my back, and I respond to his touch, his taste, his heartbeat that's pounding out of his chest. His fingers grip tighter and his mouth is thirst and need, and I'm a begging pile of bones, cracking open, liquefying to be absorbed into him.

Until the calmness comes and my body sags into his.

The storm inside and out stills.

"Stop and let us handle it," Eogan whispers in my ear.

His gaze switches to Colin, who's erecting blockade after blockade of mountainside with more power than I've ever seen him capable of in an effort to stop the avalanche. Eogan shoves me aside, and the next thing I know he's rushing head on into the massive landslide. Which shouldn't even be possible. *Oh hulls. No.*

He's going to get himself killed. I start running, but it's too late. The rocks and snow are bearing down on him, and then he's gone.

Except the avalanche veers off to the side, and I catch glimpses of Eogan's black body standing there. Blocking. His ability acts as an invisible shield, expanding to interrupt the surge, shifting it to Colin, who opens the earth in a crevice for the devastation to slide into, leading it away from the town.

Hours go by.

At least that's what it seems like, although it's only a matter of minutes before the rumbling stops and the danger is over. Colin collapses from the effort and Eogan sloshes over to pant with him and pat him on the back before checking the hillside to ensure the earth is sealed all the way.

When he returns, he strides directly through the snow to me.

Untouched.

Unharmed.

"Nym . . ."

I hit him.

For bringing me to this mountain. For endangering us and the town and the little boy by pressing me into something I cannot do. I *will* not do. For making me desire him. And then for scaring the litches out of me by making me think he was dead. It suddenly occurs to me that I might actually hate him more than anyone I've ever known.

Except, it also occurs to me that I'm in love with him.

CHAPTER 20

WE BREAK CAMP WITHIN THE HOUR. I PREpare supplies while Eogan cleans a shallow gash on Colin's arm and works to cool the boy's suddenly spiking fever. His red-flushed skin is so hot, it's thawing ice off the pine trees three paces away.

"His body overheated," Eogan says, "from the stress of using his ability at that magnitude. It's a Terrene thing—it'll fade over the next few days."

As our horses clip down the mountain pass, the snow on the trees continues to melt in a forest of raindrops around Colin. The bald boy is riding with Eogan, slumped against his back, with his mount roped behind. He doesn't groan, but the pain and exhaustion written on his face are enough. I can barely look at him.

Clearing my throat, I open my mouth. Hesitate.

"Don't," Colin says. "You've already apologized like two 'undred times. I told you I'm fine. It's not yer fault. You shoulda seen the trouble I caused in *my* first big disaster."

"But your arm—"

"Will be 'ealed by tomorrow. Although"—a hint of slyness creeps into his tone—"if it'll make you feel better, I'll play sick longer so you can nurse me back to health. Because holy-mother-of-kracken, did you see how fantastic I was? The way I had yer avalanche in the palm of my hand—caressin' her like a baby? Just think of what I coulda done to Bron's armada!"

"More than fantastic," I say for the eleventieth time.

"As if I wasn't already irresistible enough." He grins, then winces before leaning in to whisper loudly, "Just try to resist droolin' over me in front of Eogan, yeah?"

I gulp. Clearly he'd not seen Eogan kiss me. "Right. Got it. Although I think my horse is drooling over you, too, so you might want to move your face back."

He laughs and for a second it sounds so nice. Normal. Until it turns into a coughing spasm.

I flinch and whisper up a draft of air to ease his discomfort, while the awareness of Eogan listening to us makes my guilt spike higher. I can feel it—the still-liquefied part of my bones that echoes his kiss, blending with my craving and anger—even as I'm picturing Adora cutting out Colin's tongue when she finds out about it. My aching hand flutters to my mouth, and I press Haven to hurry ahead.

We've ridden for four hours before my muddled head registers that we're on a different path than the one we travelled up on. Eogan's got us on a sideways route instead of straight down through the town of the little boy and his mum. I consider thanking him but that would require speaking to him.

At dinnertime, we stop and eat. Eogan releases the horses and tells us to sleep a few hours for Colin's sake. I don't though. I just stare at the fevered boy and wrestle with the knowledge that I hurt people. I hurt him. Because of me, Adora could hurt him more. Because of me, Lord Myles could hurt Eogan. And because of Eogan, I could hurt a whole host of others at his whim or because of my temper. I'm like a death knell for everyone who gets near me.

I slide my hand over my sleeve, feeling the memorial scars beneath as something twisted in me itches to create another. My fingers reach for the handle of my knife, its cold steel burning into my skin like the guilt smoldering over the well-worn scars in my soul.

Eogan shifts and my eyes connect with his. As if he knows precisely what I'm thinking.

He opens his mouth, but I turn over to stare at the firefly trees blazing off in the distance. After that it's silent for a long while.

When his low voice comes, it's controlled concern—but it rumbles all the way down to my bones. "*You* are not the things you've done, Nym."

I shut my eyes.

"You're worth more," he adds, but by the time it registers, his murmur is already dissipating.

When the moon hits midnight, we get up and Eogan ties Colin on behind him. I hook the other mount's reins to mine and am relieved to leave the mountain range behind.

"Nym." Eogan's rich voice carries through the dark.

"I don't want to talk about it, please," I whisper.

So we ride through the night in silence except for Eogan's soft breathing beside me and Colin's muttering hallucinations.

Eventually, morning light shivers and splashes like paint on a canvas over the landscape in front of us. Outlines of villages come into view, followed by farms and smokehouses with cocks crowing and dogs barking to the noisy cries of children.

Colin stirs and Eogan stretches in his seat. "We'll stop on the outskirts of the next town and chain up the horses." His gaze avoids mine. "Then find a common house to eat at."

But at the next village, the outskirts have been taken over by a patchwork of blue and red tents and yellow-painted wagons with streamers flapping high above in the wind. For a moment I wonder if it's already main market day, but then I catch sight of a ten-foot-tall man swallowing a sword as he dances.

Colin chuckles. "It's a carnival." And for the first time in two days, I feel a smile surface. *Not just a carnival—it's a traveller carnival.*

Dogs race around the wagons, barking at panther-monkeys whose enormous bodies jump from roof to roof, dangling corkscrew tails to lure the hounds closer. Each time one's within reach, long panther talons flash out and the dogs jump away, making a game of it. Grab and hiss, grab and hiss—the monkeys keep it up, hoping for their favorite meal of fresh canine brains.

A tiny girl dressed in a pinwheel of colors stands below, shaking her finger and lecturing the disgusting monkeys, although it's hard to hear what she's saying amid the racket of breakfast pots, stakes being hammered, and voices shouting in thick foreign accents. Somewhere an oliphant roars, sending vibrations through the ground just as two ferret-cats race by and duck beneath a cart covered in murals. When I look up, an old woman is watching us from inside. She glares and yanks the curtain shut.

"On second thought, we'll break at the next town." Eogan nudges his horse to keep moving.

But the ten-foot-tall man has already caught sight of us. He struts closer before bending down to unbuckle loops at his thighs. He jumps and launches himself, and suddenly he's vaulting head over heels and leaving his lower legs behind. We rein in the horses as he lands in front of us, a third of the size he was before. It takes me a confused moment before identifying him as a rather tall dwarf who's been using stilts.

Colin and I cheer politely as the man bows low, and when he raises his head, I recognize him from the common house.

"Well, if it isn't my little fighting friend," the dwarf hollers, peering past Eogan to Colin. "Come to see our show, 'ave you? Sorry to disappoint, but it won't get on for another few hours."

"Thanks, but we just came for food, friend," Eogan says. "We'll move on to the next village."

"Move on, eh? Where you goin'? An' where you comin' from?" He rubs his chin with stubby fingers and eyes our trainer, as if gauging his character.

"From the southernmost point of the Hythra Crescent. We're heading back to the High Court."

The little man's face perks up at the mention of the mountain range. "Got a look at the Sea of Elisedd an' her warboats, did ya?"

"We did."

The dwarf leans back on his heels and breaks into a grin. "Been meaning to get up that way myself." He glances around. Chews his lip. "I'll tell you what." He waves a short arm to encompass the ground surrounding us. "If you don't mind eating here outside camp, you can have the honor of breakfasting for a half hour with Allen the Fabler, Travelling Baronet." He bows.

The curtain in the nearby cart jerks aside and the wrinkly old woman scowls down at him. He waves her away, muttering for her to mind her own evil business.

Eogan retreats his horse a few steps. "That's kind of you, but—"

The dwarf jumps forward. "I won't take no for an answer. I'm a bit starved for normal folk, if you know what I mean." He juts a thumb over his shoulder at the cart. "The old woman's paranoid, but don't let 'er scare you." He waves us down from the horses. "You'll eat an' tell me a bit of your travels and the war, and then be on your way."

Without waiting for a reply, the dwarf trots off after our food with the old lady's gaze following him. "Leave it alone, Mother!" he yells.

If Eogan cares that he's just been bossed around by a dwarf, let alone one who recognizes Colin, he doesn't mention it. Instead he gives us an unnecessary reminder to avoid offending *Allen the Fabler, Travelling Baronet* and his people. I peek at Colin. He's busy giving a flirty wave with his injured arm to the old woman.

She slams the curtain shut again, and I smother a laugh.

When the dwarf returns, he brings bowls of who-knows-what drowned in spiced yellow gravy with blood-colored bread for sopping. We eat while the dwarf drills Eogan and Colin about the ships we saw and how soon we think Bron soldiers will breach the barren cliffs. I focus on my food.

"You seen the plagues yet?" the dwarf asks over the sounds of barking dogs and monkeys.

Eogan shakes his head. "Not up close."

"Nor us. But we passed a traveller three days ago come down from the Fendres Mountains. Said he'd stumbled upon a tree village in Litchfell that 'ad black sheets hangin' from every one of their doors. The stench was terrible. He gave it a wide berth and avoided hunting anythin' in the forest just in case of contamination."

I freeze. *The plague is in Faelen? In Litchfell?* Setting down my bowl, I discreetly edge away from the dwarf. "I didn't know the plague had passed beyond the coast."

He shrugs gravely. "It was on the western side of the forest, where most don't dare roam. He suspected it either originated from there or else travelled down from the pass. Said the bodies were covered in boils and he found some animals like that too. Whatever the disease is, apparently even the bolcranes left the dead alone."

Maybe that's why the bolcrane and wolves were on the move. They're being starved out.

"Folks say the Lady Isobel arrived yesterday," the dwarf continues, "an' there's hope maybe she's brought a cure."

Eogan goes rigid across from me. "Doubtful."

I raise an eyebrow, but he ignores me.

The dwarf studies him. "Why? You think it's hogwash? Or you think she won't 'elp even if she could?"

"Both."

The little man rubs his jowls and nods. "I agree. It's been so long since our elders have been in Drust. All we know is rumor these days. But I'll tell you what—anyone comin' outta that place can't be trusted. Mark my words, that woman's a Mortisfaire."

He stands and takes our bowls. We scramble up and thank him.

"No need for that. It's how I keep my ear to the ground." He waves us off to our horses. He waits until we're riding away into the morning sun before kicking his heels and traipsing back to his stilts.

Back on his own horse, Colin looks at Eogan as soon as the dwarf's out of sight. "You gonna tell Adora that the plague's in Faelen?"

"Of course."

"You gonna tell her the Lady Isobel might have a cure?"

"I'm sure she's heard it."

Colin nods his head. "Right. Considerin' Isobel's probably already roomed up at the estate."

I wrinkle my forehead in his direction. "What?"

"Isobel. She's stayin' at the estate while she's in Faelen. Weren't you listenin' in the kitchen the other day?"

I look at Eogan. His expression is stone. "Apparently not."

"Breck's actin' scared as a ghost about it," Colin continues. "Afraid the lady'll put a spell on 'er or some such nonsense." He turns to Eogan. "What do you know about her? Is she really Draewulf's daughter? Is she a true Mortisfaire?"

Eogan keeps his gaze on the horizon in front of us. "I know that she's arrogant, powerful, and deadly when she feels like it. And yes, she's his daughter."

"But isn't that dangerous?" I interrupt. "Having her here in Faelen? Having her near our king?"

"Yes. Although, what level of dangerous will depend on what she wants."

"You ever met 'er?" Colin asks.

"I have."

Colin cranes his neck to look Eogan full in the face. "Really? Did you get up close? Can she really change a man's heart to stone just by her looks?"

"Not by her looks. But it doesn't matter, mate, because you're not to go near her. At all. Same goes for you, Nym."

"What?" Colin narrows his gaze. "Why? She as gorgeous as they say?"

"Not in the least."

His tone's firm, but I look over. Because he's just fibbed clearer than I've ever heard him. I stare until he glances up at me. *Liar,* I mouth.

He purses his lips and kicks his horse to move ahead.

And suddenly I'm sick of it. Sick of his secrecy while he has such reckless consideration for the rest of the world going to hulls.

"So how do you know her, Eogan?" I call after him.

"I met her as a child."

"Was she a Mortisfaire then?" Colin asks, but Eogan's only answer is to holler back that it'd be nice to get home before dark. He spurs his horse forward, leaving dust to settle over us.

CHAPTER 21

WHEN WE FINALLY MAKE OUR WAY ONTO Adora's estate, it's twilight and our horses and bodies are ready to give out from the day's pace. Eogan sends Colin off to wash and rest. As soon as he's gone, Eogan and I brush down the mounts and work to avoid each other's eyes in the barn's buttery lantern light.

Haven flicks her head, grunting for more as soon as I've finished. When I don't give in, she catches her halter chain around her leg and winds herself up in protest. And glares at me.

"You're such a baby," I murmur, and bend to unwrap it, struggling when I realize my crooked fingers are stiff from riding.

Eogan is instantly behind me. "I'll do it."

"I'm fine. I've got it."

"You're not fine. You're putting your face next to an exhausted, half-starved horse like a lunatic. Let me do it."

I don't move. Mainly because I'm so tired that if I stand, I'll either dissolve in his closeness or lash out at his face. Either way, I'll make a fool of myself, and I'm not in the mood to be mocked tonight. "Look, just go take care of whatever it is you have to take care of, okay?" I whisper.

He doesn't argue, but he also doesn't budge. Just stands there, leaning over me, being attractive and holding out his hand. Finally, he sighs and reaches around to grab her harness and hold her head while I struggle with the metal rope.

"Thank you," I mutter when I'm done.

He unhooks her halter and pulls it over her head, then coos her into the stall. I walk away without looking back at him.

Adora's voice carries across the yard and makes me jump. She's yelling my name.

"Tomorrow we'll be training up at a lake while Colin stays behind to rest," Eogan says coolly just as I reach the barn door. "Bring a water satchel and cloak."

I nod and rush off to the house.

When I reach my bedroom, the door is ajar and Adora's shrill voice is emanating out along with the pungent smell of soap. I push it open to find Breck on hands and knees scrubbing the wood floor and Adora standing at the window.

She turns, and I swear the entire drapery moves with her, as if her pantsuit was made from it. She's wearing the highest pointed heels I've ever seen. No wonder she yelled across the grass instead of stomping over to get me. "Ah, there's the deaf girl. I was beginning to think you were being defiant."

"I was brushing down the horses."

She arches a brow. "I hear Colin is hurt."

I nod and glance at Breck. She doesn't turn. Just tucks her

auburn hair behind her ear and keeps scrubbing. She looks weak hunched over like that, and the skin above her collar is yellowish. I peek closer. It's sporting what looks to be a half-hidden gash. There are smaller ones on her arms.

What the—?

"Breck!" Adora snips in a loud whisper.

The servant girl looks up and something's clearly wrong with her. Her face is puffy and there's bruising around her eyes. She's either been beat up or in a fight. She stands. Bows to Adora and mumbles that she'll be back later to finish.

As soon as she's gone, Adora's gaze is back on me. "And Eogan? How was your time with him?"

"Fine. What happened to Breck?"

"Fine *how*?"

I stare at her straight on. "Like I-despise-him fine. What happened to Breck?"

The first part seems to please her because she instantly smiles and swaggers over to me. For a second she looks as if she'll brush a hand across my hair, then pulls back and wrinkles her nose, taking in my outfit. "I'm glad to hear it. I trust you'll keep it that way. It'd be a shame to . . . cause anyone grief." She walks over to where Breck was cleaning the floor and taps her foot, drawing my gaze to the stained wood.

Wait . . .

My lungs fold.

Even from this distance I can see it's blood. Dried into two tiny separate pools.

I snap my head up. "What did you do to her?"

She lifts her hand and studies her sharp, green-painted

fingernails. "It's so reassuring to know I have your continued gratitude and commitment to my rules." The foot tapping ceases. "I trust your skills have almost reached their full potential?"

I clench my teeth. She beat Breck without any idea whether I'd followed her rules or not. And now she wants to talk about my skills?

Of course she does.

"I'll take that as a yes. Good, because I have a job for you and Colin. A way to . . . alter the disappointing course of this war, if you will. We've a small window of opportunity three days from now that I believe to be our chance to save Faelen. I spoke with Eogan before you left, and he agreed. In the meantime, Lady Isobel is visiting the next five days, and you're to stay out of sight. Except, of course, for tomorrow evening's party. Understood?"

I stare at the bloodstained floor through my anger and slowly force a nod.

She's careful to avoid brushing up against me on her way to the door. "Oh, and before you dress for bed, wash the filth off yourself."

As soon as she's gone, I walk over to stand beside the blood. A servant being beaten is nothing I'm unaccustomed to, but Breck . . . The smell of the soap stings my nose along with my own sweat. It turns my gut. *This was because of me?*

My hands ball into fists even as my legs grow shaky and my vision narrows in anger, disgust. I slide to the stained floor before my knees give way. It's always because of me.

Colin. The little boy's village. The wolf. And now, Breck.

Five. Ten. Fifteen minutes I sit as the fury inside builds,

inflicting pictures of the latest life I've destroyed—even if only a wolf. And of the lives I'm on the brink of destroying.

That I'm being conditioned to destroy.

I hate this, hate all of it.

The sky outside begins rumbling the same way my fingers are quaking, and suddenly that twisted thing inside me is aching, churning. I tug one of the knives Eogan made from its sheath and look around for my mugplant jar even as Eogan's gaze drifts through my head.

I shake it off. How dare he invade my private space. Especially when part of this is his fault.

I press the blade against my skin to add a mark, a branch just beneath the bluebird. But that face, his gaze, won't stop. And for whatever reason, I can't shut it out. It comes again, lingering a moment before slipping a path all the way through me. And then abruptly there's Adora's face smirking down at Breck.

I stop.

Adora. I raise my shaking chin and glare at the bloodstain on the floor. I clench my jaw. From somewhere the determination emerges that, whether because of me or not, this insanity of Adora's has to stop. And no mark of guilt is going to do that.

I lower the knife even as everything in me screams to continue—*needs* to continue.

But I won't.

I don't.

My hands are shuddering as I resheath my knife, just before I hurtle a roar of thunder to shake the entire house.

CHAPTER 22

S O AM I TO HAVE THE PLEASURE OF DEALING with your attitude *all* day?" Eogan watches me dismount from my mare. "Or are you just ignoring me to make a point?"

His tone is overly polite. Same as it's been ever since we left the High Court's lengthy shadow this morning to travel east toward a lake I'd never heard of. Two hours of riding with a wall of tension between us, and there's still nothing I care to say.

"It's more convenient for both of us, don't you think?" I mutter, struggling to release Haven from her bridle.

I pat her rear before turning to follow Eogan up a trail covered in traipsy trees leaching honey into the air. Above us, the cerulean sky hovers like an ocean, and I wonder if he's taking me to look at more warboats. Or wolves.

"You mind at least informing me of *why* you're ignoring me?"

My fingers flit to my mouth even as I glare at the back of his head and try not to notice how nicely his broad shoulders taper down to his waist. Or how stupidly gorgeous the rest of him is. I drop my hand and press up the path. "You had no right to do what you did on that mountain."

"Are we talking about the wolves or the kiss?"

"Both."

"As your trainer, I do my job in whatever way I see fit. And believe me, both were necessary." He tosses a glance back, his tone hardening. "Although neither is in danger of happening again, if that's what you're worried about."

I flinch but pretend it's the sun in my eyes. One moment he's taking my breath away and the next he's gouging holes in my insides. Like he's multiple men rolled into one, and none of them make sense but all make me insane.

"Let's just do this daft training session and go home," I mumble, shoving past him.

"This *is* part of the lesson. Today we're going to get out all this pent-up anger you have and teach you to let go."

"In that case I'd rather go back to Adora's."

"Annnd that would be the pent-up attitude I'm talking about."

Is he jesting? "My attitude has to do with the fact that you endangered us, and yet you don't seem to care."

He actually laughs. "Believe me, you were not in danger from those wolves."

"No, but we *were* in danger from *me*. I almost destroyed that village because you pushed me into something I couldn't do."

"Look, if it makes you feel better, I never would've pushed you in so fast if I'd had any idea you'd react like that. Even though whatever resulted from the session, Colin and I would've handled it just fine. As we did."

I stop and turn to stare at him. *Is he an idiot?* "How could you not know I'd react like that? You're training me to kill, and people almost died. Does it even occur to you what it *does* to me? To know that *every* time I erupt, I see more blood on my hands?"

Something flickers through his expression and his tone frosts over. "You think I don't know what it does to you? Why do you think I blasted Colin after your little common-house exploit? That's exactly why I set you up with the wolves. To show that you can do this. To let you prove to yourself *how* in control you are."

"Except I'm not in control! The only reason those people survived is because of you and Colin." The sky shudders and my eyes start to fill. I blink the tears away before a dumb storm hauls in.

His face pales. "You were in control, Nym. You could've taken out that entire wolf pack and you didn't."

"Right, I just almost took out a portion of Faelen instead. And now Adora's got some brilliant plan to use Colin and me for more destruction."

He closes his eyes and pinches the bridge of his nose. "Look. The other day you asked what happened to the others I trained for Adora."

He runs a hand down his jaw and exhales.

"What happened is I trained them too well. To the point they outgrew their consciences. They became assassins, killing when it was faster rather than finding a better way. You heard me say the other day that killing is a part of war. But it's not the *only* part. It should always be a last resort."

My bitter chuckle slips out. "And yet you and Adora can't wait to use me. 'Train harder, Nym.' 'Are you ready, Nym?' 'Faelen's going to fall without you, Nym.' Except I don't want to be used that way."

"Which is exactly why I've been working with you. Because if it wasn't me, Adora would've found someone else or tried to train you herself. Your power is like none we've seen, and they would've ruined you, Nym. I've known from the beginning you're capable of learning control—but what I needed to know was, when you achieve control, if you'd have the conviction to reserve death as a last resort rather than an easy solution."

I open my mouth to argue, but his words spread over me like a blanket soaking into my soul. It brings a flavor of freedom that I'm too numb to taste.

He smiles but it doesn't reach his eyes. "That test proved what I already knew. That you're not like them. You're not like *me*. I'm not training you to be a weapon. I'm training you to hone your abilities so you and you alone will have the choice to protect as far as you're able. So you can live with your conscience. With those wolves, you made a decision and found a better way." He hesitates, and I'm abruptly aware of an urgency in his demeanor I've not caught before. "Which means we can now finish the lesson."

Forgiveness for him emerges at his confessed intentions even as my curse rears its head at his ignorance. *If only it worked that way.* I shake my head. "No matter how much control I learn, it'll never be enough."

He peers down at me. "We'll see."

Turning, he resumes his lead up the trail until we've gone

another half terrameter, then veers us off the path toward a wall of hedge and trees.

"Through there." He pulls a bough back and waits for me to duck the overgrown branches. I keep my gaze straight as I slip past him—acutely aware of how warm his body radiates and how perfectly his eyes match the landscape.

I step through the scraggly opening and out onto a rainwater-tipped field overlooking a vast, glittering valley.

Mother-of-kracken.

I stall.

The air is wet and cold and drippy and enchanted.

And it tastes of magic.

I drink it in along with the magnificent forest spinning around us. It's one from another era, much older than Faelen, and gracefully woven in and around hillsides of pale meadows meandering all the way down to touch a slumbering gray-jeweled lake. And it's completely undefiled by hovels or roads or chopped-down trees.

My skin tingles with the concentration of old magic drifting in the air, and I half expect the breeze to carry songs up from the wood folk or the cries of the ancient elfin battles. My lungs fill with its delicate melody as wisps of fog trail along the skyline, like translucent fingertips lacing through the trees, spreading their aura and the scent of the day's summer storm.

The warm earth reaches up through my boots, as if it's alive, pulsing. This place is so unlike anything I've ever sensed or seen, and yet something within my cracked soul says I've been here before. That I know it just as I know the song it's whispering. It invokes a homesickness I don't understand, and my heart is threatening to weep, to stay, to live and drink and drown in it, leaving the world and war behind.

"What is this place?" I whisper.

"The Valley of Origin." Eogan sounds as in awe as I am. "A place used centuries ago to worship the Hidden Lands' creator. Until the five kingdoms divided and most people forgot about it."

He stands there allowing me to soak it in until all too soon our silence grows full of self-consciousness. I can feel it—the charge in the air thickening. I search for something to talk about, aware that from a foot away he's watching me, not the landscape.

"Tell me about your parents, Nym."

Not the topic I was searching for. I shrug like there's nothing to say.

"Do you . . . ?" His voice catches. As if he doesn't even want to ask. "Do you remember how they . . . died?"

Yes. I glance at my hand. "It doesn't matter."

"Did they have other children?"

I fake a laugh. "I think their hands were too full with me."

"I'll bet they were."

My sharp glare is met by that breathtaking smirk of his. *Oaf.*

"They were older. My mum said they tried for years to have babies, and when they finally did . . . they got me. The world's anomaly."

"Were they happy toward you?"

"Yes," I answer slowly, unsure of what his point is. "Well . . ."

"Well?"

Until I murdered them. I shift away from him and kick a pebble in the grass. *Can we just get on with the day's lesson already?*

He stares down at the lake. "Has it ever occurred to you

that maybe you were born for such a time as this? And not just because of the war, but for the people who need you?"

I frown. "Has it ever occurred to you that I'm sick of talking about this? Let's just train."

His smile turns stubborn. "You don't have to talk. But you can't deny that for as long as the war has been going on outside Faelen, her society has waged its *own* internal war on its lowest-caste citizens. You should know. You've been a victim of it."

My stomach clenches. I've no interest in reminiscing about what I've been a victim of. I turn away, but his hand grabs mine. "Look, all I'm asking you to consider is that you have the power to change things. What if the reason you were given that power is to defend those without any? Both from external and internal harm. Like a shieldmaiden for your people."

"A shieldmaiden who's spent the first half of her life as a monster?"

I tug away, but he won't release me. Instead he steps closer and looks down with eyes full of pity. "You didn't know what you were doing."

I don't want his blasted pity. "Right, and that makes it better."

"No, but it's a far better explanation than simply assuming you're cursed. And it's a hulls of a lot better than wasting your life regretting the gift you've been given. Right now you're striving after a redemption you don't even believe is attainable."

I doubt "gift" is what my parents were calling it as they burned alive in their beds. "It's not a gift, and there is no redemption for me." I jerk my arm until he releases me to walk away.

"And that right there is why you can't fully control your ability. Because you're afraid to believe better about yourself."

"Because I know myself, and I'll continue to hurt people. I'll hurt Faelen, and I'll end up hurting Colin and you. Just like I hurt Breck."

"Breck?"

I close my eyes. *Litches. Why can't you just shut it, Nym?*

"What do you mean? What'd you do to Breck?"

I swallow.

"Nymia."

Fine.

I don't look at him. "When I got to my room yesterday . . . Breck was . . . scrubbing blood off the floor. I think it was her own blood, and something was wrong with her—like she'd been beaten. Adora made it clear she'd had something to do with it. Because of me."

"Adora hurt her? In *your* room? Why didn't you tell me? What was she trying to do—threaten you?"

I open my eyes and look miserably at the ground.

"Nym," he growls, "did Adora threaten you?"

"Everyone threatens everyone." My voice is a tired wisp.

He catches my chin and tips it up, anger pasted across his features. "Who's *everyone*?"

I blink tears away and start to shrug him off, but those emerald eyes filet me one piece at a time until I'm naked and exposed. And it hurts like litches because I'm starving to tell him all of it but terrified of the ramifications. Not just that they'll be hurt— that *he'll* be hurt—but knowing that two hours from now Eogan will be back to his mode of pretending that I don't exist as anything more than a tool for war.

I clear my throat and force a casualness I don't feel. "Adora ordered me to stay away from you except when training, or else she'll hurt Colin. And Lord Myles, he . . ."

Eogan raises an eyebrow. Waiting. His gaze darkening. "Myles what?"

I shake my head.

His fingers slip from my chin as his eyes slit into pure, unadulterated ferocity. "Myles threatened you *how*, Nym?"

His expression instantly smoothes. He straightens. "Look . . ." He runs a hand through his hair. "I'm not going to force it out of you, Nym, but if there's something I need to know—you have to tell me. I've been at this a lot longer than you, and I don't want you worrying, and I certainly don't want you doing anything about it. I'll take care of it."

I want to argue, but his expression says I'll only make it worse. So I just nod. But all I see are Breck's puffy eyes and Eogan's slit throat.

He leans in until his bangs sweep my forehead. "Promise me."

I don't say anything. Because I won't—*I can't*—promise not to try. Because I'll not have him getting hurt because of me.

He tips his head back and sighs, then studies me. Until that appealing half smile emerges. "So Adora told you to stay away from me, eh?" His gaze slides slowly down my body, then back to my face. "And how's that working for you?"

My mouth drops open. *Fine. Good. None of your business. I'm failing miserably.* But none of my answers come because my throat has just collapsed. *Stupid bolcrane.*

He chuckles and makes some unnecessary comment about me blushing. I twitch my hand and send a single hailstone through the air to slap his head. He lurches and laughs harder.

I start to smirk, then frown as I look from him, to my hand, to the hail remnants in his hair.

His expression turns quizzical.

"How come your block didn't stop that from hitting you just now?"

He shrugs. "Lucky aim."

Daft answer. "Why?"

"I told you—it works differently with different people."

"Okay." I bite my lip, examining him. "So you can use it to calm me, but . . . it doesn't *protect* you from me?"

His expression turns careful. "Like any ability, my block has its weaknesses."

Against my will, the edge of my heart ripples. *Am I a weakness for him?* "What, like it only protects you from certain people? What about the avalanche—does it work against anything trying to kill you?" My relief soars. Maybe it will protect him from Lord Myles.

"It's usually more an issue of when than who. It doesn't guard me permanently."

"Usually?"

The look on his face shuts me down. Then he's grabbing my arm and tugging my sleeve up and sliding his fingers along my deformed hand. "So how about we do this thing?"

"What thing?"

He smirks. "Close your eyes."

He presses down as I comply, and there's an immediate thickening in the air as the damp, magic-soaked atmosphere rushes into my lungs. The next thing I know, it's launched through my veins, singing through my blood and muscles, infusing them with that ancient melody I swear I know and yet have never heard.

That feeling of homesickness returns, and if I concentrate hard enough, I can almost hum the enchanted refrain from another time, another spectrum, as it blends earth and sky and water into a heartbeat that is pulsing with my own.

"Feel that?" he murmurs.

I hardly nod. With my eyes shut, I've come from this ancient time, this ancient place. I was created out of its elements, and now those elements have returned to awaken everything around us—the ground, the valley, the lake—they're in my mind and in my breath, as if they're the original version of me. The thing I was intended to be.

"What's it doing?" I gasp.

"Reminding your heart of who you are, and what your Elemental race is for. What *you* were created for." His chin brushes my hair as he leans in, sending goose bumps down my skin. "Now this is the part where you let go."

What? How? I start to panic, but something inside of me shifts, as if the magic filling my lungs is speaking and I should listen. And I know instinctively that it's stirring me, inhabiting me even as it's whispering that it's incapable of inhabiting evil. The thought emerges that, therefore, there must be a goodness within me that predates my curse. I exhale and cautiously allow the siren within me to respond.

I brace for it. But instead of my power exploding like a thunderstorm, it comes as a gentle tide. A heart surrender. Almost painful in its approach, beckoning tears to my eyes as it renders my defenses nonexistent. And suddenly I can't remember why I ever needed them anyway because the very power I've spent my life cowering from is, at its core, pure.

A mist forms on my face, my neck, my lips.

Eogan's hand slips down to mine. "Open your eyes."

His face is the first thing I see. Tiny, jeweled water droplets cling to his dark eyelashes. The drips shiver as he smiles before they release to join the millions of others floating around us—around the entire valley—in rainbow-lit colors. As if the world's gravity no longer holds sway over the elements.

I stretch out my hand and the rainbow mist collects on my skin, molding to me like a colored suit of glass. I lift my arm higher and the water ripples into place along it like crystalline armor. Then I'm reaching farther, toward the distant lake, where I can feel the energy flow as I pull at the air. The lake waters churn and move, no longer gray, but brilliant and alive as a geyser shoots up out of it to follow the arc of my hand. I tug it harder and, like a serpent, it rises into the sky, ready to do my bidding. Beside me, Eogan swears.

I release the water in a giant splash and turn to the storm clouds lacing the valley. With a flick of my wrist, they crack and release a lightning bolt, but before it can land, I tug it closer. It hits down ten feet in front of us. The static from it stays in my fingers as it zaps back and forth on the watery shield. I lift my hand to show Eogan.

He starts to touch it, and when I pull back because it'll kill him, he smirks and grabs my hand, then presses it to the center of his shirt-covered chest.

The energy releases a glow on his body, and suddenly his skin is fire and lightning and northern night skies, igniting the air around us. He grins, eyes brilliant as they smolder down at me, his heartbeat alive against my hand, sending my stimulated lungs lurching into my throat.

I swallow and try to relegate my emotions back toward some

level of safety while the storm in his eyes crackles in amusement. "You have no idea how extraordinary you are," he murmurs, and suddenly I can feel the hunger pouring off of him as thick as it's leaching from me.

My jaw drops. The clouds in the distance roar and the floating droplets ascend to create new clouds of their own as a gale picks up, whipping my hair back.

Eogan raises an eyebrow, and his eyes blaze. As if the same lightning storm assembling above us is now poised at the edge of his gaze, determining whether or not it will engage. His breath shudders as my mind forms a definition for the look in his eyes: Craving. Conflict. Apology. Written in colored-light reflections across his handsome face. The pulse in his neck quickens. His inhale is hesitant as his gaze slides down to my lips.

My rib cage curls. Wavering. Terrifying me with how badly I want him to kiss me again.

He pushes a hand along the side of my neck and into my hair, then runs a thumb down my jawline as he tilts his face to hover an inch from mine. His finger stops beneath my trembling lower lip.

My world pauses.

His eyes flicker. An agonized smile, and suddenly he's clearing his throat. But his voice is still husky when he says, "Look up."

Confused, I trail his gaze up to the storm surrounding us.

The winds should be ripping the ground up from beneath us and tearing the forest and the sky from its very axis because the hurricane is stronger than anything I've ever created. But instead, everything remains untouched, seeming to move in time with the chaos, in a wild cyclone of light and water and rainbows, a shield of lightning and snow with us directly in its eye. Abruptly,

I am falling, swimming, flying apart inside as the siren within me finds the door to her cage flung open and deliverance to be near. *Deliverance. Freedom.* The words sear themselves to my heart.

I smile at Eogan. I can feel control emerging.

"Now do you believe you were created for better?" Eogan whispers.

His body trembles as his mouth grazes my skin just before he rests his chin in my hair. I close my eyes.

When he sighs, it's one of self-control.

After a moment, he pulls away and his face has already transformed into his very official, disgustingly polite self. "Come on. We need to get you back, or you'll be late for Adora's party."

CHAPTER 23

"HOW 'BOUT THIS ONE?" BRECK SAYS IRRITABLY, and holds up the filmy blue dress Adora nearly busted her panty seams over a few parties ago. She runs her hand down the material and tries to suppress a cough in its sleeve, her chest sounding tight even though her skin's a better color today.

I crinkle my brow. "Breck, you sure you're all right?"

"Fine. Other than waiting for you to decide on a dress."

I drop my hairbrush and take the garment selection from her arms. "I told you I can get myself ready. You should go rest. Or, at the least, go check out that hippo they're roasting in the kitchen," I add with a teasing tone.

Her hazy eyes don't change expression, but she licks her lips and rubs a hand across them.

"Go. Adora'll never know you weren't here."

She wheezes into her palm. Tucks a ragged hair strand

behind her ear. "Well, in that case, you just be sure an' curtsy at the king for me, miss." She hustles from the room before I can reply.

Miss? I watch the door close. *What the bolcrane did Adora do to her?*

I press a hand to my pounding head, pathetically aware that whatever game Adora is playing, I'm losing. An hour ago, upon returning from the valley, I asked Breck flat out about Adora while we recolored my hair brown. She actually snarled at me and said we weren't "goin' to be talkin' about it. Ever." When I queried if it was because of Eogan, her expression turned confused, then angry. "I said it's none of yer business. An' if yer smart, you'll stop askin' an' just do what Adora tells you to win this war."

I didn't have the heart to tell her I'm not sure I can do that—not if Adora's plan proves anywhere near as twisted as our owner. And whatever role Eogan's playing in it . . . between the two of them, I'm beginning to feel like an asylum patient. *He wants me, he wants me not. She despises me no matter what, and she'll hurt people anyway.*

I stalk over to the mirror and hold up Adora's hand-me-down dresses one at a time. The last one in the pile is a billowy satin the color of gray stormy skies. Uneasy. Dangerous. I swag it under my chin, and whether it's my imagination or the magic still haunting me, my eyes flash. As if the valley's enchanted melody is still there. *You're stronger than them*, it whispers.

Yes. I am stronger. Even if I doubt the *than them* part.

I decide to wear the poofy dress, thanking the stars that there are minimal buttons. Even so, it takes three times as long to put it on due to my gimpy fingers.

The first trumpet rattles the mirror while I'm attempting to fix my hair like Breck does. But within half a minute, I've conceded that the best I can do is to leave it down in its long, saggy curls and hope Colin won't tease me too badly. I'm shutting the door and hitching up my skirt when the second trumpet blast comes. It sends me running for the stairs, and by the time I reach Adora's ballroom door where the bald boy is waiting, I'm breathless.

"Cutting it a little close," he whispers.

I ignore his admiring glance at my attire until my search of his face satisfies me that his health is almost back to normal. His body heat's still high—I can feel it—but his smile says he's good. And the fever's put a shine in his eyes that matches his brown doublet handsomely.

Colin's grin widens. He winks and opens the door just as the third trumpet erupts and, with his hand on my waist, shoves us into the miniature ballroom. I pull us around guests swathed in more glitter and perfume than anyone should safely inhale, interrupting the attendees' excited murmurs with my apologies as we make our way to stand opposite Adora, who's frozen in a curtsy with her hand aloft. She looks like some morbid version of a tree nymph in an amber-colored twig dress. Especially with the carcass of a dead squirrel attached to one shoulder.

Without turning, her eyes snap offense at our tardiness before meeting my rueful smile with loathing. I swear the room's air drops just as King Sedric strides up, and we bow with the rest of the guests.

Then the king's taking her hand. "Lady Adora, I'm looking forward to this evening's party as well as the negotiations to follow."

The squirrel head on her shoulder jiggles as she laughs. "Your Highness flatters me. The idea that anything I do could help ease the kingly weight you carry humbles me. Of course, I'm always entirely at your service. To ease . . . whatever troubles you may have."

My brow goes up. I lift my fingers to hide my giggle as the king's expression freezes. His gaze turns awkward a moment before he releases her hand and steps back.

"Is there really no limit to her flirting?" someone behind me mutters.

No. No, there's not.

"Allow me to present the Lady Isobel to Your Majesty," Adora continues, and on cue, a woman unfurls like a flower from a mound of fur cloaks beside my owner.

A gasp shreds through the room.

How I didn't notice her two seconds before is beyond me, because now her presence permeates the entire suffocating space. Tall and willowy, with black eyes and raven hair set off by a tight, nearly see-through gown, she's the picture of power and intimidation and seductive delicacy. If Adora can control a harem of men, this woman could dominate a horde of warriors. And she can hardly be four years older than me.

Jealousy slips up my throat. *Eogan fully lied.* I jab Colin in the ribs to make him shut his gaping mouth before he gets drool on me.

Lady Isobel glides forward, surrounded by five female masked guards, and offers the king her gloved hand. She doesn't curtsy or bow or show the least bit of deference beyond a cor- dial nod, but if the king is intimidated or impressed by her, he doesn't show it. In fact, he may be the only person who's not falling over himself to stare at her.

A host of introductions are made between the lady and others of the High Court's esteemed council—including Lord Myles, who pulls his attention from Isobel long enough to smirk at me. I narrow my gaze and tip it to his cravat, as if he's got some unsightly stain on it, then bite back my amusement when he actually looks down. His responding glare is murder.

I smile innocently and return to studying Lady Isobel. And not just because she's gorgeous and unlikable and Eogan was clearly less than forthcoming about her physique, but because I've never seen a Mortisfaire before, let alone Draewulf's daughter. *What must it be like to have that kind of ability? To have that kind of heritage?*

I shiver just as a cheer erupts in the crowd. Adora and her dead squirrel are announcing she's arranged a special dance before dinner in honor of our guests. The three harpies pick up singing their mystical waltz harmonies as I pat Colin on the back and start for the side corner to blend in with the gaudy wallpaper.

"Wait! Dance with me," he says. But his eyes are still on Lady Isobel.

I'm saved from replying by three salivating ladies-dressed-as-mermaids who pounce. No doubt thrilled to have a handsome, very young man to fight over. I wave him off as they twirl him to the center of the room where Adora leads the waltz with two male guests, one dressed as a sin-eater and the other a fern.

"Excuse me, miss, would you—?"

"I'm flattered but not feeling well."

Two, three, thirteen offers later, and I don't even glance at the gentlemen before responding. My head blurs Adora's guests, who sound alike as they chatter about how the war has affected their access to frothy dresses and turned their servants into ninnies. But there's a tightness in their voices I've not heard before, and their tones dip at the word *war*. As if whispering it will make the reality less terrifying. I listen and keep my eyes on Lady Isobel.

I'm working to decipher the thoughts behind her smile as she converses with King Sedric and Myles when a number of generals near me pick up discussing the battlefront. I edge closer at the mention of the hundred airships that came into sight off the coast yesterday, floating above Bron warboats. Fifteen minutes of eavesdropping informs me where the likeliest strikes will come (to the northwest of us to gain control of the water pass), and how soon (any day), and how the infantry units have been repositioned.

Then the men move on, and after a brief moment of watching the group around Isobel, I make a decision.

I head for Lord Myles.

He catches my eye and excuses himself from the king and Lady Isobel's company. Not that he seemed to be a part of their conversation anyway. When he strides over, his snarled expression does nothing to hide his intrigue.

"Well, if it isn't the little Elemental seeking me out. I'm flattered."

"I want to speak with you."

"Of course you do. Truly, it's a wonder you haven't committed suicide from sheer boredom in this place."

"From the looks of it, your chat with Lady Isobel wasn't quite the thrill you'd hoped either. I wonder—was it your awkward flirtations that repulsed her or the stench of traitor?"

His lips pucker as he leans back to assess me. "Nymia. I swear I've misjudged you. That *sss*arcasm. Please tell me you employ it often. Because there's a shortage of sharp-witted women these day*sss*, and I find it positively entertaining. But here, how rude of me. Did you want to dance?"

"I don't dance. I want to talk."

"Hmm." He runs a glance down me. "Tru*sss*t me, talking should be the furthest thing from our minds. But no worries, we can do both."

"That's not—"

He slides a cold finger up my arm. "Tsk, tsk. It wa*sss*n't an invitation, love."

My feet trip over each other to keep the rest of me upright as he clamps one hand on my waist and the other over my owner circles and presses me to the dance floor. I'd slap him if I didn't think he'd out my Elemental status here and now to the king. Instead I step on his foot, hard, just as I catch Adora's scathing glare that's challenging me as to why I'm not cowering against the wall like a squashed fly.

Then Lord Myles is in my face. "You know, I think anger is an excellent attribute on you. You're practically glowing." He spins me close. "Perhaps I'll infuriate you more and see what spark*sss* we set off together, hmm?"

I frown. "My sparks get violent."

"That's exactly what I'm hoping." He pushes me out and twirls me until I'm dizzy, with only his fingers gripping mine, and in that moment Eogan is there. Stiff. Glacial. Watching us from the sideline. Then I'm back in Myles's arms, inches from his perfect teeth. "I believe you wanted to ask me something?"

"What do you know of Lady Isobel?"

"Such boldness. Let me gue*sss*—jealous of her beauty? Because, in point of fact, it's her political cunning that will take her far."

I ignore his slight and try to keep my eyes from Eogan and Adora, both of whom I can feel staring at my back. "But what's she really here for? And what can she do as a Mortisfaire?"

"Ah. I see." He keeps his hand on my waist and glides us around another couple. "Those, my dear, are the golden-egged questions, aren't they? Look around—everyone's dying to find out and yet terrified. So consider it an honor I happen to know more than them, and that I've, thus far, allowed you to live long enough to ask. Simply put, she's here to offer the help of the Dark Army she's been putting together right under Bron's nose. As far as being a Mortisfaire, I'm certain you've heard she's a descendant on her mother's side of that particular Uathúil lineage. A certain sect of maidens able to kill a person by turning his heart to stone. Very intriguing. And quite useful."

A shiver skitters down my spine. "How does she do it?"

"A whispered word, I'm told."

"So even *you* admit she's dangerous. And King Sedric thinks it's wise accepting her offer of an army supposedly made of monsters?"

"My dear girl, wars are won by taking risk*sss*. And monsters? Where *do* you get your information?"

"So you admire her, and King Sedric interacts with her. A little ironic considering your intolerance for Elementals, don't you think?"

"Perhaps because Elementals are rumored to be the more

212

dangerous. But tell me, is that a confes*sss*ion I hear? An official admission that you are, in fact, an Elemental?"

I clear my throat and try to keep my voice steady. "I'd like to know when and where the Bron airships will strike."

He startles a second before breaking into laughter. "What makes you think I know?"

"You're spying for them. I trust you've got your own backside covered enough to avoid the explosion areas. Like the High Court or Castle, for instance—when do they plan to hit those?"

"Oh my dear, what incredible spunk you have. It's a shame you're working with Eogan. But for amusement's sake—because truly, you do amuse me—let's *sss*ay I knew." He twirls me beneath his arm until I'm an awkward mess of arms and legs. "Why in Faelen would I tell you?"

"To spare unnecessary deaths. To recant your patheticness before I tell Adora."

"Let's see . . . the first does nothing for me. And the second will only get your boy over there killed. Speaking of which, he seems quite interested in u*sss* this evening. Shall we give him something to wonder about?"

"Leave him out—"

His icy lips press over mine in a slippery kiss. But before I can push him away, he's already grabbed my wrist and whirled me in the direction of Eogan. Then reels me back in with a smug expression aimed at the trainer.

"Are you trying to set me off?" I say furiously. "And I swear if you so much as touch Eogan, a hail of—"

"How perfectly delightful it would be to set you off," he whispers, and a mental image emerges of the two of us standing side by side, crowned and robed, beneath a lightning storm raining destruction on all five kingdoms. He smiles. "Imagine the fun we'd have together. And Eogan knows it. Just look at how he's watching u*sss*. So cold. So callous. Disapproving of such brazen fraternizing between an old student and a new." He shakes his head and sighs. "Once a trainer, always a trainer."

I start in shock.

"That's right. Didn't he tell you? I was his first and most powerful pupil. Until we parted ways many year*sss* ago. Then you came along." He runs an icy finger down my cheek. "I wonder . . . are you more powerful than me?"

He's a Uathúil too? Keep him talking, Nym. "What's your power?"

He leans so close his mouth touches my ear. "Sometime I'd like to show you. But for now, if you'll excu*sss*e me, I think Princess Rasha has just arrived. Which ought to be fascinating watching her and Lady Isobel paired next to each other in Adora's hou*sss*e, don't you think?" He spins me away and strolls off, leaving me to regain my balance in front of Eogan.

CHAPTER 24

EOGAN'S FACE IS A MASKED WALL AS HE WATCHES Myles stride away.

I dust off the lord protectorate's clammy slime from my arms and mutter, "You didn't tell me he was your pupil."

Eogan shifts his cool gaze to mine. His eyes drop to my lips, and a glint of irritation flares, then disappears. "There are a lot of things I don't tell you. And, clearly, there's no need seeing as you've quite an effective way of soliciting information on your own."

I frown. "He kissed *me*. And I believe soliciting information was the reason for us attending these parties."

"That's a bit daft considering today's conversation and the fact that I specifically asked you to leave Myles to me."

An instant later his expression brightens with fakeness. "Ah, Colin! Perfect timing. I think Nym was hoping you'd keep her company for a while. If you'll both excuse me . . ."

He walks off as Colin bumps my arm and chuckles. I paste

215

a grin on my face before I'm tempted to rip his off and hope to kracken he doesn't notice me shaking. "So you survived the love-struck mermaids." I nod to the dance floor. "For a minute there I thought we'd see blood and limbs flying."

He flexes. "I was like music for those ol' gals. So, you gonna tell me what you an' Master Bolcrane did today? And please don't let it be that you destroyed half the Bron armada without me."

"Only a third of it," I correct, and then smirk when he can't tell I'm teasing. I start to fill him in on our trip to the valley but stop when it's clear he's never visited the place and his only interest is whether violence was involved. "So what'd *you* do all day?" I ask instead.

"Slept in the library most of it. Until Adora caught me. She wanted to go over her plan for me an' you savin' the world. It's a pretty good one actually."

I'm immediately all ears. "Go on."

He scratches his bald head before ducking close. "Okay, so here's the thing. Rumor has it that the top Bron generals really 'ave taken the pass just above Litchfell Forest. And there's goin' to be a meetin' in a keep there in two days time. Right around the same place that the dwarf said the plague hit. Good cover, huh?"

I wait, with a premonition that says I'm not going to like the rest.

"All we do is sneak in an' assassinate—"

I'm shaking my head before he finishes. "No. No way. I'm not killing them."

"Nym, you can't be serious. Don't you get it? Like Eogan said—they're going to wipe out Faelen if we don't."

"Like Eogan said." And yet he seemed to say differently today. I shake my head again. "How about let's not talk about it tonight?"

I say to Colin. Mainly because I don't want to fight about it. My head hurts and I don't know what to think, and Eogan's got me confused again.

"Tell me about Princess Rasha," I add with my sweetest smile, hoping he'll take the drift in topic.

"Did you see her? She's got reddish eyes. Talk about strange. Bet it'd scare the bloomers off Breck to know I stood near her."

I follow his hand to where he's pointing, but the crowd blocks my view as they're abruptly moving toward Adora's banquet hall. Someone's just announced it's time to eat.

"Did you see Breck today?" I ask hesitantly. We trail behind the flow of guests to the wide doors until we hit a wall of bodies caught up in conversation.

"Nah, Lady Isobel's been too busy bossin' 'er around." Colin presses us forward to see what the interruption is just as I catch my name spoken unusually loud.

"My precious nephew and twice-removed niece," Adora is saying as the crowd shifts, revealing the twisted grin plaguing her face. "You'll have to forgive Nym though. It's hardly been over three weeks since I rescued her from her horrendous life—what with her parents and the favor house."

I stall as my stomach hits the floor.

"Accidentally set the house on fire with the morning coals. Literally killed her parents in their beds. I've always chosen to believe she didn't know what she was doing, poor thing. Can you imagine murdering your own parents?" The words—even as they're spitting from her mouth, I'm silently begging her to reel them back. *What is she saying? What is she doing?*

She turns to stare straight at me, as if surprised I'm standing there, except her glare makes it clear she knew. Her dress swishes as she steps aside for her listeners to get a complete look at her subject of humiliation. "You can imagine how unstable she still is because of it. I'm only glad I found her in time to save her from the favor-house life she would've gone back to."

Lord Myles's smirk is unconscionable, but it's not him I'm seeing. King Sedric, a woman I presume is Princess Rasha, Colin beside me—they all blur together as my gaze comes to rest on the one person I can't bear to hear this.

Eogan.

I watch his face blanch as my soul slides open in front of him. My chest shaking and my eyes freezing in place in confirmation of Adora's words. I killed my parents. The only parts she's left out are the Elemental aspect and the fact that my time at the favor house lasted less than five hours before I destroyed everything within a half-terrameter radius.

My mouth turns acidic, and my legs begin to quake so hard it's like they're echoing the crumbling inside of me. I can't breathe. How she found out about those things is inconceivable. I don't even bother to excuse myself. I rush off to find a servant's passage to die in.

When I reach a hallway, it's occupied, and just as I'm hurrying past to find another corridor, it dawns on me that the people standing in it are Lady Isobel and Breck. I pause, and they both tip their heads up. Isobel's expression turns to annoyance. *Has she been lecturing the poor servant?*

"I expect those things washed by morning," I hear her say loudly, then she turns on her heel and strides for the door leading outside. Not even bothering to look back at us.

"Breck?"

She ignores me and feels her way into a side hall that goes to the kitchen.

I lean against the wood-paneled wall and slide to the ground. If I shut my eyes, perhaps I can pretend this evening is just a trick of the light and I'll be back in the valley with Eogan, with the magic and crystal shield and his whispered breath in my hair. What's going on with Breck . . . What Eogan thinks of me . . . I have no idea. Not that it matters. Because I don't want it to matter.

But it all matters.

One minute, three minutes, ten minutes go by. I don't move.

"I don't know what you've done to infuriate Lady Adora, but that was unkind of her."

I spin to find the Luminescent, Princess Rasha, watching me. *What'd she do—follow me?*

I glare at her. Maybe eighteen or nineteen, her hair is the beautiful color of the cocoa stone and her skin like a rich sunburn, and Colin's right—there's a peculiar red hue to her gaze as she takes in my face, my shame, my Elemental eyes.

"What do you want?" I mutter.

She steps forward and stares harder at me, and for whatever reason I can't look away.

"She's not your aunt," she says, and it's a realization, not a question. She nods. "Explains her attitude."

"She's my owner," I say, so we're perfectly clear.

The Luminescent nods again. "Owner of your body perhaps, but not your spirit."

A rush of tears attacks my throat. I stifle them back and ask again, "What do you want?"

"To offer friendship, I think. For a time when you'll need it. The spirit in you isn't broken, just unbelieving. But in order to fly . . ." She holds out an airy hand. "You hold the key to your own cage."

Is she on some sort of herbs? I pull back as if she's offered poison. *She sounds like Eogan.* "Excuse me," I mutter, and, stumbling to my feet, I practically throw myself down the hall and out the servants' door, gulping in the cool air against my hot face.

I find the path that leads toward the barn and start down it, head throbbing under my fingers. Somewhere ahead of me a woman giggles. Whoever it is I hope she chokes.

When the pouty laugh surfaces again, I look up.

And come to a full stop in front of Eogan, who's entwined in the arms of the Drust ambassador, Isobel.

"You always were more stubborn than your Bron brother," she says as he lifts his gaze to meet mine.

CHAPTER 25

E OGAN'S FACE IS STIFF AS STONE AS ISOBEL SLIDES her hand across his chest. And even though he's not reciprocating, I'm fully aware he's not stepping away from her either.

She covers her mouth in mock surprise and, edging around him, winks at me. "Ooh, looks like we've been caught. And by the slave girl training to be a soldier."

My eyes flash to Eogan. My throat goes dry.

"Oh, don't worry," she soothes. "He didn't rat on you. I already knew what you were the moment I saw you. Eogan always was the best at training others to do the dirty work for him, weren't you, darling? Although . . ." She climbs her fingers up his chest, and a pang of jealousy shoves against my ribs. "It's only recently I heard you'd surfaced to trade in real soldiers to train Uathúils." She looks back at me. "Which begs the question, what kind are you?"

Eogan pulls her hand off him. "That's enough, Isobel."

The lady laughs. "Oh come now. Surely the girl can speak for herself. Or has King Odion's twin lost his sense of patience?"

My gaze darts to Eogan's face, and I'm abruptly coughing on my own air as I take a step back from both of them. *King Odion's twin? Is she jesting?* But no, she's not. Suddenly my tongue's forgotten how to move and my head's reeling like a swing because that blasted spasm of jealousy has been joined by confusion and pain gouging my gut. *What the hulls, Eogan?* I can't speak even if I wanted to.

His expression is furious and he's abruptly peeling himself from her. "Isobel, enough. Nym, go inside."

"Well now, you've just made it awkward." She pouts. "Is it because I spilled your little secret, Ezeoha? It's not as if they won't find out once Odion comes tromping through. And look at her—she won't tell anyone. I'm sure the poor thing's got secrets of her own. Anyway, someone in her position's just grateful to be alive, aren't you, dear? From the looks of it, she's far too weak-minded to consider betraying an heir to the throne."

"Eogan—"

"*Eogan*, is it?" The woman's lips curl. "On a first-name basis, I see. How interesting." She sharpens her gaze, giving me a once-over through the lantern-lit dark. She puts a hand on his shoulder and leans up to his ear, watching my reaction. I steady my chin and hope the rising anger hides the raw jealousy now eating its way through my skin.

She steps forward but pauses when I square my shoulders and glare.

"Oh Ezeoha," she purrs, "I do believe her secrets are even more entertaining than I thought. This Uathúil has a thing for you." She reaches toward me, but Eogan's hand is swift as he pulls her back. Her tone twists clear as death. "Trust me, sweetie, he's only capable of one love interest, and you're not his type."

If I strike her with lightning, can I take them both out? I let the sky overhead rumble as Eogan issues a warning, but, abruptly, Colin's running over, waving his arm. He stops when he sees Lady Isobel, then blurts out, "A messenger just told King Sedric that the Barren Cliffs have been breache—"

His sentence is cut off by a deafening explosion.

It sounds exactly as if the sky's falling.

Eogan grabs Colin and me and shoves us down as the ground shivers. The air fills with roaring and my gut drops into my knees. The sound keeps going, rattling my teeth, my head, my fingers. Isobel also stoops just as another eruption hits and my eardrums nearly burst.

Then Colin's shoving Eogan off of us, yelling something. We follow his pointing finger toward the valley between us and the High Court.

It's bathed in orange flames.

I start running, but Eogan lashes out for my hand. It takes a moment before I stop fighting him long enough to decipher his moving lips. "Go inside!"

I shake my head just as more mini-explosions catch my attention, farther off along the mountains. They're travelling down the entire Hythra Crescent. A chain of tangerine glows spark up in the distance, and my heart ignites with grief and fury all in one beat.

Eogan's grip firms as he turns to Colin. "Both of you go change into your leathers." He presses us toward the house as

Adora's guests spill out in a scene identical to the one my first night here.

Except this time the bombs aren't trial runs.

Abruptly, Adora is beside us, yelling commands before turning and saying, "Eogan, please join me in my chambers. The High Council wishes your presence. Colin and Nym, go to your rooms. Lady Isobel, you'll understand if I graciously ask that you get comfortable in *your* room until we have an assessment on the situation. After that, we'd appreciate your presence and input as well."

Isobel smiles. "Of course. I suddenly feel a headache coming on anyway. You'll send the blind servant up with tea, I expect." She presses fingers to her temple and, shooting a seductive smile at Eogan, struts through the excited crowd to the house. From the corner of my eye, I catch Myles standing in the center of the frenzy, staring up at the blaze with a twisted grin on his face. Then Colin and Adora are following Isobel. Eogan clamps a hand on my shoulder to push me after them.

"The world's going to hulls and she needs a cup of tea?" I say in a withering tone. "Nice girlfriend you've got there."

He propels me faster. "Don't, Nym. This isn't the time."

"Right. Because then we'd have to talk about what a complete liar Eogan, King Odion's twin, is, wouldn't we? Does Adora know?"

He catches the servants' door and holds it open as another blast ignites the dark in the distance, mirroring the blaze in his eyes. "No. And we'll discuss this later. Go to your room and wait for me." His voice lowers. "Don't make me lock you in."

The look I give him when I step through the doorway could

raze an entire water kingdom. I walk in the direction of my room, slowly.

Growling, he pushes past me, and I wait until he's far enough ahead before trailing him up the two flights of stairs and slipping into a hall recess. There, I pause for the various council members to file by. When the last disappears into Adora's study, I bolt for the door and slide my hand in the way to keep it from closing.

"We need to send help to the wounded," the king's voice muffles through the opening.

"It's unlikely there are many wounded left. You saw those explosions!"

"Besides, we don't have enough people to spare, Your Majesty. If we don't use the soldiers for battle, we'll seal our *own* fate."

"We can't just leave them! Those were villages they targeted. And can someone please explain to me *how* Bron knew where each of them was located?"

"I'll take Nym and Colin and start at the closest village hit." *Eogan.*

"No," Adora snaps. "I think it'd be better to have the two of them wait a couple days, Eogan, and then follow through on what you and I have planned. Even you told me—"

I curl my hand into a fist and I swear the magic from the valley sparks through it. I head for my room, shaking so hard it's near impossible to open my door once I reach it. *A couple of days? No rescue for those people? How can they be so callous toward their own citizens suffering less than an hour's ride from here? And Eogan . . .*

I can't stay here. I can't sit in my room and wait for who

knows what—more betrayal from him or Lord Myles? *Are* both *of them spies?*

I change into my leathers, nearly tearing my dress in the process of getting it off, and slip downstairs, listening as messengers run through the halls shouting orders above the servants' clatter. I pull my hood up and leave through a side door to put Haven's reins on.

The place where the bomb hit is less than three terrameters away, but every road between Adora's and the High Court is swamped with fleeing people and soldiers trying to hold back the panic. Riding bareback, I move onto the smaller farm paths, but even there, some of the guests from Adora's party have gotten their coaches stuck in the mud. I keep my face hidden and continue riding.

It doesn't take long to reach the ridge I'm looking for. When I do, the area on the hillside opposite me isn't just bathed in fire. It's spewing a blasted inferno of destruction as wide as the village that stood there. Flames lick through wood structures, billowing black smoke so hot and thick that Haven bucks and refuses to go farther. Tying her to a fence post, I sprint the rest of the way on foot, but even as I'm getting closer, it's obvious why they're not sending soldiers to help. There's nothing left to rescue.

I run for it, the magic from the valley surging through my veins. Surprising me with the ease at which I can pull down the rain and pour it over the demolished structures and boiling dirt, sizzling as the smoke rises to darken the clouds. Not until I reach the village edge does it occur to me to try to draw in more clouds from the coast and send them down the crescent. Maybe it'll deter the airships, or at least put out the fires at the other bomb sites.

With the rain stamping the flames out in front of me, I whisper in enough clear air to breathe. Then, tugging my cloak over my nose and mouth, I head toward the first smoky ruins to search for anyone left.

Then the second.

Then the third.

The higher up the hill I go, the more slippery the ground becomes and the thicker the smoke wraps around my throat—the steam and billows rising almost as fast as I can push them away with the rain-soaked breeze. I'm coughing by the time I reach the fourth home attached to what probably used to be a marketplace.

Searching through the dark, my burning eyes almost miss the hand reaching out from a charred doorway. My chest tightens at what I'll find, until I hear the feeble groan.

An elderly man. Trapped beneath a roof beam. I rush over and kneel, then bring in fresh air to keep the smoke off his face. He lifts his hand—flopping it around until I catch it in mine. "It's okay. I've got you."

He lifts my fingers to his cheek and sighs, and I sit there and watch him stare at the tears tumbling from my eyes, drenching my face, my clothes, the ground until, eventually, the light in his gaze fades, releasing his soul along with his breath.

I press his lids closed. "Go with the creator."

Wiping my cheeks, I force myself to stand, to move on in search of others. Except I rise too quickly because suddenly the world is spiraling, and two seconds later I'm bending over to vomit.

When it's finished, I wipe my face on my cloak and continue forward, using light cast by the cloud-ringed moon and what's left of the quickly fading flames. But each home I come to is filled only with the dead. Men. Women. Children.

I'm halfway through the village and hacking and coughing and calling in more wind when a strange noise emerges above the rain and sizzling buildings. A loud whirring. I look up and flick away the smoke high enough to see another one of the Bron airships.

It's heading for the High Court.

Anger. Fury. I don't know what it is, but I don't even think. I flick my hand and watch a lightning bolt strike the hull. One moment apologizing to those inside and the next cursing them for what they've done to this village. To Faelen.

Within seconds the airship explodes midair, as if a pocket of gas was ignited, and the entire thing is flying apart in an ear-piercing, fiery ball of red. Parts and debris disperse in every direction, and then, abruptly, it's all coming down. Except instead of falling for the fields, half of it's thrown right above the village, and right above me.

Run.

Enormous chunks of wreckage slice through the air, and I'm scrambling back the way I came just as one lands two feet in front of me. I jump and keep going. Another lands to the side, and then more, followed by splintered fragments that rain down like metal daggers.

I lunge beneath a barn's overhanging roof, but not before a shard slices my elbow and another rips open my leg. I cry out and cover my head, as if that will save me from anything else crashing through the rickety, burnt wood. Nausea rises again and the smoky coughs are chugging up my lungs, shredding my throat. I pull in fresh air from the valley and wait until the sounds of falling debris lessen. When I look up, small fiery bits are all that's left. They float to the ground, burning out one by one in the pelting rain.

Fiery bits of ash that used to be people—I try to squelch that thought, but it seeps in anyway. I killed them intentionally, in anger. *Before they could kill others*, I tell myself. But their lack of innocence doesn't make it okay. Just like Eogan knew. Just like he trained me for.

With a cursed sob, I pick myself up and start dragging my leg in the direction of Haven.

The ground's too slick and I slip once. Then again. Then I'm back up, coughing and stumbling forward, only to squint at what I think is a shadow walking toward me through the wreckage.

A shadow with emerald eyes.

Eogan's gaze smolders, taking in the scene as he crunches across broken glass and smoking wood to where I'm standing. I stagger forward and look down at the dribbles of dark blood oozing from my elbow. They patter on the dirt like rain.

Eogan's exclamation is not meant for female ears as I crumple to the ground, and the next moment he's at my side. Even though I despise his lying, traitorous self, my aching heart says his face is still the most beautiful thing in my world as he's poring over me, searching for injuries. He grabs my hand and inspects the blood, then pulls my chin up to examine my face.

"How bad are you hurt?" But before I can respond, his gaze falls to the torn leathers on my thigh. His expression churns.

Waiting for it . . . For him to yell. To scold. To do whatever.

Instead, he pulls his shirt off and rips it into lengthy shreds, grimacing when I cry out as he binds my leg and elbow.

When he's finished, his gaze meets mine and sticks a moment.

"I killed them," I whisper. "In the airship."

"You did what you had to."

"I should've found another way." But even as I say it, I know there was no other way. This was different from the redheaded girl. The grim set of his mouth says he knows it too. *This is how I will live with my conscience.*

"How'd you know I was here?"

Another explosion of falling timbers, and Eogan grabs his sword and slips his arm around my waist. He pulls me up before muttering heatedly, "Because I know you. Really, what the kracken were you thinking, Nym?"

I shake my head and try to draw in more air, but suddenly I'm not focusing well. "I had to help the people."

He starts walking with me. "Who, Nym? Look around. They're all dead!"

They're all dead.

In the fire. The smoke. The rain.

And I killed some of them.

I *do* look around.

And abruptly I am five years old with my storm raging overhead.

And all I see is my home in flames and my parents in the old man's dying face as my blood soaks in and makes a spattered mess all over the binding on my arm.

I jerk away from him. They have to be here. I need them to be here.

"Nym, you're exhausted and we have to go. Come on."

But I can't leave again. Maybe I can save them. Maybe I can tell them I'm sorry and show I have control now.

I reach out, but it's Eogan's hands, not theirs, that find me and start dragging me back. Because he doesn't care—for me, for them, for any of us. I squirm—pushing, pressing to get away. "You don't understand. I have to save them!"

"Nym, you can't save anyone. They're all dead!"

What? For a moment my head swims, my thoughts melting into shadow. *No, he's wrong. He only wants to take me away from my white, snowy world.* My five-year-old self is kicking and screaming and I'm half blind pushing him off again. "I have to find them! I have to help my parents!"

And then he's yelling, too, but his words don't make sense and, abruptly, the pain from my leg hits the raging torrent in my head. My screams cut off as my lungs suffocate from the smoke.

He yanks me against his chest and pins me there. And for one moment I swear I hear grief break his voice when he murmurs, "Your parents are dead, Nym. Because I helped kill them."

My entire world dissolves into darkness.

CHAPTER 26

S ILENCE.
    I open my eyes to four stone walls and a drippy ceiling
    that, at some point during the night, spread its dampness
to the blanket covering me. My breath rasps and when I try to sit
up, my lungs catch fire. The resulting coughing fit sends the cut
on my thigh screaming and my mind lunging into last night's
disaster:
The flames.
The dying man.
The falling airship.
    I hack harder—until I'm scared my lungs are going to rip
out—and end up on my side just as the door opens.
    I peel my swollen eyelids up.
    Adora.
    Arms crossed, mouth set in a gold-lined frown framed by per-
fectly erected hair and a gaze bloated with anger. "You're awake."

I'm dying, my brain whimpers.

She crosses to stand beside the bed, lips pressed, and taps her fingernail on her arm. "I doubt you can imagine how worried I was when Eogan brought you home last night. All of my time, all of my investment in you, almost vanished down the drain. I actually had to wonder if you'd survive the night with all that wheezing. And yet . . ." Her voice pitches as her fingers brush down the blanket covering my throbbing leg. "Here you are."

Her hand stops over my wound.

"Which is what I like about you, Nym. Your determination to live—to survive—no matter how much trouble you cause others, nor how dreadful you treat me after everything I've given you. *You. Still. Fight. To. Survive.*" She mutters that through her teeth. Then she smiles, and it's so fake it makes my gut flip.

"The physician informs me you'll be fine enough within a couple days. The leg injury's not too deep, but we'll need to keep up with your medicine to hold off the sepsis. Although as far as anything to ease your pain . . ." Her fingers press on my injury. "I have opted to forgo that."

Abruptly, her hand is digging into my wound.

I scream. She pinches harder until I'm writhing and my curse is flaring, except there's no charge in the air to pull energy from. *How deep is this room beneath her house?* Water droplets collect in a pool along the ceiling, as if I could somehow manipulate them against her.

One, two, three more agonizing seconds and, mercifully, she relents and steps back. "You see, I need your head clear, Nym. Free of this ridiculous draw you have on Eogan, and from everything but the job I have for you."

My entire body is pulsing. Fading. *Where is Eogan?* I consider asking, but the throbbing is jumbling my thoughts.

"King Sedric has met with Lady Isobel to negotiate the loan of her army, but in all likelihood, it's too late. Three Bron generals have already taken a portion of Litchfell Forest and are currently holed up in a fortress there, commanding their armies. I believe our only hope is to have you and Colin buy us time by destroying that fortress and the generals within."

My mind's growing hazy.

"I'm giving you the choice, Nym. Save Faelen, or spend the rest of your days in this cell—which won't be long when I decide to misplace the medicine and allow the sepsis to set in."

If she slams the door on her way out, I've no idea, because everything slips from consciousness.

Drip.

Drip.

Drop.

I brush a splash of moisture from my cheek.

When I open my eyes, the ceiling is still dripping and the lantern is dimmer. Eogan is standing there studying me from a spot against the stone wall.

From the looks of his damp shirt and tangled bangs, he's been here awhile.

King Odion's twin brother.

I turn over and stare at the mattress. I've a million questions to ask, but no motivation to start. *How long did he say he'd been with Adora—three years?* The same time period during which

Bron grew bolder. And here he's sat, privy to Faelen's most precious secrets.

The thought makes my stomach curdle.

"How do you feel?" His tone rings so official I could spit.

I don't respond.

A hesitation. His fingers pick up drumming against the wall. "The physician believes you'll be steady on your feet in two days' time. After that—"

"I don't care," I say hoarsely, eliciting another tortured coughing spell that forces me into a sitting position. It lasts half a minute before abating, and I look up to find his sterile attitude has caved to concern. It grates against the massive, aching chasm in my chest. *As if he has any right to worry.* "How *should* I feel?" I mutter. *Crazy? Infuriated?* "And who in hulls is asking? Eogan the trainer, or Ezeoha—Bron's heir?"

Eogan's jaw shifts. Tightens. "Both."

Right. I glance away. "Does Colin know who you are?"

"Only you."

"And Isobel," I point out in a raspy voice. "Who, by the way, I would've assumed was the love that broke your heart, except you didn't look too heartbroken in her arms last night."

His coloring fades in direct proportion to the hardness materializing in his eyes. The finger tapping slows. "I'm aware you won't believe this, but my heritage and past relationship are actually of little importance. What *is* important—"

He's right. I don't believe it. "Are you a spy?"

"I'd think you know me better than that. Although, considering the volatile situation, you'll understand why I'd wish to keep my identity private."

"An interest Isobel clearly doesn't share."

He frowns. "She won't reveal it at this point."

"Except to me because—let's see, how did she put it?—I'm 'just grateful to be alive and too weak-minded to be a threat.'"

"That's only because she actually views you as a threat."

"Bolcranes," I scoff. "Why would she, unless you're a spy?"

His harsh gaze flickers to my lips, where it pauses before dropping to the floor. He says nothing.

"Is that a yes? Because for kracken's sake, Eogan, at least have the guts to admit it! What were you doing—scouting? Trading secrets?"

"I think you've read enough of Adora's history books to know that most of my kingdom thinks I'm dead," he says bitterly. "I chose to leave Bron rather than fight Odion for my right to rule, not expand my dominance, so don't even attempt to judge my intentions."

"Right. And would those be the same intentions you had wrapped around Isobel's body last night?"

He utters an oath and pushes off the wall toward the door. "You're being ridiculous."

Then stalls.

He plows a hand through his black messy bangs as he turns back to me and sighs. "Look . . . Isobel was—*is*—a part of my past. Our fathers hoped to make a marriage of it, but clearly that didn't happen. I've not seen her in the four years since I left Bron." His glare narrows. "Now can we move on to why I'm down here?"

"What'd she do to you?"

A strange grief flexes across his face even as his lips curl. His breath wavers audibly, as if he's trying to decide whether to confess or curse at me. "Let's just say there's more than one way to turn a person's heart to stone," he finally growls.

I cross my arms. *Not good enough.*

He dips his head. "Fine. I was six. My father asked Isobel to *change* Odion and me. Guessing accurately that our blocking abilities would protect us physically while her curse hardened our emotions. Thus making us incapable of feeling and, in his mind, the *perfect pair*—relying on logic rather than the influence of sentiment. He then proceeded to raise Odion in politics and me as Bron's war general—assuming whichever of us was strongest would succeed him after his death. Except Isobel's curse worked too well on me. By the time he died, I didn't even care enough to fight for what, by rights, is mine as firstborn."

A hurricane of images slips through my head. Eogan's closeness, his coldness, his repeated withdrawals from me.

"It wasn't until I hit my coming-of-age that I realized the only emotion Isobel left me with was a desire for her. Something I eventually came to disrespect. Four years ago, when I left Bron for Faelen, I thought that perhaps if I lived among the people I'd slaughtered in my youth, it might . . . fix me."

A desire for her.

The people I slaughtered in my youth.

I narrow my gaze, not even attempting to hide the hurt and venom I feel. My fingers tighten into fists even as something from the smoky scene last night niggles at the back of my mind. Something he said . . .

Something made hazy by Adora's medicinal herbs.

His gaze drops to the ground. "Not until I discovered the Valley of Origin did something alter in me. It didn't break the curse completely, but . . ." His voice shudders. "It made me feel things. Remember things. And then . . ."

He lifts his eyes to mine and the niggling abruptly thrusts

up the dim recollection of his arms around me last night, dragging me away from the burning buildings.

"Then I met the girl from the Fendres Mountains whose home I helped my father destroy in an undercover training session at the age of ten," he whispers. "And I could still remember her white Elemental hair and her screams."

His admission snaps through my mental fog so fast, it draws a breath up my raw throat that sends my insides heaving, yelling.

My parents. My home. I realize too late a cluster of tears are sliding down my cheeks as a tremor surges inside, his words carving up my heart like a piece of meat.

He killed them. He destroyed my world.

Reluctant inhale. Hardened exhale. "You . . ."

I can't even get the words out.

And he let me believe it was me.

"Nym, I swear to you—"

"Don't."

"You have to understand—"

"Understand what? That you killed them? That you let me believe it was *me*? This whole time, Eogan, you *lied* to me! While you trained me! You lied *while you touched me!*"

And I thought I was the monster.

I scoot as far against the wall as possible.

"Nym, if I'd told you the truth at first, you never would've let me help—"

"Are you insane? I don't want your excuses! You had no right! You've not been helping me—you've been *using* me."

"I saved you! And yes, maybe I have used you. But you'd be under Adora's thumb right now if it weren't for me. Or worse—in

238

the favor houses. And I *did* help—I kept you from becoming one of Adora's war machines."

"Oh, cut the bolcrane—you just turned me into a more civilized monster! But the blood on your hands is still the same." I fight to keep my voice steady as the tears thicken up my throat. "Is this what Isobel did to you? Turned you heartless? Taught you to make people desire you in order to use them?"

He rubs a hand across his jaw and stares. And says nothing. He doesn't have to. His silence says that's exactly what she did to him—removed his ability to truly care about anyone but himself.

Hunger yes. Callousness yes.

Self-serving . . . ultimately.

It's a single, raw realization.

But it rocks through me like a hurricane tearing a hole in the fabric of my skin, exposing affections and cravings for him bound around heart-bones that, until weeks ago, had barely existed. I hate myself for it. For the feelings. For the aching my own desire brings. For the lies I let him use on me.

I turn to the wall and tuck my knees to my chin.

"Just leave," my voice snarls before a mangled sob erupts, and the quaking sets in and expands until the rest of me is cracking into a hundred wretched little fragments. Each one smaller than the last. Each one stabbing every inch of my flesh as anything left that matters is, bit by bit, swallowed up in the agony and anger.

The bed shakes beneath my chest until the only thing left is a fundamental need to breathe.

Eventually, even the breathing slows.

And at some point, my tears stop.

When they do, I discover that somehow I'm still here. Still me.

Still the Elemental I've been all along.

Just better trained and broken. Like one of Adora's warhorses.

I wipe my eyes. Clear the husk from my throat. And when I turn, Eogan's still standing there, his jaw working to speak.

"You were right, you know?" My voice sounds dead. A curse uttered from the lips of a ghost. "About our little game? You warned me you'd win."

Eogan's body solidifies as aching flecks of apology splay in rapid progression across his face.

I swallow. "And you did. So you can tell Adora I'm ready to speak with her."

When he doesn't move, I lift my chin. "I suggest you hurry if you want us to win this war."

The aching in his expression deepens. A millennia of seconds goes by before he squares his shoulders and nods. "In the future, when you aim for their airships, use wind instead of lightning. You might be able to force them down without frying the occupants or exploding the bombs along their hull."

"Right, and you know that because you're *not* a spy."

"I know that because I designed them. Six years ago."

Then he's gone.

I sag back on the bed as the lock clicks into place.

My mind clicks *out* of place.

And abruptly I'm lunging in a panic for the door, like a broken bird in a caged room. Fluttering to find the latch. To find air.

To breathe beyond the grief wrapping its talons around me as it pulls me to the floor.

CHAPTER 27

WHEN ADORA LETS ME OUT OF THE STONE room, it's into the hands of one of her fancy, perfume-doused men who clearly views walking a stumbling, puffy-eyed girl up five stairwells to be the worst form of torture. When we reach my bedroom door, he prods it open and grumbles about following me in.

My hand is on his chest so fast he can't recoil before a thunderclap rattles the wood hallway.

His eyes bulge and narrow.

"I need to change," I mutter.

Straightening his vest, he shakes me off before airily peeking into the room, as if to reassure himself I'm not planning some elaborate escape with my leg split open. He finally retreats, saying, "Fine, but you'll hurry if you know what's good for you. And if I hear anything funny, I don't care how naked you are, I'm coming in."

Right. Try.

I slam the door, then limp to the window and push it open to inhale thick gasps of the cloying, damp air. I exhale relief at the sight of the Castle and High Court, both still very much intact, gray and glittering on the hill. Only to drop my gaze at the sight of the torched hillside with its broken buildings and obliterated families.

I cringe just as a whip of rainwater slashes over my cheeks and chin, bringing with it the bitter scent of loss and grief and urgency. As if the elements themselves are furious at the lives destroyed. I can almost hear them whispering approval of my choice. Nudging me to move. To change all this.

I turn toward the armoire.

A knock sounds.

"Go away," I growl, but the door opens anyway, and Colin is there. He says something to the guard before pushing it shut, and even from where I'm standing, I can tell he's jittering all over. Adora must've met with him.

"So are we gonna go before there's not any Faelen left to save?" he says, bouncing on his toes. "I've got the map and Breck's gettin' the food. She'll be ready when you are."

"Adora's sending Breck?"

"To help with meals and keep an eye on my fever—even though I'm *fine*. Also to help with your leg since you're not yet 'ealed, an' apparently she needs Eogan for somethin' else. Except between you an' me, I think Adora's just tired of Isobel takin' free rein bossin' Breck around and is lookin' for a reason to annoy her."

I allow myself a smirk, and not just because it's a chance

to irritate Isobel, but because it'll also save me worrying about what Adora might do to Breck while we're gone.

"Besides, I asked if she could come," Colin admits. "Isobel's taken to bossin' her too far and I think maybe even hit 'er. When I saw the bruising . . ." His hands clench into fists and his voice shakes. "Adora had to hold me back from killin' that witch. Breck's keepin' a stiff lip about it, but still . . . between Isobel an' the airships, she'll be in more danger here. I'd rather she be with me than have to worry."

I nod but keep my mouth shut as to the real cause of those bruises even as a chill ripples down my throat.

"In that case I'll be ready in half an hour," is all I can say.

Turning back to the rain-slopped window, I allow myself one last look at the water coming down in sheets, coating the white Castle and far-off mountains in a rhythmic pulse that I swear matches the one churning in my veins. Bracing for what we're about to do.

Colin moves to stand beside me. He stretches his hand out and lets the drops splat on his fingers. "It's been like that since Eogan brought you in, you know. Like the sky's cryin' and won't let up for anything."

My skin freezes. I don't glance over at him. Just keep my gaze on the storm-swept landscape.

"That's because it *is* crying," I whisper. *Because my insides are crying.*

He's silent so long I finally look up to see what he's still doing here. He's examining my puffy eyes.

"They say it's the only thing keepin' the airships from makin' more strikes," he adds.

And then he's grinning and turning and bounding for the door, calling behind him, "I'll go saddle the horses."

Shaking myself alive, I drag my shrieking leg to the armoire and pull open the drawer where I've seen Breck keep the hair- and face-coloring products, including the comb and bottle of liquid used to counteract walnut-root juice. Both in hand, I climb into the basin still full of freezing water from yesterday's preparty bath and work quickly, stripping my hair back to its white.

Stripping my soul back to its creation.

Back to the Elemental I came into this world as.

When I'm done, I struggle into my blue leathers and strap my knives around my calf. I glance in the mirror on my way out the door, only to pause at the changes the past few weeks have wrought. *Has it been so long that I hardly recognize myself anymore?* I smile at the hair. Something within whispers how much I've missed that little bit of the old me. Like familiar friends that have spent too much time apart.

I grab my cloak and give way to another coughing spasm before hobbling out the door.

If Colin notices my hair beneath my hood when I reach the barn, he doesn't comment. He's too anxious to leave. "Breck's waitin' for us by the house." He pushes a tiny wood box into my hands. "I stole it for you. Open it."

Inside are a handful of small, odd-shaped tablets.

"Took it from Adora's room. There's enough medicine in there to dull the pain while we're gettin' to the fortress. It'll help you ride faster."

I refuse to cry.

Instead I thank him, then yell at him when it hurts like hulls as he helps me onto Haven. Once up, I feel over the bandages to ensure the wounds didn't reopen, before pulling out two of the medicine tablets and swallowing them, hoping the herbs won't just numb my leg and elbow, but everything else in me as well.

Tugging our cloaks around our faces, Colin and I canter out of the barn and across the yard where Breck's waiting by the servants' door. Our horses snort and shy when we get close, and judging by Breck's tight frown at my greeting, I can't really blame them. She's clearly less than thrilled by this adventure.

Colin laughs. "It won't be that bad," he promises, yanking her up behind him.

We exit the gate through the pouring rain—and maybe it's that we're heading toward battle, or toward the deaths I'm about to cause, but a shudder ripples across my shoulders. And as much as I'm tempted, I don't look back—for Adora. For Isobel.

For Eogan.

I gulp down the ache and, pressing Haven into a gallop, take the lead—weaving us through the mossy paths along the main road. It is cluttered with waterlogged carts and terrified-looking people, half of whom seem to be heading toward the High Court and the other half away from it. We slow a few times to cross paths between them, but then I'm right back to pushing our pace until, after twenty terrameters or so, the interior valley stretches out clear before us.

Soon the rain is the only sound aside from our horses' hoof-beats as the sky pours out on the black dirt and wheat fields shooting straight through the heart of Faelen. We ride past farms and empty markets and people who've nowhere else to go but in their homes while they wait and listen for airships overhead or the metallic tromping of Bron feet. The downpour runs rivulets off the roofs and front doors of every hovel we pass, glinting with the slivers of candlelight from inside. Ushering us on toward the gnarled emerald forest and white mountains that, even from here, whisper haunting reminders of my parents and my past.

At midafternoon, we stop beneath an abandoned sheep shed for a meal. I take another two pills and tug back my hood to look over the map Colin's pulling out.

He steps back and accidentally bumps into Breck, who's shoving half a chicken in her mouth.

He clears his throat.

"You look . . ." He's staring at my hair.

"Elemental, yes." I hold my hand out for the map.

He passes it over and keeps gawking as it occurs to me he's never seen my hair white before. Once I've unfolded the paper, he focuses long enough to point out a southwestern spot below Litchfell Forest where a sketched fortress is marked by a swirl of Adora's ink. I nod and use my finger to trace the various roads and spots where Adora made notations of soldier encampments. From the looks of it, Bron's forces are creeping along Litchfell and down on Faelen's southern ridge. The airships must've destroyed our forces in the Fendres Pass days ago for how much of the area Bron now controls.

Colin leans over my shoulder. "What do you think?"

From her spot on the ground, Breck hooks a nappy chunk of hair behind her ear and says, "We need to be there by tomorrow afternoon." As if neither of us were aware of the fact.

My thanks to her is canceled out by a coughing spell that rattles my entire body. When I'm done, I shake off Colin's look of concern and show him the path I'm considering, which is the same as Adora's with one exception. "Adora's right. This is our best bet. It's the fastest and will invite the least interference—both from our soldiers and Bron's. Until we get to here."

I indicate a spot on the forest's edge, then move my finger farther north from her red line. "If we cut through Litchfell at this point and travel along the side of the Fendres range, we'll arrive sooner. It'll be more dangerous since we'll be walled in, but if I remember correctly, it shouldn't last more than a few terrameters and then we can cut up the side *here*."

I glance at him. "And by 'dangerous' I mainly mean bolcranes."

He grins. "Breck?"

She wipes her mouth with a handkerchief and shrugs. "Doesn't scare me."

"Finally grew a backbone," Colin whispers at me conspiratorially. "From bein' around Isobel I think."

Breck lobs a hunk of bread and manages to hit him on the arm. I grab it and hobble off to feed it to the horses, leaving the twins to their scuffle.

I've just finished adjusting Haven's bridle when Colin is suddenly at my elbow.

"About ready then?" I ask him.

He doesn't move. Just crosses his arms and stands there.

I frown. "What?"

"Just wonderin' if you're actually gonna tell me how you're doin', or if I have to ask."

I glance away. "Better, thanks. What'd you do—sweet-talk Adora's maid for the medicine?"

"Somethin' like that, but that's not what I meant. After I left your room earlier, Eogan talked to me. Said somethin' didn't go right between you an' him and that I should look after you." He steps closer. Taking up my vision. "An' by the looks of the weather, I'm guessing there's a bit more to it."

A bark of thunder shakes the sky.

He raises an eyebrow and chuckles. "Thought so."

I pull away. "I don't want to talk about it." And walk off to help Breck with the food-filled saddlebags.

"Fine with me," his voice follows softly. "But when you do, I'm here."

The lump that clogs my fiery throat is grateful and grieving all at once. I toss him a bag and then nod and yank my hood up before allowing him to take the pressure off my leg as I climb into the saddle. We leave the sheep shed behind with a pounding of hooves.

After that, I only glance back at Colin and Breck once, and it's because his gaze won't leave me alone. I can feel it. *What does he want?* When I look, the concern I find written there is caring. It's authentic. And it's the same expression I've seen a hundred times on Eogan.

The pain it brings clobbers my lungs.

The clouds crackle, and I press Haven to ride harder, the thumping of her hooves keeping time with my screaming heart until, whether it's my exhaustion or the medicine, my mind eventually takes off to drift on its own in the rainy fog. I welcome the numb—the cold as it whittles away at me, hour after hour, until I'm nothing more than a dull pile of ice.

Shades of day have folded into black shadows of night when we finally reach the edge of Litchfell. We stop among the thick, peripheral trees long enough for the horses to feed on a disgusting nest of hornet-badgers and for Breck to help me rewrap the dressing on my leg before she wanders off enough paces to relieve herself. My leg is inflamed, but I can't tell if that's a warning of infection or just because it's been abused on a horse all day.

"You're like fresh bait for the bolcranes," Colin notes grimly. "Probably smell your injury a mile away."

I shake my head. "They can't smell. They hunt using heat visio—" I stall. And stare at him. *Ah kracken.* Adora didn't tell him.

His face turns the color of the dripping, overgrown spindle trees behind him. Their lengthy green branches poking out in all directions like giant needles waiting to impale. He shifts to peer into the thorny forest as the rain drums around us. His barely fevered body will be like a blasted bull's-eye compared to ours. I thought he knew.

"Colin, if there was any way around—"

He shrugs it off with a brave face that is false. He saw Adora's map. There's no way around Litchfell except by water, mountains, or cliffs. Which is why very few people ever visit the Fendres.

"I've been planning to keep the temperature around us at freezing. Which means you should be fine."

"Maybe we shoulda got here earlier and gone through while it was daylight," Breck says, making me jump. I didn't even hear her behind us.

"It wouldn't matter. It's never daylight at the heart of Litchfell,"

Colin mutters, indicating he at least knows that much. "So how 'bout we get this over with, yeah?"

I stand and tug my cloak tighter, suddenly aware of the sound of an airship puttering through the lessening storm overhead. Along with what I swear are hoofbeats coming toward us.

Flipping around, I glare into the dark.

Nothing.

It's nothing.

Before I think on it further, Breck pushes past me. "We need to go."

Suddenly a chorus of bolcrane screams erupts.

CHAPTER 28

THE SHRIEKS OF TORTURED CHILDREN SHATTER the night around us, echoing off the enormous spindle trees and jagged rocks, removing all doubt that the bolcranes sense our flesh.

The fact that we're still alive just says they haven't found it. Yet.

Colin stays close with Breck as we ride fast and hard past miasma clusters that lash wispy tendrils out in search of blood and by giant ticks on trees that supposedly use their teeth if you get too close. I'm trembling and sweating like a rhino-horse.

Stay to the center of the path, I tell my hands. But it's all I can do to just keep us *on* the path while trying to cool the temperature amid the heat and what I suspect might be my own injury-induced fever rising.

By the time we reach the steam swamps, spasms are wriggling up my spine, making my leg hurt and vision blurry. But even when my head sags, I'm too scared to slow down or pull out the medicine lest I drop it.

Another miasma cloud morphs, followed by a chilling screech, and I have to blink to focus on Haven as she dodges the deadly fog.

"Pick it up, boy," Breck mutters behind me. "I can feel us slacking."

When I peek back, she's nudging Colin, who's wearing a dazed expression—as if unsure whether the cries in the black woods are actually from flesh-eating animals or the innocent in need of help.

"Colin, focus!" I yell through my cloak. "Breck, punch him!"

She does, somewhat awkwardly in her blindness, and his eyes snap clear again.

"They sound so real," he says.

"Well, they ain't!" Breck barks. "So keep your fool self together."

Another shadow looms ahead through the fog. The stench grows stronger as we pass by a stream that smells of cadaver.

The second time the shadow appears I have the distinct impression of extra hoofbeats again. Coming from behind us. *Or maybe from the side?*

A shriek erupts and the forest crunches, and abruptly a body has charged onto the path thirty paces ahead. I blink twice because—*What in—?*—it looks like a man. Like Eogan. But then suddenly it's morphing into a black, slime-covered bolcrane.

We slam to a stop fifteen paces shy of it just as the monster opens his crocodilian mouth and screams, blowing chunks of drool through jagged rows of teeth. My skin crawls. Judging by its fangs, the animal is young, but it's still bigger than Haven, with jaws that could wrap around my entire torso.

He elongates his neck and tastes the air with his tongue.

Then screams again.

The horses spook, prancing to the side before lurching back as the beast moves his leathery, bloated form forward and flares his poisoned quills.

"Easy, girl." I pat Haven and prepare to pull a charge from the air, but as my fingers tingle, my eyesight blips and goes hazy, and then Colin's horse is in front of me and to the side of me, and I barely have time to hear him yell before the beast lunges.

My breath slows.

The moments slow.

Until all I see are flashes in my head, like a series of paintings in which Breck is thrown off the horse just as the bolcrane's oozing teeth come down. With a snap of its jaws, the monster clamps around Colin's chest and drags him, writhing and shrieking, off his mount.

Noooo!

I am screaming.

I can't stop screaming.

Then I'm coughing and gasping, and my lightning strike's exploding, but it somehow just misses the beast. The bolt's force ripples the space around us, wavering the atmosphere until it crackles and clears.

And with it, my vision alters.

I shake my head.

And squint.

It's as if time somehow reeled backward because Colin and

Breck are still on their horse and the bolcrane is still charging, and what I saw never happened.

The mount flips around as the beast skids past. Abruptly Colin's warhorse leans out and bites the monster on its bare haunch, ripping a chunk of flesh off. The bolcrane shrieks and lurches, but another twitch of my hand brings the next fire strike down like a knife. It severs the beast's spine, and the thing falls into a black, smoking lump on the ground.

I barely have time to look at Colin, let alone feel relief or confusion, before our mounts hurtle back onto the path. After that, it's all I can do to hold on as my feverish mind begins to slip further and the world around us enters a haze. Eventually, I get Haven to slow enough for me to beckon Colin to take the lead. He nods and plows ahead while behind him Breck's got her arms tight around his waist and appears to have passed out.

What I wouldn't give to pass out . . .

I rub my sleeve across my eyes and refocus on holding the temperature low for one hour.

Two hours.

Three.

Four hours of ice and miasma, ticks, and bolcrane shrieks.

Not until the gradual graying of dawn does it occur to me that the sounds are slowly fading and the path we're on has been climbing for quite some time. And it's lighter here with patches of morning moonlight sifting through the trees.

Another spell of listless time passes, and suddenly something cold hits my nose. The next thing I know snowflakes are falling. Like tender white kisses gifted onto such a hostile landscape. They're so eerie and whimsical, I almost laugh at the irony.

Soon the snowdrifts are thicker, mounding across the ground, encroaching on the steep trail.

Colin brings his horse to a halt.

"We can't sto—" I start to say, but I do stop.

Because even in my daze I notice it too.

No breeze. No beasts rustling or breathing other than the horses and Colin and Breck and me. Even the bolcranes and miasma clouds have abandoned their bloodthirst. Suddenly I'm leaning over to vomit, discharging what little is left in my stomach as the scent of rotting flesh hits me and clashes with my pain-induced nausea. It smells of death here.

Colin watches until I finish, then offers me his water.

I grab it and take two tablets, drowning them with big gulps before handing the bag back with a thank-you.

He nods and begins to move us forward only to be met by raucous snorts from the horses. Another minute, and they flat out refuse to go farther, and when I nudge Haven, she actually nips at me.

Colin shakes his head. "We're gonna 'ave to go around." He heads for a path no wider than a deer trail.

"That'll take us north."

"It's the only way available."

Good point.

I follow him, but we've not even gone fifty feet before the blending of trees and snow opens up on our left, and there, hardly any distance away, sits a tiny, dilapidated village. It's built on platforms high off the ground with bridges running from treetop to treetop amid houses attached to the trunks. In the morning gray light it's impossible to see the dead bodies, but I can smell them. The original path we were on would've led us right to them.

My stomach threatens to retch again.

"It's that village that dwarf was talking about," Colin murmurs.

I nod and try to keep the medicine from coming up while holding my breath from the plague-infested air. No wonder the bolcranes didn't follow.

I glance at Colin who's now holding his mouth shut too, then back at Breck, who's obliviously snoring. My words slur as I try to keep my head clear. "Let's keep moving."

It's two hours of working our way across the snowy trails with me nodding off frequently until we find one that'll return us in the direction we need. The paths still climb the mountainside, but the area is starting to appear more like the earlier part of Litchfell—noisier and darker, even with morning dawn in full bloom and the rain gone. My shoulders are drooping hard and I'm having a difficult time controlling the temperature when we finally burst from the path through the thick forest growth into a frosty clearing, which spans fifty feet across ice-covered grass before butting up to a towering, smooth wall of rock. It's the Fendres line.

"What in hulls?" Colin murmurs, staring up. The cliff face shoots forty feet above us and to the right and left for as far as the eye can see, like nature's barrier to keep the forest and bolcranes contained. One that's only partially effective as I recall, since over the years the forest has continued on up the mountain above it.

Colin rides over to stick his hand against the massive stone.

The ground rumbles slightly, and then he turns back. "It stretches in both directions for a couple hours."

The air exits my lungs. The detour took us too far north. "Can you make a path?"

"If it were a bit lower, yes. Right here? It would take quite awhile."

I grit my teeth. Nod. "Let's get going then. We can still reach the fortress sooner than Adora's way, but . . . I . . ."

Colin clicks his mount.

"But . . ."

Something's wrong with me. *What was I going to say?* My head suddenly feels like a boulder my shoulders can't keep aloft. My lungs, my leg . . .

I attempt to prod Haven forward and end up leaning over her to settle my forehead on her neck. Her heat pours off in waves.

"I think I need—" My foot catches in the stirrup, and then Colin's hand is holding me in place as behind him Breck stirs.

"What's going on?"

"She needs rest," Colin answers Breck, while the thought surfaces that Haven would be very put out if I dry heaved into her mane.

A loud rumble and tearing rips the air, and somehow it's Breck's arm holding me up and Colin is off his mount and bent to the ground.

An arcing crack appears in the rock wall, followed by a crumbling.

"I just need a minute," I try to mumble, but the words sound funny.

Another shredding noise. Colin makes a pulling motion and

a rush of stones comes tumbling out, leaving behind a neatly carved-out cave.

He really is incredible, I think just before my body hits the dirt, and I swear I hear Breck cackle.

CHAPTER 29

WHEN I OPEN MY EYES AGAIN, I'M LYING inside the freezing, earth-scented cave. The horses stamp in the dark and between their noise and the stench of sweat, I become aware that something else has stirred my thoughts awake. Like someone moving around inside my mind.

"Colin?"

From his sprawled-out position near the sunlit entrance, the boy's breath puffs up warm and steady and sleep laden. He doesn't move.

"Breck?"

No answer except for a soft cough beside Haven.

Straightening, I squint at the spot and am rewarded by a pair of blinking green eyes.

My heart lightens and plunges all in one burst. How he got here—how he found us—I don't know. My body protests when I stand, but I don't care. *What's he doing?*

Eogan strides over and brushes a hand over my arm.

It makes my skin bristle. I pull back. "What are you do—?"

"To check on you," he murmurs, moving in so that I'm wedged between his body and the cave wall. "And to warn you not to destroy the fortress."

When I open my mouth to argue, he adds, "I'll take care of it," with eyes that glitter oddly in the dim. "And when I'm done, I'll come for you. I'll take care of you. But you have to trust me. Just stay away from the Keep until I return."

The look on his face seems blurry. But it's also soft. Tender. And this time when he slides his fingers up my arm, I allow it. It feels good and I'm so tired, so cold. So achy.

For him.

A lump of misery flares in my chest. *No.*

Eogan's hand brushes my neck and he leans in. His fingers pressing hard.

I force up thoughts of Isobel wrapped around him and what he's done to me. To my parents.

No. I shove against him and end up banging my head against the wall as he slides a hand around my owner circles. For a moment, his face grows even more indistinct. Fuzzy. Like when I first thought he was the bolcrane.

"Nym, ju*sss*t calm down."

Something's wrong. "Who are you?"

Suddenly he's on top of me, with both hands around my neck, choking me so I can't breathe.

I bring my knee up, but he's too quick. His leg crushes against my injured thigh, shooting fire through me, and in the in-between seconds before my lungs explode and my lightning flashes at the cave entrance, Eogan's body wavers in front of me.

A hint of silver glimmers. His form grows smaller and paler and his eyes dim.

Until he's morphed into Lord Myles.

What the—? The lord protectorate presses harder, but this time when my knee thrusts up it lands a hit in his man-treasures, sending him backward enough for me to fall forward on him, choking, coughing, gasping, blinking in his face, grabbing for which vision is real.

Then he's swearing and clamping down on my arm, sending an explosion of unbidden images through my head—of him talking to me at Adora's party—touching my arm—of orange hair stuck to blood on the floor, and Eogan's throat being slit. And Colin being eaten by a bolcrane a few hours ago. They hit me one after the other in tangible, real-life succession until the realization settles.

He can manipulate thoughts.

"You were following us!" I shove his hand off and scramble away. Horror is dripping from every pore in my body. "Why? What are you doing here?"

The lord protectorate stands and limps toward me. "So you found your way through my ability? Impressssive. You know, the few times I've used it on you, I secretly hoped you'd catch on."

The sky sparks along my fingertips. I hold my hand up and let its energy crackle, illuminating the air around us.

"I love the white hair, by the way. Very . . . Elemental."

My hand snaps with the storm's rumble. "I'll ask again what you're doing here." I edge toward the cave's entrance.

He takes a faltering step and grimaces. "Let's just say I have a certain interessst in seeing the Bron generals succeed. And while by law I have every right to see you hanged, I thought it'd be more *beneficial* to offer a choice. You can leave the Bron generals alone and come work for me. Or . . ."

I raise a brow.

His hand flicks out so quick it's on my skin before I can move, and a vision of Isobel and Eogan passionately kissing nearly launches me off my feet. It's followed by Eogan stabbing Colin, then turning the knife on me. I squirm as the blade plunges into my chest one, two, three times before it reaches my heart. With a shriek, I fold in half from the impact.

I squeeze my eyes shut until, after a few seconds, the pain disappears. When I reopen them, Lord Myles is right in front of my face, smirking with those stupidly shiny teeth and offering me a different vision—the one of him and me standing hand in hand, raining a lightning storm down upon the kingdoms. But this time, an old, shriveled man with wolfish features is sprawled disgustingly at my feet. Dead. And there's a crown on my head and a white dress displaying my neck, my arms, my hand, which is no longer crippled but perfect and beautiful. Gone are the memorial marks and circles on my skin.

I am perfect. Strong. Elemental. And I am in control.

It makes my heart ache with a hunger I can't explain and leaves me gasping.

I stumble back and bump into Colin, but it's the noise outside that yanks my attention. A rustling of horses and leather.

He's brought others.

"The Faelen people—*your* people—deserve better," I say, finding my breath.

"Which is why I'm going to give them a *ssstrong* king instead of a weakling." The lord protectorate pulls out a knife and holds it up so the morning light glances off of it, then slides a finger on the flat side of the blade. "You can help with that, you know."

A shift behind me and suddenly I feel Colin's hand on the small of my back. I sense him hesitate, then roll over and slip away as I keep my gaze on Myles. I watch his eyes register Colin's movement.

"He won't last long out there."

If he thinks that, he doesn't know Colin. Keep him talking, Nym. "You honestly think *you'd* make a better king?"

"Not just me. *You and I together.* The most powerful Uathúils this world has seen. Just think what we'd become once I finish training you."

The sounds outside are growing louder. "And why would I want that?"

"Because I can unleash your powers and teach you control on a level Eogan can't. And because if you don't leave the Keep alone and let the war take its course, my men and I will gut you and your Terrene friend fas*sss*ter than yo—"

I lunge for him, but he touches my side, sending immediate images from his fingertips through my veins of Eogan being burned alive at Adora's house. In disgusting, excruciating detail. I whimper and grab his wrist. And abruptly, the pictures fizzle out as his body goes rigid and begins to shake.

The energy transferring from my hand wrapped around his arm begins to spark and flare, lighting up his skin like a torch. He screams and drops the knife, jerking violently. He thrusts his other hand to mine, sending fresh pictures dancing through my eyes of Breck lying dead and Eogan being ambushed and me splayed out cold and pale three feet in the ground while dirt is shoveled on top of me.

I press harder. Until the heat in my hand turns to cold and a wave emits from my palms, spreading a film of ice from my fingertips out over his clothes, his skin, his gasping face. It crackles and stings. And I know it will kill him. *I* will kill him to keep him from hurting them.

Use death as a last resort, Nym. Eogan's words slip into mind.

Myles drops his hand from my skin with a gurgle.

I stop.

Abruptly, everything stops.

The lord protectorate falls, skin smoking like icy breath, just as the ground beneath us starts quaking. Cries erupt and the commotion grows as the earth keeps rumbling. Inside the cave, the ceiling is throwing down dust and rocks the size of my fist. The horses bolt out beside me, barely missing running us over. I cough on the filth, then grab Lord Myles by the arm and drag him out while my muscles and burning leg beg me to leave him.

Then Colin's behind me. He has grabbed the horses and is yelling about Breck in words too fast for me to understand.

"Where is she?" I ask.

"I don't know! An' why in hulls is Lord Windbag here tryin' to kill us, and why in kracken did you drag 'im out with you?"

I drop Myles's arms and head for Colin. "Where'd you last see Breck?"

"She was gone when I got out here."

"What about the other men?"

"They fled into the forest after their hor—"

A crashing along the tree line cuts him off. It's followed by Breck's cry and a bolcrane scream.

CHAPTER 30

B RECK APPEARS LIKE A LAUGHING MADWOMAN
from the forest, legs racing and hair sticking straight up.
A half terrameter behind her, the tops of snow-frosted
trees are shaking and bowing to the accompaniment of cracking
limbs and uprooting trunks. The ground trembles.

An adult bolcrane.

Colin's eyes grow melon-size. He shoves Haven's reins at me
and jumps onto his mount, spurring it toward Breck.

"Nym, let's go!" he's yelling. "Breck, what in hulls?"

I reach for a stirrup as the bloodcurdling cry of a grown man
explodes from somewhere close in the forest. Colin races for
Breck. The assassins' heat drew the monster right to us. *Fools.*

I strain to get my aching leg up on Haven, but before I do,
Colin's already reached his sister. He leans down and yanks
Breck up behind him, and I'm at once relieved and terrified as

the forest screams grow louder. I'm also suddenly aware of Lord Myles lying beside me in a faint.

I look from Colin and Breck to Myles and back.

"Nym, what're you waitin' for? We 'ave to go!" Colin hollers.

I bend down to feel Myles's pulse as my legs quiver and threaten to give way.

"You can't be serious!" Colin dashes up to me while Breck's hanging on to him for dear life.

"We can't just leave him!"

"That thing's comin', and if you bring Lord Myles, he'll probably just try to kill you when he wakes!"

The shuddering in my thighs moves up my body, making my head feel dizzy and my skin cold. I slip out the medicine box and swallow the final two tablets, then tuck it away and yank up my hood. He's right of course. I can't bring Myles.

I look at the cave, which, while still bellowing smoke and debris, is miraculously still intact. "He betrayed Faelen to Bron, but we can't just let him die." I lift the man's arm again and, clamping my lips shut, try to drag him back into the cave, while my own leg and gut revolt.

Colin just glares as he jumps down to help. "You want to save all them too?" He dumps Myles's body inside before batting a hand back at the forest where more cries are erupting.

"His men came knowing what they were getting into, and they left the same way. But the lord protectorate isn't even conscious enough to defend himself," I say, limping for Haven. "Just seal the entrance enough so the bolcranes can't get him. Please."

Colin doesn't bother responding. He simply lifts me onto Haven before turning to thrust his hands over the snow-speckled ground, drowning out all noise with an earthquake. A thick wall of dirt shoots straight up, and within seconds the entrance is mostly covered. The bald boy lunges for his mount, pulls himself up, and tugs Breck's arms around his waist.

My mutter of "Thanks" is claimed by the wind as our horses take off in lengthy strides, ears flattened, dirt flying.

A wail from the charging bolcrane, and suddenly the treetops are flapping in a forward motion, and glimpses of enormous black leather flash between the white and green branches we're rushing past. The monster is keeping pace just inside the forest edge.

He's hunting us.

I put out my hand and jerk down four lightning bolts in succession. Breck says something I can't understand as I watch the bolcrane slow, then stumble and appear to fall. I turn my attention back to Haven and, putting my head low, follow Colin close to the mountain wall, praying the gradually climbing space we're in meets up with a path soon. Or that the wall tapers down enough for him to cut a trail.

His attention stays trained on the sheer-faced mountain where green tufts are sprouting out and farther ahead is an overhang of snow. The air begins getting colder and eventually the cliff drops down until it's only fifteen feet above us before quickly turning into a slope that eases upward into a tree-spattered, steep meadow.

Colin veers off to guide us up through the clear space, which increasingly narrows into an actual path. We push the horses, leaning forward as they fight for their footing on the snowy ground, and over the next couple of hours, Colin has to hop off multiple times to create a line of ridges deep enough for their hooves to dig into. In between those pauses, I find myself slipping into semiconscious sleep on Haven's heated neck until, finally, we reach the lowest peak and I force my head to clear.

I'm home.

That is my first coherent thought.

I push it away. I don't want to imagine it. I don't want to think it or care about it.

But the sickening in my stomach stays.

I peer around to distract myself and see the sun is almost at center sky even though it's doing nothing to warm the frigid air. The rain-washed atmosphere is already showing new, thin lines of smoke drifting in from the entire southern border, and more trailing in from the west. A low hum echoes across the mountain range. At first I think it's from bees, except it has a distinct metallic ring.

We're nearing the pass.

Another ten minutes of riding, and the sparse smattering of trees becomes thicker with snowdrifts caked to them.

I press forward to where Colin's riding. "How you holding up?"

"Tired. But I'm not the one riding with an injured leg. You?"

I hold out my water skin to him. "Fine. As long as we keep moving."

His breath comes out in foggy puffs as his face morphs into a grin. He gulps mouthfuls and hands the bag back as, behind him, Breck snores with her hooded face ducked onto his back.

He squints at my eyes. My trembly hands. And clicks his mount to keep up with mine. "So, you gonna tell me what's really goin' on between you and Master Bolcrane?"

I shift in my seat. "Doesn't matter."

"It does to me."

"It shouldn't."

"Anything botherin' you matters to me."

My eyes well up for no blasted reason. I lift my chin and smooth the crack in my throat. "It's fine."

"Maybe I should be the judge of that. Especially if there's somethin' I need to know."

Fair point.

He waits.

I let him, until it becomes awkward.

"Eogan is King Odion's twin brother," I finally say in a steady voice.

His head whips around. "He *what*? Did he *tell* you that?"

"He and Isobel."

"Yet he fights for Faelen."

"So it would appear."

Colin's gaze turns challenging. "What, you think he's a spy?"

"You don't?"

"No," he says without hesitation.

I look away.

Me neither.

"But that's not what's bothering you. Yer upset 'bout somethin' else."

I glance up at him. Open my mouth. Close it. And there it is: the admission that this bald boy knows me better than I have ever given him credit for.

He watches me in silence, and for whatever reason I recall that night at Adora's party when he told me about his mother and father and Breck and his home. When he told me his story.

Something in his eyes says now he's waiting for mine.

But apparently I've not been paying attention to where we're going because the trail abruptly splits in two, and just as we set in on the higher one, we round a bend and a boulder and emerge near an enormous field. It's surrounded by fir trees and snow and a mossy stone outline of what used to be the foundation of an estate house.

I slow.

Smoke drifts across the horizon and the breeze carries in its burnt, violent scent as crocus heads rustle across the white meadow.

My blood shivers.

Haven stops.

It's a full minute before I work up the nerve to slide off. When I do, I press my booted toe into the icy ground as if to make sure this is real. That the heartbeat and lung-breaths thumping inside of me are the same as those that ripple beneath the earth here.

They are. I can feel the energy, the familiarity of its steady life-rhythm in this place. It is old and purposeful and deep. Not like the Valley of Origin, but . . . it's a rhythm that has kept going even after everything that existed here was destroyed.

A chain jingles and Colin dismounts beside me.

I ignore him and stare at the mound of flowers pushing up through a snowdrift. The meadow's now filled with baby saplings and new life, belying the violence done to it. I scan the area until I see it—the little spot where I stood and watched my world fall. I can almost picture the blood spatters in the snow.

Colin stays quiet. Still waiting.

"Do you believe a person is born for violence?"

He looks surprised. I watch him consider it a moment. Then,

"I like to think we're all born to do good, but dark things sometimes get in the way. Why?"

One breath.

Two breaths.

Five breaths.

"Because Eogan helped kill my parents here when I was five."

His silence reveals his feelings more than the quick jerk of his arm against mine.

After a pause he says, "I'm guessin' he didn't know what he was doin'."

It's a hopeful statement more than a question, to which I respond, "He didn't know who they were, but he knew what he was doing. Just like he did with all the people he murdered. And his spending the last few years trying to be sorry doesn't make it better."

"No. I doubt anythin' would." Colin rubs his neck. "But makin' a hurtful choice is different than being born for violence—than being truly evil—isn't it? Just like the things you and I did in our past don't make us evil."

I kick the dirt with my shoe. "Eogan believes you and I were born to bring deliverance to Faelen."

"So?"

I stare out at the smoke-whispered valleys and forests covered in death-eating birds and shrug. "How can you say it's not a person's fault when he harms others, whether intentionally or not, but then say it's honorable when he chooses to help? I mean, what makes a person evil? If you believe a person was born to bring help, then were others born to bring destruction? Was Eogan born to kill my parents?"

Was I born to destroy life, or to defend Faelen?

Colin bumps my shoulder. Then does it again. Until I look up and that bald-boy smirk emerges. "I think some have to fight harder to choose good over evil because the evil's got it out for them. And maybe it's because those're the ones evil knows will become the strongest warriors, recognizing true wickedness when it rears its head."

Something, a wave, a feeling, a force, tingles up through my feet as if the earth beneath is agreeing with his words.

He slips his arm around mine. "Maybe the ones who've struggled with true evil are the ones meant to make the biggest difference against it, you know?"

He hands me Haven's reins. Pauses. Then plants a kiss on the side of my head and winks. "You ready to go be not evil with the most attractive male friend you've ever known?"

I feel a smile edge the corners of my mouth. One last gaze around the sun-drenched meadow and I slip my hand into his. "Thanks."

With a deep breath I turn to Haven, and I find Breck has been listening. She's wearing an expression halfway between a smirk and disgust. But when I blink, it's gone and her look of tired annoyance is back in place.

"By the way . . . what were you doing in the forest earlier, Breck?" I tip my head at her.

Her blind eyes stare at nothing as her lips peel back into a wide, toothy grin. "Hunting."

"Yeah, about that, Breck," Colin erupts. "What the kracken? What's with you? You coulda been killed, you know."

I don't wait for her reply to him. I don't want to know. I just mount up and, taking the lead, let them hash it out in their snappy sibling way while I hurry us along toward the ridge that gives way to views stretching from the valleys of Faelen to the Sea of Elisedd.

When we get close, I swear the ocean sparkles and sings my name with salt breezes that stimulate my tongue. Clouds drift in with the wind, moseying their way toward us, and toward the small fortress I assume is the Keep, which is jutting up through the smoke and fog about a terrameter below. With three buildings, a courtyard, and an exterior wall made of stone, it's carved right into the mountainside—gray like the dulling afternoon sky and topped with shake shingles crusted with snow. The Fendres Passage splays out like a string far below it, spanning from the Litchfell Forest east of us, through the mountains and out to touch the open sea.

Beyond that are the ships. Bron's. Ours. Covered in such a shroud of smoke that it's impossible to tell which is which. And above those fly the airships—I can hear them clearly now—droning like murderous gnats, making their way in an advancing column toward the pass and Faelen.

The closest airship pushes through a cloud not far from us and my mouth goes dry. It's enormous. Like a tin castle floating beneath a giant, rippling pale balloon that is the size of Adora's house, with insect-larvae-like wrinkles and a huge dragon painted on the side. Even Colin's breath seems to catch at the sight. The monstrosity it's carrying looks like a metal tube with pipes and gears and a bladed thing that appears to propel it forward. And underneath—the bomb.

The closer it moves, the more it stirs the air, sending wisps of eeriness up from the fortress.

I shudder.

There's something dark down there. Another presence. More insidious even than the Bron army.

The thought emerges that the unseen things that haunt this world have taken residence here, and it would only take one rip in the atmosphere to release them. A form of evil colliding with the skin of our Hidden Lands. Seeking to soil and own it.

A wolf howls in the distance, and the minstrels' songs about Draewulf slip into mind. Colin's horse shies. Even Haven gives a slight tremble.

Colin gulps and looks at me. He feels it too.

Let's just get this over with.

I peer at the fortress, at the tiny men roaming around it like ants, and imagine it going up in flames. Poof.

Just. Like. That.

I lift my arm and it shakes. I don't want to do this.

Use killing as a last resort, Eogan's voice whispers in my chest.

I try to ignore it. *This is different. There's something wrong with this place.*

Colin stretches out his hand and the earth rumbles.

My chest flinches.

Curses.

I move my fingers over to stop Colin's. "What if we can halt the war without killing them?"

"What?" Both he and Breck turn in my direction.

"What if I can get to the fortress and find another way to stop them?" I hate the words even as they're coming out of my mouth. I don't want to go down there, but I also can't bear the guilt.

"Are you jesting? You want us to go down there? That place is crawling!"

"Not you, just me."

"Stop bein' an idiot," Breck says. "Just do what yer suppose' to."

"Nym, your ability doesn't protect you," Colin says. "Those men'll kill you in a heartbeat."

"I won't get caught. I'll be quick, and if I'm wrong, then I'll come back and we'll do what Adora asked."

He stares at me as if this is the worst idea I've mentioned in his history of knowing me.

"Look, if we're going to take a bunch of lives, I need to be sure it's the only way. I have to live with mysel—"

"You're not 'ere to investigate!" Breck explodes. "You're 'ere to obey the order you've been given! How dare you think—"

"Breck," Colin says firmly. He turns and chews his lip at me. "I know you. Once you see the person you're supposed to kill, you won't be able to, Nym."

"Exactly!" Breck murmurs.

I ignore her and keep my gaze on Colin. "I promise you, I will do what needs to be done when the time comes."

His gaze is worried. For me. For my safety. I can see it in the flexing of his brow.

"Please. I need this."

His sigh is slow. But when he utters it, I know I've won.

It's followed by a grin. "You're lucky I like you, storm girl."

I reward him with my own sad smile. "Thanks. If I'm not back by dark, take the fortress down anyway."

CHAPTER 31

O NCE WE FREE THE HORSES, IT'S A SWEATY, hour-long descent down a treacherous goat path, which Colin maneuvers with ease even as he's angrily shifting dirt around to help Breck. His fury at her insistence on coming with us just about matches her mood at me, making the already-painful hike even more awkward.

I bite my lip.

Stay above and demolish a fortress of men I've never met.

Or drag my friends closer to danger . . .

I look at Colin. *He didn't have to come.*

Swallowing, I pull from the wide fog bank that's accumulating along the cliff, cloaking us, and just concentrate on descending with my dull-aching leg and cramped hand as the sound of the airships grows louder. Their noise ricochets off the valley floor along with the clanking war preparations.

As we near the tiny gray fortress, I see it's made up mainly of a parapet between two turrets—one attached to a slightly lower, round building, the other to three stone lodges all crammed into a giant courtyard. At first glance, the outer surrounding wall appears wide, until I realize that the courtyard is almost level with it—a design of convenience allowing the guards to easily peer over the side and down the hundreds of feet it drops, where the only point of entry is up the steep, narrow stone walkway. Or down the mountainside we've just come.

When we reach the wall, we wedge ourselves against an ice-dusted rock to watch the guards walk by without being seen. At this level, the atmosphere feels as if it's crawling with that dark presence.

"Close enough for you?" Breck growls to Colin, her ear tilted, listening.

I give her shoulder a reassuring pat, which she yanks away from.

Colin puts his hand to the ground and slowly raises the other, as if to say he's counting the number of guards he feels through vibrations in the earth. His fingers come up, one, two, three. Fourteen guards he indicates, but that's not what's got my attention. Through the fog, one shuffles by. He's wearing the cloak of Faelen.

I frown and look at Colin, whose expression turns confused.

Let's get closer, he mouths, beckoning toward the frosty, shingled top building farther along the mountain from us. He pantomimes to ask whether I think I can jump to it if we move closer.

I shake my head. *Not with my leg burning and the medicine wearing off.*

I point to an open window near ground level of the closest round turret. "What if we drop into the courtyard and climb in?" I murmur.

He glances from the window, to me, to Breck. Chews his lip. His agreement only coming once he's certain we've got the guards' routine down and he's begged Breck to stay put. She consents, but that queer smirk is on her face again. It makes me twitch.

When Colin's ready, I wait for him to jump before easing myself into his arms. Then I press him toward the window.

He uses his fingers as a stirrup to help me through before creating handholds for himself—quickly joining me inside on a shallow loft that overlooks the sunken, circular room. The place is empty except for a desk, three chairs, and a lit fire. I push my hood back.

Colin's just leaning forward when voices float in from outside. The speakers' sharp comments go back and forth, incomprehensible. Then fade.

When we're sure they're gone, we sneak down the creaky set of steps leading into the large room.

Colin listens at the first door while I head for the desk on which sits a quill pot and a scroll, both smelling of fresh ink. I glance at the bald boy, who's moved on to the second door, before I open the lengthy, tightly written paper.

I narrow my gaze.

It's an agreement of some kind. With King Odion's signature.

"Colin, come look at this," I whisper.

Suddenly he's beside me, grabbing my arm and shoving me toward the stairs. I toss the scroll on the table and scramble up the shadowed steps. I bite my tongue as a shock of pain wells up my leg. Climbing down a cliff wasn't my brightest idea today.

Colin slips his hand to squeeze mine just as the door opens and four men enter. Two knights, neither of whom are wearing identifying surcoats, are followed by two men in brown cloaks shrouding their faces.

The knights each move to guard a door while one of the cloaked men strides to the fire. The other moves to the desk and bends over the scroll, tapping his fingers on it. One minute, two minutes. Colin nudges me and gestures. *Those are the Bron generals. What are we waiting for?*

The tapping stops. "As you can see, our position is more than generous to the Faelen people," the man says, turning our direction.

Beside me, Colin gasps. My chest deflates as if a storm of needles has just slammed into it.

I swallow and count the reasons I shouldn't kill the beautiful man right here and now. Until I peer closer and realize there's an arrogance to his green eyes that Eogan doesn't have. A cruelty. Which means it's King Odion standing here, not his twin.

But Odion? What's he doing here?

I lift my hand and feel the atmosphere spark. *It doesn't matter why he's here. This is better than Adora or Eogan could've even imagined.* It will be quick for him. For them. My stomach knots even though I know I can prevent the horror that is to come when Bron takes over.

King Odion turns away.

I stand. And wait. At least he should have the honor of seeing his attacker's face before death. The static in my blood is just snapping when the man at the fireplace glances right at me.

He freezes.

I hesitate.

Slowly, he reaches up and pulls back his hood. Revealing the sandy-brown hair and young, tired face of King Sedric.

He raises a brow at me but hurriedly directs his words to King Odion. "I need more time to consider. An hour, if I may, for such a decision," he adds, as I retreat into shadow.

King Odion clears his throat and, after a moment, clicks his heels together. "I will hold off my forces *one* hour. If your signature is not on this treaty by then, the blood of your people is on your head."

Without waiting for a response, he turns, and one of the knights follows him out the door.

"You may go as well, Rolf," King Sedric says to the other knight, whom I now recognize from Adora's parties as his captain of the guard. The door has hardly shut behind him before the king's voice rings louder. Sharper. "Come here, both of you."

We obey, bowing when we draw near, my gaze meeting his scrutiny of me even as I take in the wrinkles and exhaustion sunk into his skin. *How did he get here? And when?*

"Have a seat." He holds my stare before moving on to eye my hair. "I must admit that I've heard rumor a female Elemental existed. However, I wasn't aware she'd been in my presence quite regularly."

I dip my head. "My king, I apologize for the deception."

"Are you a Uathúil as well?" he asks Colin without moving his eyes from me.

"Yes, Your Majesty. I'm Terrene."

He nods. "Of course. I should've known Adora would reach beyond the bounds of normal assassins." He walks toward the fireplace, then back. "And what are you both doing here?"

I swallow. "We were told Bron's generals were holed up in this Keep, directing the war, Your Highness."

"I see. And you were thinking to . . . ?"

"Destroy it."

He stops pacing. "Who gave this order?"

"Adora."

"I see," he says again, and this time his face pales. "I assume she didn't inform you I would be here?"

"She indicated it was only Bron's generals inside this Keep, sire. We were to destroy it from the ridge."

"And do you often disobey your authorities?"

"Nym wanted to be sure," Colin says, and there's a measure of pride in his tone.

"Defiance is not normally a desired trait," the king says evenly. "However . . . in this case, I see it is one that clearly bene-fited me. Although . . . now that you're here, the question is what to do with you. Which I think will greatly depend upon whether your plans have changed."

"Of course they have, Your Highness," I say quickly. "I swear we didn't know. We would never—but Adora, did she . . . ?"

"If you're wondering whether Adora knew I was meeting Odion here, she did. As well as my three war generals and the knights who accompanied me. If you're wondering why Adora betrayed me, you could probably guess better than I."

A knock on the door makes me jump. The king glances over, indicating we should stay seated. "Come in."

Rolf draws his sword the moment he sees Colin and me.

"Stay your hand, they're with me. What is it?"

The knight's glare remains suspicious. "Your Highness, you

asked me to inform you when Bron's airships were heading into position. They are. As is their army. But seeing as you've not yet eaten this day, I had Sir James prepare you a bit of bread and wine. May I beg upon you to take it in your rooms as you consider Bron's proposal?"

"I'm not hungry, but thank you, Rolf. Please see the food is brought for these two though."

A hesitation. Then, "Very good, sire."

With a last wary glance, the knight backs out the door, and King Sedric turns to us. "I'll have more to speak to you about when this is over, but for now, I have one question." He looks squarely at Colin, then at me. "I assume Adora's had her man Eogan, who I'm now aware to be King Odion's brother, and who—"

"He knew nothing of this, Your Majesty," Colin interrupts. "I swear it."

"Who I'd assume to be a traitor," the king continues warningly, "had I not spent enough time with him in the war room to reserve judgment. Has he been training you in your abilities?"

He hardly waits for us to nod. "From what you have told me, Adora believed your powers great enough to take down this Keep, which suggests they are quite advanced. My question is, are your abilities vast enough that you would be capable of halting this war, should it come to that?"

"My powers will mainly be of use with the ground troops, Your Majesty," Colin says. "But Nym's . . . Nym could do it."

I glance at him and raise a brow.

King Sedric's attention settles on me. His voice softens. "Then the question goes to Nym. Will you fight for your people?"

I peek at my hands. At my booted feet. At my leg that is

thrumming dull pain. "Even if I could, you're asking an Elemental slave to rescue the people whose laws would see her dead, Your Majesty."

"I'm aware of the irony."

I clear my throat.

"Then forgive my forwardness, sire, but while *I* may deserve to be hanged or enslaved, many others do not. I would fight for Faelen, Your Highness, if you would commit to do the same. Fight for *all* our people. Otherwise . . . you may not like what you get from me."

Colin's gasp is audible, but I don't really care. It's a fair challenge, and one I'm quite aware I can't lose at this moment while it's just the three of us in here and the static is rumbling across the late afternoon sky.

If the king is shocked at my boldness, he doesn't show it. He just walks over and picks up the scroll from the desk and situates himself in the chair opposite us, from which he continues his study of me. An elongated minute tramps by. He taps the scroll against his leg, then holds it up. "Do you know what this is?"

"A peace treaty. But you've not decided whether to sign it."

A tired smirk tweaks his features. "I'm still undecided as to whether I can trust King Odion's word. And whether doing so is in the best interest of our people."

I nod, keeping my gaze on him.

"On one hand, this treaty will mean the survival of our nation. On the other, it will mean unlimited access for Bron through our kingdom and waterways, and a way for them to make war against Cashlin and Tulla." He suddenly turns to Colin. "You are from Tulla, are you not?"

"I am, sire."

The king rubs his day-old scruff that is thick enough to belie his young age. "So you see, it comes down to sacrificing Faelen and our sister kingdoms in the name of saving them, or else fighting a war we cannot win. Either way, Nym, the innocent *will* suffer. There is little I can do about that. However, seeing as there is something *you* can do, I'll ask you to consider your own responsibility while explaining such a bold challenge to your king."

My misshapen hand tingles.

I scratch my palm. My fingers.

"In truth, Your Highness, I've been asking myself if this version of Faelen is even *worth* saving. If we actually deserve to survive—particularly when our last war treaty was at the sacrifice of our own people."

Uncomfortable inhale.

Just keep going.

"Your Majesty, if I fight for Faelen, there's no guarantee of victory. My power is still . . . maturing. But what you choose to sign or not sign with Bron, as well as the laws you allow or revoke, will determine the true heart of Faelen and whether what we value as a people is worth defending. And that is something no one can do but *you*."

My stomach is clawing its way up my throat as I watch the king chew his lower lip. But to my relieved surprise, he doesn't look angry. Just small and weary. A boy with the weight of the world on his crown.

Suddenly I want to reassure him, to tell him it'll be all right.

But when he gazes up at me, somehow we both know it won't ever be all right, no matter what he decides.

Another knock taps on the door and Rolf enters along with another knight—this one wearing a Faelen surcoat.

King Sedric stands and beckons us to do likewise. "Behind me, you'll find a door and stairs that lead to my rooms. You may lie down in the first, for in truth, you both look like death warmed over. When I'm ready to see you again, I will call for you. In the meantime, my knights are alerted to your presence. If you try to leave or complete your mission as Adora laid out, they will be forced to kill you on sight. Although, I choose to believe we have reached an understanding. And, Nym," he adds quietly, "I trust we'll both do what needs to be done when the time comes."

Without waiting for a response, he turns. "James, take them to the apartment next to mine and see that no one leaves or enters."

Bowing low, Colin and I follow Sir James out. Colin brings up the rear on the stairwell—to ensure I don't fall, I suspect, as my leg has me limping and grasping for the wall. When we reach the apartments, we're ushered through the nearest door into a scarcely furnished room. Sir James leaves us, but I hear him settle against the wall outside, and a few seconds later another door closes. The king's, I assume.

Colin helps me to the bed before moving with an ill expression to the room's only chair. "Adora lied," he mutters, a splash of anger blooming on his cheeks. "Question is, why?"

I shake my head. I'd have guessed she intended to hitch her plans to Lord Myles's, except he was trying to prevent our attack. Standing, I ease my way over to open the window through which I can hear the airships hovering through the incoming storm clouds—the droning engines pounding into my head the reality that none of this makes sense.

"It's bizarre how much King Odion looks like him," Colin says after a minute.

I'm saved from commenting by a sudden knock followed by Sir James's entry with a cold meal. He sets it on the bed, then departs, and Colin and I set upon it like wolves.

It's a good twenty minutes after we've finished and are try-ing—and failing—to rest when I first notice the commotion outside. Muted yelling. Metal clashing. Colin and I head to the window, but we can't see into the courtyard from this angle, so we stand there straining our ears to make sense of what seems to be the beginnings of a fight.

Shivers ripple up my spine. The clouds crackle overhead.

The disturbance continues, growing louder with men running and armor tinning, and then the noise has spread inside—into the stairwell. When the next knock hits our door, Colin is halfway across the room by the time it opens.

Except it's not Sir James.

"Breck?" Colin stalls. "What're you doing here? You're sup-pose' to keep hidden and safe!"

"How'd you get *in* here?" is what I want to know. "And where's the guard?"

Breck tips up her sightless gaze. "I don't know, but Adora's just showed up. Where's the king?"

Adora has what?

"What do you mean Adora's here?" Colin says. "She's a trai-tor! That's why she sent us!"

Breck ignores him, demanding again, "Where's the king?" And this time there's an annoyance to her tone.

She tugs a chunk of hair behind her ear.

286

I stare at her blank eyes. "How'd you get inside the Keep? How'd you find us?"

She says nothing. Just turns on her heel and exits the room as fast as she came.

We scramble after her only to hear the door lock as we reach it.

"What in hulls?" Colin shouts. "Breck, what's going on?"

From beyond the door there's a yell followed by a choking sound, and Colin is immediately clawing the wood frame. "Breck! Breck!"

"Here, watch out." I push him back and, tugging a lightning charge through the window, use my hand to slam into the door. It takes three tries before the bolted thing flies open in a rush of smoke, but when we step out, Breck is gone, along with Sir James who was stationed there.

In his place is a puddle of blood with smudged footprints leading down the hall.

"Come on." I grab Colin and half-run, half-limp for the king's room.

A knight is laid out on the floor. More blood. He moans. His face and body have taken a beating. "Where's the king? Where's Breck?" I ask, as Colin helps him sit up against the bed. He doesn't talk. Just points out the door.

Colin and I run.

When we reach the split in the passage at the bottom of the stairs, I don't even pause before veering up the adjacent stairwell. "You search the room we entered through, I'll check the terrace."

"Find her, Nym!"

When I reach the top of the steps, the door's ajar. I fling it open and lunge onto an empty terrace, scarcely taking in the Bron soldiers and commotion in the courtyard below in my haste to cross the walkway leading to the other turret. When I do, there's another Faelen knight strewn awkwardly across the stone floor. He's staring up at me with a graying expression and a knife in his chest. Beside him, a Bron guard is crumpled facedown in a puddle of blood. *What in kracken is happening?*

I bend over the Faelen man, but he pushes me away, murmuring, "Get to the room below."

Then his head lags.

His arm drops to his side.

I let out a choked cry and take the spiraling steps two at a time.

At the bottom, I burst through the door only to be jerked to a stop by a rough arm and a sword at my throat.

I swear my heart fails and restarts itself twice before Rolf releases me and shifts aside to check the passage and seal the door.

"Nym?"

In the tapestry-lined room stand seven more knights, Princess Rasha with her strange reddish eyes, and King Sedric.

And behind them, Eogan.

The *real* Eogan. Black skin and emerald eyes. Forest of jagged hair beneath his hooded cloak. His gaze is pained, but not as bitter as Odion's. Nor as blurry as Myles's.

It's unreadable though.

I glance away before my heart dissolves into a puddle of ash.

"Where's the boy, Colin?" King Sedric demands.

Oh hulls. I turn back to yank the door open, but Rolf stops me. "No one leaves or enters this room now. The king's been betrayed."

Is he dense? Of course he's been betrayed. "By Adora, and she's here!"

"By King Odion." Princess Rasha's airy voice quivers and floats as she steps forward. "It's why Eogan and I came. As soon as he heard King Sedric was here, he knew. And as soon as I heard Adora tell Lady Isobel her plans to follow Eogan, I raced to warn him." She smiles at me. Sad, regretful. "We made it down the cliff minutes ago, just before Adora rode through the gate swearing allegiance to Odion. He means to kill King Sedric, but we believe she intends to kill them both."

"My brother would never settle through a treaty something he can take by force," Eogan mutters. "And in this case, I'm positive he means to do so, Your Majesty."

"Is Lady Isobel with Adora?" a knight asks.

"As far as we know, she's still at the estate." Rasha looks at King Sedric. "Supposedly awaiting your decision regarding her Dark Army. Although it's clear she's supporting Adora."

The king nods but I'm not certain he's heard. He just keeps looking at Eogan. And Eogan just keeps looking at me.

Blood pools in my lungs, echoing my trainer's name from a cavern that is still screaming his betrayal, his guilt. I straighten my shoulders and move toward the high-up window just as something very large rams the door beneath.

CHAPTER 32

"Y OUR HIGHNESS," ROLF CLIPS, "I RECOMMEND we attempt to move you to the back quarters until we can clear an escape route."

The battering ram thunders against the door again, making the wood squeal just as a man's sharp whistle erupts from behind us, beyond the door I came through. The captain of the guard solicits the king's nod before releasing the handle, and another Faelen knight comes tumbling inside. The sounds of shouting and sword fighting ricochet around the room, dimming as soon as the wood's slammed shut and the plank dropped in place.

"How many are there?" demands King Sedric.

"At the moment, forty to our twelve." The newcomer sweeps an eye over me. "Thirteen if you count the girl."

"Count the girl." Eogan pulls two knives from his boot and glances at Rolf. "How fast are your men at climbing?"

"We have to help Colin and Breck," I say.

The captain ignores me. "Fast enough, but the cliff is blocked."

"It won't be for long. I'd advise you to pick your two best guards to send with King Sedric and Princess Rasha up the ridge," Eogan says. He looks back at me, his gaze gentle. "Are your horses up there?"

"They are. But what about Colin and Breck?"

"We'll help them as soon as we're able, Nym. Right now we've got to protect the king."

He tips his head to King Sedric. "Your Majesty, I've no time to make apologies nor assurances other than to say I am not my brother, nor do I condone his actions. But I suggest you prepare to scale the mount—"

"I'll not scuttle from a fight," the king interrupts. "Especially one for my kingdom."

"Your Highness, I respect your courage, but if you fall, so does Faelen. As long as you're alive, your people have hope."

King Sedric looks to argue further but instead turns to Rolf, who dips his head in agreement. The king pauses, followed by a firming of his jaw, and he turns me a look that seems to convey his agreement to our earlier conversation. "Fine. Let it be done."

"When you reach the ridge," Eogan says, "Princess Rasha will know how to find our warhorses. Take them and ride."

The princess nods as the clamoring outside grows louder. She draws a knife from beneath her cloak, as if ready to take on the entire Bron force herself, and steps near the king.

She flutters a smile my way.

I swallow and nod, and try to ignore the sudden fear lurching up my spine.

"Aen, Frederick, you're with the king and princess." Rolf

beckons two of the knights. "The rest of you come with me. We'll hold them back until you're safe, m'lord."

He strides to the door, then peers back to ensure we're all with him. The pounding outside is deafening.

I pull a knife from my boot and catch Eogan's attention long enough to wish I hadn't. Because what I see there looks very much like an emotion I don't want to feel.

He tips his head at me and then stoops as the captain wrenches the door open.

As if on cue, the battering ram thrusts into the room along with four Bron soldiers. Eogan puts a knife through two of their throats before either gets beyond the first step. The other two are dispatched by Rolf's men as three more appear with swords drawn. The captain and Eogan take them down.

Abruptly, the entire courtyard breaks into chaos.

"They're over here!"

"It's the king's men!"

"King Sedric is over here!"

Clattering footsteps reverberate off the stones as excited voices ring out and the clang of steel shifts our direction.

In one morphing unit, our group scrambles over the battering log and dead bodies, surging out into the cold just as the evening sunset flares and flecks my vision with white and black spots. Half blind, I launch through the door only to feel a metallic edge swipe at me. I lash my blade out, but Eogan's broadsword has already felled the man by the time I can see again. I jab my dagger toward another, but this time Rolf is there first. A helmet cracks above a chain-metal chest, and a spurt of red blossoms out on the fortress's stones.

Oh litches, I don't know how to do this.

I don't know how to fight this way.

I glance around.

I don't want to fight at all.

Ducking back, I suck in a frozen, salty-aired breath and shove the blade in my boot. *Come on, Nym. Get your bearings or you're going to get yourself killed.* I gag as a spray of hot blood sweeps over me from a living, breathing, dying person.

I think I'm going to be sick.

Then I notice the hundreds of giant airships hastening past us through the gorge. Carrying those bombs in their undercarriages . . .

Just focus on those.

A sharp wind whips up and draws in more clouds.

I step out and lift my hand.

A crackle of air thrusts back the larvaelike balloon of a ship just as something whizzes near my shoulder, barely missing me. *What the—?* I turn but can't even see the man's face through his helmet. I just feel the madness rolling off him. I swing my palm over and touch his body with a shock of heat that crumbles him like straw.

But there's another man behind him. Then another. I stoop. My leg screams. I scream and begin crawling along the soldiers' feet, using my deformed fingers to tap their boots.

And all the while I'm shuddering and hearing myself yell that I'm sorry and I'm begging for them to stop.

But they don't.

They just keep coming.

When I can't take the horror anymore or the bodies toppling

over me from the fighting going on above, I scramble back behind the defensive line of Rolf's knights and work my way into a clearing. And stand.

The storm clouds there are churning and condensing, casting the entire valley in deeper shadow. Reacting to me. Waiting for me. I pull them closer and, grabbing one quick lightning stream, rip it along the outer edge of the Bron horde, cracking the air and sending the whole courtyard into smoke and confusion.

An echo of my thunder bounces off the valley walls, followed by a breaking, then a roaring, and somewhere along the mountain range, an avalanche of ice splits free. An eruption of metal and exploding gas says it slid into an airship.

"Archers!" an authoritative voice yells. "Take her down!"

Thump, thump, thump. Two of our knights in front of me drop dead before I realize the arrows are even in the air. I hit the ground and watch the rest rain around the stones and bodies.

"Move back!" Rolf calls to his men.

"Nym!"

Eogan's running at me and pointing. I follow his hand to where the archers are and my next lightning thread takes one out. The other men dodge before turning to send up another volley.

Abruptly I'm thrown against the turret wall, and Eogan is holding me there, covering me as I hear the arrows land and another Faelen knight cry out. When I glance up, Eogan's already stepping away as he nods to me.

I twitch my hand and the dimming courtyard ignites with a flash and the atmosphere roars.

Except, when it clears, the archers have moved and I've missed my mark.

Eogan nearly knocks the wind from me as he crushes me to the wall again. The arrows launch a third time but I'm suddenly having a hard time focusing on them. I'm too busy asking myself what kind of sick person notices a man's breath on her neck or his mouth grazing her forehead when she's scared speechless and men are dying all around and he's a liar who killed her parents.

A sick person like me apparently.

The rain of arrows overreaches and thuds against the cliff, all except for one, which skewers a Faelen knight through the throat. I utter a cry but Eogan's hand is on my pulse, evoking an immediate sense of ease as his less-attractive twin appears, walking toward us from amid the Bron knights.

King Odion raises his sword and the fighting around him halts.

Eogan disengages from me, murmuring, "Finish them." And moves toward his brother.

I crumple my fist then flick my wrist, and the archers on the low wall erupt in gargled yells as a broad hail of ice knocks them off their perches—bringing a distracted expression to Odion's face and, I know, a grimness to mine.

When the two men reach each other, Eogan yanks off his cloak, and a collective gasp rises from the paused soldiers.

CHAPTER 33

KING ODION POISES HIS SWORD HIGHER AND, taking a step forward, sends his voice barking across the courtyard. "Tell the ships full attack, and bring me the Faelen king!"

"Stand your ground!" Rolf counters, as the horde of Bron soldiers rushes forth in a recharged, bloodthirsty wave. They've gone rabid with their sharp metal swords and angry faces.

Angry, stunned faces.

Stoop, weave in, roll away. Stoop, weave in, roll away. One, two, three men I send unconscious with my fingers before I've worked my way far enough back to stand and teeter on a leg I think has gone numb from adrenaline or terror.

Someone shouts over the battle clamor and I glance up to see Eogan and Odion locked in their own battle on the edge of the writhing, fighting mass. My stomach cramps. *Eogan's neck.* A red line runs across the side of it, leaching blood.

Before I can respond, a hand grabs my shoulder and shoves me aside, cutting off my view of Eogan.

Rolf meets a Bron sword with his own. "You trying to get yourself killed, girl? Move!"

I retreat farther behind the Faelen knights, tripping over body after fallen body toward the two brothers, twisting away beneath oncoming blades before taking out their owners with a shock of charged air and smoke. I can hear my own grunts as their weapons knick and cut me, but it's all happening so fast and so bloody that, at some point, I forget about the pain. I forget the horror.

I forget feeling anything at all except the sickening realization that Eogan is about to die.

I edge closer as Odion lunges forward with an expression of hate. If Eogan would move I could end this insane fray.

Odion's sword glances off his brother's before he dips to swipe at his legs. Eogan jumps and parries, then brings his own blade down, catching Odion on the arm, then arcs his foil to land a hit on the chain mail guarding his twin's rib.

Odion stumbles back and leaps onto the low wall. He jumps down three feet away before charging and swiping at his brother like a madman. He forces Eogan into a Bron soldier who thrusts a blade out.

My hand is up just as the sword tip bounces away midair. *Eogan's block.* Without looking back, Eogan takes the man down. Then he rolls out of the way of his brother's next strike.

But not far enough.

Eogan's cry says the blade has connected with his shoulder.

My lash of fire tears so swift and loud, it's a whip cutting through the wall and bursting apart the bricks beside Odion. I yank it back before it can hit Eogan and aim to bring the next one down on his brother's head when a heaving ripple of stone nearly jolts me off my feet. It gives Odion pause and topples half the regiment.

My relief rushes up and bursts.

I spin round until I see Colin standing near the back side of the turret without a shirt on and covered in dirt and blood. He hops up on the wall by the cliff and grins at me through the growing dim, then points at the gate where more Bron soldiers are plowing through the narrow fortress entryway.

He bends down, his eyes still on me. I nod.

The courtyard begins to undulate. It takes me two strikes at the fortress's gateway before I finally meet Colin's efforts with a hit big enough that, together, we shatter the arch into a smoking slump of mortar and stone. It won't keep the Bron army out long, but it'll slow them.

I yank down two more fire bolts around the mass of soldiers, and Colin sends another small earthquake that, for a moment, seems it will unhinge the entire fortress from the cliff. The churning wave of fighting slows as both sides pause then dive for cover.

Except for Odion.

He looks straight at me and smiles in that way politicians do when they see something they want.

I whip an enormous hailstone at his face, but he ducks in lunging at Eogan.

A trembling thread erupts along the ground and the next thing I know, there's an explosion of rock and dust directly behind Odion. I look down to discover Colin crouched beside me. He glances up and winks. "Hey."

"You're alive."

"'Course. Just took a bit to deal with the guards inside. You seen Breck?"

I shake my head as Odion's voice rises. "Looks like you've found yourself some unique ones, big brother. Seems you forgot to tell them their abilities won't work on—"

Eogan stabs his twin in the shoulder and sends him toppling backward over Colin's open fissure behind him.

Odion fumbles at the air. Sways. Slashes. Before jumping over it to scramble back with his disoriented men.

"Get King Sedric and take him round the turrets!" Eogan yells.

The three nearest knights yank the turret door open and usher the king and Princess Rasha out. When they emerge, even from where I'm standing it's clear the king's only been kept inside by physical force. His gaze is deadly as it sweeps over the bodies, the Bron men, the fallen Faelen knights. Over the blood covering it all like a wretched crimson blanket.

The atmosphere slows.

Like the very air itself has its breath hinged. Waiting on the king.

Waiting on the dead . . .

For a moment, the only sound is that of the droning airships as Princess Rasha's grieving eyes find mine.

"Your Highness, stop!" a cold voice rings out.

Beside me, Colin gasps.

I glance over at the speaker and watch Breck appear through the smoke, her wrists bound. And behind her, Adora.

Breck stumbles, and Colin starts for her.

I grab his arm just as Adora swerves her eerie smile our direction. She's got a knife at Breck's neck.

"King Sedric," our owner's shrill voice calls. "You'll tell your men to step away from you, or I'll slit this poor girl's throat."

She steps closer and even in the midst of battle, the insane woman's makeup is perfect, as are her clothes. Only her hair appears to have caught fire at some point.

She laughs.

My neck bristles.

Suddenly Princess Rasha hollers what sounds like a warning, but whatever she's saying gets drowned out by the sound of metal wrenching and bombs falling. The Keep starts shaking and the sky blisters, and the interior of Faelen appears to explode in fire.

The first wave of ships has made it through the pass.

CHAPTER 34

THE SKY DIMS BRIEFLY, THEN THE CLOUDS ERUPT into what looks like a mirrored image of the ground. They light up and explode in orange bursts and angry heat, their thunderous noise rocking the valley.

With a flick at those clouds, I rip a lightning streak through one of the airships, taking it down before a renewed war cry rings out and the Bron soldiers rush us.

Colin snaps the stones underfoot, effectively knocking the men over before launching himself toward Breck just as Rolf and the king charge Adora. I swerve my hand to aim at her, but she's suddenly slipped away and somehow Breck's hands are free and the serving girl is lunging for the captain of the guard.

What the—?

She flips him in front of her, and Adora's knife is now glinting in her fingers. Breck raises the blade to Rolf's neck and smiles, and then it hits me: Breck's smirk.

Breck's smirk is toothy.

Oh good-mother-of-Faelen.

I drop my hand as my friend's face flinches and twitches and for a moment takes on the persona of a wolf. Her body lengthens and mutates, until she looks taller and older. Sharp teeth and a flat snout sneer down at us from an ancient man's fearsome face before she shivers and relents back into the form of Breck. Complete with those brown eyes set above freckled, rosy cheeks.

The boots of thousands of marching soldiers rise up on the wind.

The drone of the airships.

From somewhere King Odion laughs. Rich. Deep. So like his brother's. "Well, this is an interesting twist!"

But all I can see is Breck with her bruised and disjointed face, cleaning up a pool of her own blood on my bedroom floor. A half-hidden gash on her back. Not just a gash, a clawed incision.

Adora didn't just betray us. She's condemned us.

Colin shakes his head and takes a step toward his sister, as if not fully comprehending.

Breck's body gives a final, eerie shudder, causing her to drop the knife and release her grip on Rolf as her skin shimmers and tears at the seams, her flesh becoming a diaphanous wisp that dissolves into a thin pile of skin and clothes on the ground. She leaves behind a monstrous half-man, half-wolf with fur and claws and teeth as dark as the demonic atmosphere that owns this place. Draewulf.

I hold back a brokenhearted gag as black air eeks up from the stones beneath Breck's remains and swirls like ghostly guards around the monster. Slowly, he lifts a claw and tucks a chunk of straggly hair behind a hideous, pointed ear.

And every drop of blood I own freezes to my bones.

"Noooooo!" Colin's yell echoes out over the pass, blending into the clanging metal and falling bombs. He grabs a sword from the ground and charges the beast, lunging for its stomach.

The beast dodges with a snarling chuckle. "Didn't you think your sister a little strange lately, boy? Or did you not care enough to notice? Too busy wanting to save the world, and yet you missed saving your own sister. So pathetic."

A half-choked cry and Colin thrusts again, but his sword strikes air and then ground.

Draewulf's foot comes down on the blade, snapping it at the hilt, while his other shoves up to gut Colin with those long, spindly claws. I snap down a lightning stream, causing Draewulf to lurch away, and King Sedric is there with a strike that slices the monster's leg open.

The beast roars.

Colin scrambles away, flips over, and places both hands to the ground. A crack shreds through the courtyard and almost rips open beneath the animal.

Draewulf jumps, his grin widening as if it's a game. "She didn't even cry that day in the Elemental girl's room. When she sensed what I was right before I took over. Just swore and punched me a good one. Might've landed it too if Adora hadn't stopped her."

I shut his words out. *He's sick. He's insane. It's not my fault what he did.*

I launch three icicles that barely miss impaling the beast,

and then King Sedric's lunging in again just as something wraps around my throat.

I'm yanked back. I can't breathe. Gagging, I kick and scratch, but whoever's got me is bigger and stronger and my thigh is hurting like blazes.

Hands shove me to the ground and my face tastes stone and blood, and my warped fingers are being crushed by the man whose voice sounds so much like Eogan's. "Touch another one of my ships, girl, and I'll rip your arm from its socket."

He flips me over.

I gasp and choke. And then spit in his face.

He slams his fist into me and I taste more blood.

"I wonder what it would take to break you enough to work for me, hmm? Watch Draewulf kill your friends? Kill your precious king?" Odion glances up. "Or maybe kill my brother?"

My eyes narrow. He laughs as if he knows his words hit home. I twist my wrist beneath him. Bend my fingers just enough to grab his hand. *If I can just . . .*

I let loose liquid fire straight into his veins.

He jerks back, eyes widening in shock, in horror, at the impossible realization that I can reach through his block and kill him. And he can't let go.

Abruptly, there's a blade in his other hand and he's bringing it toward my chest. But I can't release him and his body's too heavy to push away.

The knife hesitates.

His mouth falls open.

He utters a curse followed by a gurgle, then slumps on top of me, and the blade clatters to the ground.

Eogan's standing over us, sword in hand, stained with his own brother's blood.

He shoves Odion aside and pulls me up. I shriek as the pain in my leg rushes in and nearly cripples me. I limp forward, but Eogan's warm hands are sliding along my arms, my shoulders, my throat. My bruised face.

"I'm fine," I say, trembling more from his touch than my pain. I push his hands off. I don't want to feel him. I don't want to pretend he cares for anything more than winning this battle. "He's going to kill them," I say, swerving my attention back to Colin, Draewulf, and King Sedric.

They're still locked in a fight, and Rolf and the other knights are now working to hold off the Bron soldiers along with Princess Rasha, who's swinging a sword more skillfully than I've ever seen a woman do.

Eogan nods once, grimly. "I'll go around behind him. Distract him from the front?"

Oh, I'll do more than distract him.

With a hitch of my leg, I step forward, refusing to allow my gaze to fall on Odion because something tells me if I look I'll lose it, and then the backstabbing, the betrayals, Breck's death—they'll all become real. And right now, Colin and Faelen need me.

"Nym." Eogan's voice dips. "This isn't like the airships or the wolves. Draewulf . . . he's more dangerou—"

"I know," I say coldly and keep walking. *Let's just get this whole sick thing finished so I can go home. To wherever home is now.* I glance over and hurl an angry blast of ice at the Bron soldiers, half blinding them, before I focus my energy on Draewulf just as he backhands King Sedric into the turret wall.

Colin's creating fissure after fissure beneath the monster's feet at the same time he's yanking rocks from the cliff and throwing them at the beast's head. It's a wonder the whole fortress is not falling down under us.

I bend low and focus on releasing another flash of ice, this time along the ground to create a slick surface on Colin's already-uneven stones. It works, and Draewulf's claws clack and clatter on the frozen bricks. He scuttles forward, and I bring down a lightning bolt, which he dodges before shifting his enormous body to face me.

His eyes zero in on mine over his flat, disgusting, part-man, part-animal snout.

He growls.

With one bat of his hand, he's knocked Colin aside like a leaf and is crawling this way.

My stomach drops. *He's just been playing with them.*

It's me he wants.

Draewulf slips and claws his way toward me, with an expression wavering between hate and mockery, as I send ice picks, followed by lightning, followed by thick chunks of hail, followed by everything I think I am capable of.

It's as if he's a ghost walking—the way he avoids them, his movements so fluid. His glare never falters as he approaches with those thick lips and pointed teeth.

I swallow. Images of Breck fill my mind—what he did to her. What he'll do to the rest of us.

"The prized slave who just couldn't do what she was told," he snarls. "All you had to do was take down the fortress and you and Colin would've survived."

"While you hid like a pathetic weakling beneath the skin of a blind girl."

His eyes flash. "Why stoop to the dirty work of taking over two kingdoms when I can have slaves do it? And as far as the blind girl—what better way to know another's weaknesses than to serve right under her Elemental nose."

He erupts with a roar and springs for me.

I shove forth a wall of fire between us that I'm not sure is from the sky or my hand. He leaps through just as my knees are kicked out from behind. I drop and Adora's insane laugh fills my head along with the stench of Draewulf's smoldering flesh. I look up in time to see his claws coming down to rip my chest into a million colorful shreds.

I lash a hand out, except suddenly Colin is standing in front of me.

Abruptly. Horrifically.

He screams as the sharp nails pierce his flesh, carving through the muscle and bone before he falls.

I slash another lightning bolt at the beast, cracking it through his arm.

A howl erupts, and then Eogan is behind him and has landed his broadsword directly into Draewulf's back. The monster staggers and roars, rips the sword from his wound, then jumps and grips the side of the turret.

He scampers up it, leaving a bloody trail as he climbs to the parapet and disappears into black shadow.

And then I'm hovering over Colin. To shield. To help.

Except there's no amount of helping to fix the torn boy in front of me. I let loose a moan that becomes a yell so loud it shatters the sky, fracturing the clouds above into a hundred ignited thunder bellows.

Colin. The precious bald boy. My friend.

The life pulses out of him in red ribbons, and I'm pressing on his chest, covering the wounds with my hands, trying to stop the flow as the *thump thump thump* of his beautiful heart weakens and drains.

"What have you done?" I whimper to him, and I am both horrified and wrecked. My tears drip down to mix in his blood. "You should've let him take me. *Why didn't you let him take me?*"

Rain begins to fall. It patters his face with caresses and misty wishes I can hardly see because my tears are pouring so thick.

His hand slides over mine. "They need you."

"*I* need you. You and me—this was *ours* to do. Oh hulls— someone *do* something! Someone help him!"

"I never did this for Faelen, Nym," he gasps. His body shivers.

"*No no no no.* I can't lose you. You're my friend." My voice is crumbling into broken shudders, like the bones and skin from his chest now barely holding together as it heaves beneath my fingers. "We need you."

"For me it was never 'bout them," he whispers. "It was . . . for Breck. For givin' her a better life." He inhales and coughs. Quivers. "You an' her deserved to be free."

I'm crying harder now. "Don't talk. It's fine. You'll be fine. Just don't go. Don't leave."

His eyes are growing hazy. He's looking around as if trying to focus.

I move closer, and his gaze latches on mine. His breath is thinning.

My world is thinning.

"It was for you, Nym."

He's slipping. Becoming incoherent. "I couldn't let him take you." Another cough.

"Colin . . ."

"Don't let him take you, Nym. Don't let him take who you are. Make him . . ." His head jerks, his lips forming and reforming the words he's trying to get out. "Make him fear who you'll become."

I can't breathe. I don't know how to breathe, and I'm losing him, losing him—*oh please no*—I'm losing him.

His pupils widen and his brown eyes deepen, as rich as the Faelen earth, as his hand slips up to my heart. He presses in, and suddenly I swear I can feel my insides trembling as he's carving, creating one last fracture.

He's inscribing my soul with his beautiful name.

Then his hand slides from me.

His chest shudders beneath my fingers as the last breath leaves his body and drifts hot across my cheeks. A kiss of warmth as his last good-bye.

And I am left. Alone.

In the rain.

Covered in the bald boy's blood.

CHAPTER 35

COLIN'S EYES STARE UP AT THE STORM-cloaked sky.

Clashing swords. Bombing airships. King Sedric's voice. They emerge and fade with the wind, only to be replaced by the death cries of the soldiers also departing from this place. To join Colin and Breck and my parents.

Everyone dies.

Everyone is betrayed.

"Take me with you," I whisper to them, as a wisp of the black, demonic air slithers from where Draewulf was and tumbles around me like a thick strand of ink. It roils and stirs the rain, rustling over my skin, a thousand teeth from ghostly mouths, gnawing. As if the evil contained in it could feed off my living heart. Burning and boring into my flesh with the insinuation that there is nothing of worth left in this world.

I swipe it away and reach down to shut Colin's eyes.

Press a kiss to his rain-spattered brow.

You should have let him take me.

My shoulders begin to shudder. The evil mist presses harder.

This time I don't push it back as it comes scalding in to smother me in black folds, crowding over my eyes with a darkness that is full of plagues and loss and hopelessness.

The clouds won't stop pouring. My tears won't stop pouring. Even the rain on my lips tastes salty, as if the sky's given way to the sea, like in the minstrels' "The Monster and the Sea of Elisedd's Sadness" ballad. *"And the big sea, she roared and spit up her foam at the shape-shifter's trickery and our foolish king . . . Begging for blood that will set our children free."*

"Except there *is* no freedom, is there?" I scream at the sea. Because the innocence that exists in this world gets stolen by the same sickness that's claimed my parents, my Elemental race, my friends, and now . . .

Perhaps it will claim me too.

Because I don't want this anymore. *Redemption. Atonement. Empty hopes promised by a manipulative owner.*

I swallow.

A hand touches my shoulder, evoking a soothing that can only be Eogan's.

I jerk away.

I don't want his fake comfort. There *is* no comfort. "Leave me."

He hunches beside me, staring at Colin. Eogan wants me to get up. Wants me to fix this.

"Our world is unfixabl—" I start to tell him, but when I turn, his expression says he's all too aware of the depth of brokenness that exists. His hand is stained red with the blood of his brother.

His fingers go to the side of Colin's head. "You were a good man, mate." Then slowly they move to my chin to tip my face up.

Forcing my eyes to look in his. "He didn't do this so you could fix things, Nym." And for a second, I swear I see a teardrop mix with the rain flecks on his cheek.

Then another.

They drip off and land on my skin.

I glance away. "So says the man who's incapable of anything but using people."

But as soon as I say it, I know I'm wrong. Because suddenly it's not calmness flowing through his fingers but jagged emotions that are grieving and messy and completely his own. Telling me his heart is growing perfectly capable of becoming undone. I feel it the same way I can feel the rain and the rhythm of the war, and Draewulf roaring. And Adora laughing in lunacy from wherever she's hiding.

Eogan's voice is husky as he holds my face. "He gave his life to protect who you *are*. Not because of what you've done or might do."

Don't let him take who you are.

His words . . . they blend in with Colin's and settle like heat within me, soothing, scorching, touching my core. Wooing my battered heart with the truth of Colin's one simple offering that encompassed everything: Love. Freely given. For someone he believed could also be free.

Abruptly, the heat of that truth grows sharper, like static, forcing clarity through my veins, carrying with it an illumination of Colin's statement back at the meadow. That this tragic war that's been waged in and around each of us, this battle that's gone on in our souls—that's ravaged us and beaten us down and clawed away our humanity—has simply been evil trying to destroy who we are.

Because evil knows what we will become: Stronger. Wiser. Unstoppable.

Don't let him take who you are. Make him fear who you will become.

Somewhere beneath my skin, the melody from the Valley of Origin begins singing—louder, sweeter. Clearer. Until it's yelling. Then it's shouting its refrain to the siren in my bones to awaken the real me that is not a curse, but a true Elemental.

I look over at the bloodied wall by which Draewulf escaped. At Colin and the bodies around me. At the airships bombing the hulls out of Faelen. And I know exactly what this world is capable of.

But I also know what *I* am capable of.

I glance at Eogan.

What we *are capable of.*

I'm trembling when I touch his hand with my deformed one and, for a second, watch the rain spill off my pale fingers to his black ones in the same way forgiveness spills from my soul. He knows what it is to rise above evil perhaps more than any of us.

His breath clouds through the rain like a wild summer storm. I lean against him and inhale as my whole body shudders. Something's shattering and being set free. As if the melody thrashing about inside of me is breaking me apart in the process.

Eogan tries to steady me, but I shake my head and place my other hand on the ground. I close my eyes and let the ice creep out from my fingertips until, shoving it harder, I spread it onto every surface of stone and wall and brick and cold flesh. Immediately, I hear both the Faelen and Bron men begin slipping.

From somewhere, Adora utters an oath.

I open my eyes and swerve around to stare straight at her. She's crouched against the wall with that knife in her hand again.

I smile.

Her eyes widen.

Eogan already has his sword out, but it's the cold energy snaking from my shivering fingers that knocks her blade away. I whip the ice current farther as she launches herself at us, hissing obscenities—about my mother, about my status as a slave, a favor girl, a murderer—and wrap it around her like a thread.

She drops to the ground and bursts into hysterical laughter mixed with screams.

I wait for Eogan to bind her hands before I release her. Leaving her alive. Barely injured.

Cursing.

Let the Faelen people deal with her.

The rain is turning the slick ground into slush. King Sedric and his men, bruised and bloodied, are tramping through it, making their way toward us. One of the knights steps ahead to seize Adora from Eogan. "We're taking His Majesty and Princess Rasha. Rolf will stay be—"

His words are cut off by a loud whistle followed by another blazing detonation, this one closer. The whole fortress sways with the sensation that half the mountain is slipping away.

The group whips around.

"Nym!" the princess beckons urgently. "Come on!"

I look at Eogan and that perfect emerald gaze posing a silent question amid the growing vibrations and sounds of cracking rock.

My body's shaking too hard to answer him with anything more than a nod. *Let's finish this.*

I try to wave Rasha off. "We'll be right behind you," I yell above the noise.

She hesitates only a second, assessing me with those reddish irises as the rain pours off her brow. Then she tips her soaked head with a look of understanding and hurries after King Sedric and the few guards left, toward the back side of the Keep. To the cliff. While Rolf stays, sword in hand, to assist us.

I wait until they've disappeared, then, blinking back the ache of tears, I drag my leg across the courtyard, which is beginning to wobble as chunks from the mountain start falling.

I step up onto the low wall and into the water puddles.

And brace for the storm that is taking over from inside me.

CHAPTER 36

THE ENTIRE WORLD IS ON FIRE. THE CLOUDS, the night air, the raindrops that are
falling
falling
falling
in perfect little drips through jagged lightning streaks that are spreading, like yellow fingers, to tear open the sky overhead. Just like the jagged melody that is tearing up everything inside me.

I stand on the low wall overlooking the courtyard, unable to move or breathe as the entire Keep shakes from the corroding mountain and bombing ships.

"Nym." Eogan's voice has a funny edge to it.

"I don't think I can do this," I say, even as I force myself to turn to him.

His gaze is burning up the thin space between us. Alive.

Strained. His jaw tightens and I catch the flex of his shoulders stiffening.

What the—?

The avalanche. He's barely holding it back as his block expands. The fiery rocks and snow brought down by the bomb are hitting midair and collecting on the invisible barrier, dipping lower as if weighing it down. Weighing him down. "Well, clearly you're going to have to," he murmurs.

I stretch out my fingertips. They burn. I scream. *Hulls, what if I can't do this?*

But in one spasm, I've coiled the ocean's breath and yanked it through the pass. The air currents howl as I throw them against the boulders, whipping the rocks away from the fortress, the cliff, and the king's ascending group of ragged men until the ice and stones are gone and the mountain's no longer breaking.

And I'm shivering at the ease with which I did it.

Eogan's sigh is audible as his hand connects with the pulse in my wrist, but it's too late for soothing. Something's broken loose in me, and that song from the Valley of Origin is pushing up its magic-soaked atmosphere to burn through my lungs.

Here it comes . . .

I gasp. My flesh, my arms. *Blazing.* I begin clawing at them—at the Elemental energy lighting my skin up and leaving me alive and terrified because this power forcing out of me is bigger and more dangerous than who I am or anything I've known. As if the Hidden Lands' creator himself is singing the enchanted refrain inside me, and I am a conduit for his voice. A harmony to blend earth and sky and water.

And suddenly I have no idea how to control it.

"You can do this." Eogan's whisper is startlingly close, tangling in my hair. I wonder if he can see how badly I'm quivering—how the water's flying off me in sprays.

No, I try to tell him. *I can't.* But my words won't move. Because this song that's in my lungs and in my breath and forcing my mouth open is binding the elements to me. I can feel each raindrop, each thunder bellow beating in my veins as the melody abruptly escapes free as a bird.

Only to discover that the music has the power to destroy an entire kingdom with one wrong note.

Oh litches, what have I done?

The song flows from my mouth and enters my shaky hands. They spark.

I squeeze them into fists but more sparks leak out anyway. Like the airship bombs dropping around us—one, two, three, ten. The ships aren't just racing out to demolish Faelen. They're now taking out the pass as well.

Eogan points to the airship that caused the avalanche, and the twenty more behind it heading for us.

I shake my head. "Eogan, this thing in me. I won't be able to control it."

His voice is gentle—almost proud. "Just focus. You know how to do this."

"I think you mean 'Please don't kill us,'" I mutter. And hear his responding chuckle just before I release the clouds to roar and howl down toward us. At the last second, I propel them against the ballooned contraptions, pressing them backward, upward.

The airships bob and swirl through the rain, moving faster and farther, curling around each other before sailing out to land in the ocean where the Bron warboats are moving through the breach.

I exhale.

A gale picks up out at sea, and now I can feel its friction in my blood. My neck tingles, and the next moment the melody surrounding me is reaching for the cerulean water, pulling it up in thick waves until it's churning and coiling, creating miniature cyclones that lift higher and higher.

They pause.

I flick my wrist and twist, and the waters plunge. Giant waves roll up like the famed Elisedd dragons. Curling. Sending the Bron ships dancing back toward the open ocean, like paper boats in a puddle, with only two of them capsizing.

I send in another gust that spins and thrusts them even farther. Just like that.

I'm violently shuddering. And yet, somehow, even with the power coursing through me, erupting beyond me, I'm controlled.

Abruptly, Eogan's hand is on my neck, and I can feel the calm flow through him, just as I swear I can feel a sudden tension surge up from Faelen. Through her valleys and snow peaks. Through the fields and black earth. Through her people's blood and sweat and voices, as if carrying up on the wind.

"They're about to launch," Eogan says, and at first I'm confused until I realize he's not talking about the boats. He's eyeing the hundreds of airships that are now tiny specks hovering over Faelen. Some already creating explosions, while the rest are lining up, taking position.

"They're going to take it out all at once," he says quietly.

Suddenly his hand drops to my waist, holding me steady as

the courtyard rumbles with an ungodly growl from somewhere behind us. It's followed by a shout. Eogan's other hand reaches for his sword as we both spin around to discover Draewulf crouched fifteen yards away. His teeth are curled around Rolf's shoulder while black wisps zip and flit around the beast's feet.

He's watching me.

His eyes are saying he's returned to finish what we started.

The next instant, he flings the captain aside and is on all fours, foaming and snarling, then bolts in our direction.

The weather ripples, and immediately the rainbow mist from the valley slides along my skin, coalescing into place. The crystalline armor. It is diamond and light and a string of thread on a knife's edge as I stretch out my hand.

"Make him fear who you'll become."

I flex it and slam two ice picks through his arm.

Draewulf yelps but keeps coming until, at the last second, he veers off and launches sideways. For Eogan's throat.

Only to be met by Eogan's sword.

The wolf swipes at him with his huge foot while attacking with his teeth. Eogan ducks, flips around, and is shoved against the wall. He nearly goes over it except for my next ice pick ripping through the monster's shoulder. It throws him back.

Draewulf swerves his dust-gray eyes at me and snarls.

The lightning ripples. Sharpens.

I don't even blink before igniting the ground beneath him in flames.

He lurches aside and shoves a black haze writhing through the air at me.

It fogs my vision as it presses in, choking, blinding me. My hand goes up with a lick of fire to dissolve it.

When it clears, fifty more wisps like it are surrounding Draewulf. Who is leaning over Eogan.

A crack of thunder brings hot liquid fire down on the monster's back, forcing him backward even as the dark wisps protect him and absorb it.

I hear a moan and my gaze darts to Eogan. His face winces.

"Eogan!" I've crossed the distance between us in three steps as his shoulders slump, tremble, then straighten to reveal three claw marks that have torn across the front of his chest. Not fatal, but enough to stun, as the sick realization dawns: Eogan's block doesn't fully work against Draewulf.

"The airships," he murmurs. "Nym, you have to take them *now* or there'll be nothing left."

I nod, but before I can do anything, Draewulf lunges.

I reach out and touch Eogan, pushing my shield to slide over his skin just as the monster's claws come down on him.

They slip off and then grab for me, but the liquid armor stays in place over both of us.

The beast doesn't move away. He stands inches from my face and narrows his gray eyes at me. He twitches his finger, drawing up more threads of black around him. Around us. Until they're nearly covering the atmosphere overhead.

He bends forward and opens his mouth in a hideous, toothy grin.

And waits.

Suddenly, the rain ceases and the sky falls dim.

The winds stop. The lightning stops.

The world goes silent.

Except for that blasted droning and sickening explosions from the airships.

I look at Eogan in horror. My ability—I feel it withdrawing from the elements to protect him. As if unable to fuel two things at once.

Whatever dark magic Draewulf has, it's powerful enough to interfere with the Elemental energy.

I can't use it for Faelen while it's touching Eogan.

Eogan's fingers slip over my arm just as the beast's lips snarl up into a smile. "You can't save them both, girl. It's Faelen or your trainer. Your choice."

I swear I can feel the airships picking up speed without wind to block them.

The blackness grows thicker.

My shield wavers.

"Nym."

I'm just calculating how to release it fast enough to follow with a strike at Draewulf when I catch Eogan's movement. He's slipping a blade from his boot.

I look at him. At his brilliant eyes. At the last of the raindrops shimmering off his skin. His breath slides out and mixes with mine as he tips his head toward the ships, then drops his gaze to my lips.

Abruptly his mouth is against them, pressing in, soft and insistent—as if he can draw out every bit of broken in me and repair the pieces with his own calm, his own heart that is beating and blurting out a confession:

That I am his weakness.

I have always been his weakness.

An image flashes of my five-year-old self being dragged through the snow from my burning home. My screams muffled

322

by his unfeeling boy-size hands so his father wouldn't hear. Those same hands that had minutes before set fire to my house.

Oh hulls. I stare up at him. *I have always been his weakness.*

He leans back and brushes a hand down my neck and my shoulder. I swallow a sob. I don't want to be his weakness, I almost tell him. I want to be his strength. But he traces a quick finger over my jaw and raises his eyes to mine. "I think this is the part where you let go, Nym."

Then he steps away. And before I know it, he's pulled back from my touch.

The shield releases just as he slashes the knife through the monster's gut.

Draewulf falls two paces backward. Swipes at the air, at Eogan, at the empty space behind him, but even the ghostly fog drifts aren't able to hold him as he stumbles toward the cliff's edge.

I turn and hurl the rainbow-mist shield toward the sky.

Crack! The sound is ear shattering as the atmosphere fractures like broken glass and explodes into a thousand pieces of night. Dissolving the inky wisps in a cyclone of air that rushes over Faelen. Pushing the airships back, shoving, throwing, heaving them past the borders of our island and over the Sea of Elisedd in one enormous wave.

The entire fortress rocks from it.

Just like the others, the airships dip and bob, looking like a horde of fireflies as they disappear into the night. Along with the remnants of Draewulf's black haze that fades, as do all traces of the storm.

I glance around for Eogan, but I don't see him.

I'm just about to call for him when the next moment I'm

scared the stars are falling off their fiery hinges, knowing it was me who broke them.

But it's not the stars. It's just a few of the broken airships here in the pass, burning up before hitting the ground. And when they clear, I'm certain someone's taking a paintbrush to the world's ceiling, swathing it in pure beauty before splattering it with tiny golden dots. They've even strung up the giant silver moon low enough to touch.

I reach out and imagine touching it just as my name is spoken. It's followed by shouts and tumbling bodies coming from the direction of the crumbled fortress gate. Some of Bron's men have found their way through.

I hear Eogan's voice demanding to speak with their generals in a tone that reminds me these are *his* people. His army that he used to command. And I'm simultaneously sighing with relief he's all right and swerving round to see him standing on the wall, being approached by official-looking men whose clothes are a tad too clean to have done any fighting themselves. Especially next to Eogan, who looks like he's been in a bloodbath.

My stomach cringes at the amount of bruising and gashes he has on his arms and face and back. He looks exhausted, sallow.

I step toward him.

My name is called again.

I shake my head at whoever it is, only to jerk forward and stagger, and abruptly my teeth are chattering and every one of my own cuts and scratches feels too warm, and my leg wound is scalding as if I'm going into shock.

I reach out and grab the wall. Then the courtyard is spinning, and suddenly there's a pair of hands on my arms pulling at me. I think they want me to come with them.

"I need to talk to Eogan. I need to see him."

But they don't understand. The hands just move to my waist and start to lift me.

I bat them away. "Draewulf . . ."

"Went over the cliff," the voice attached to the hands assures me, and then he's hoisting me over a shoulder covered in blood and Faelen colors. Rolf's face comes into focus for a second. "It's all right. Eogan asked me to look after you."

"I don't want to go." I want to see Eogan. "Put me down." But Rolf must not be hearing right because no matter how loud I yell, he just keeps telling me it'll be all right and complimenting me that I have done my job well.

That I have saved Faelen.

CHAPTER 37

We are flying. Skimming somewhere between sea and sky. I hold out my hand and watch the buttery sunlight trickle through my fingers with the wind. Warming my skin as it spills across my arms and face through the airship window. Like the foamy ocean spray wafting from below.

The ship rises and dips on the air currents just as Eogan steps in front of me, blocking my view of the distant coastline as he runs a hand through his hair.

"What do you think?"

"Of?"

"Of you becoming a delegate and moving here to Bron's court." That self-assured look in his eye glints his amusement even as I swear his tone sounds nervous.

"Is that where we are?" I ask, craning to see past him to row upon row of shimmery buildings on the horizon.

"Not yet. That's Bron's outer coast on the left. And that over there"—he points to our right—"is the famous fault line."

"Separating your people from Drust and Draewulf."

"Silly Storm Girl. Draewulf's gone." And before I can argue he leans in close, flashing me that unfair smile. To which I chuckle and present him with a kiss.

He raises a suggestive brow, causing me to laugh, and in that laugh, to inhale a world of beauty. Every smile, every friendship, every bit of goodness I've seen. Every bit of goodness I've hoped existed within me. And just like the ship I am fluttering, dipping, soaring . . .

"Nym?"

I jolt awake. Rub my eyelids. And open them to find myself in the window seat of my newly designated bedroom up at the Castle, which doesn't look that different from my room at Adora's. Except for the fact that Princess Rasha is staring up at me from her stomach on my room floor, in what has, apparently, become her preferred spot in the Castle these past few days.

"I think they're starting." She kicks her legs up behind her and toys with a set of throwing knives.

I smile my thanks and scoot my leg over. "Do you want to watch?"

King Sedric strides out onto his white stone balcony in direct line of sight. The crowd's roar surges through the enormous Castle courtyard—a thousand voices of energy, lifting on the late-evening breeze, in rowdy waves of emotion.

Joy. Pride.

Relief.

Mixed with a few hints of bitter anger at what Bron has done and distrust over what a truce could still bring.

Princess Rasha shakes her dark head. "I often prefer to listen rather than see. Otherwise I sense too much and my head gets full." She shifts the knives in front of her in order from smallest to biggest. "You were dreaming the future again, you know," she adds in her airy, matter-of-fact way that is, in fact, confusing.

I freeze. Swallow. I want to ask what she knows of the future, just like I've wondered how she knew I needed a friend. But any reply I have stalls when King Sedric is joined by a familiar face that sends my insides blushing before searching for composure beneath my gaudy, pearl-white dress. Neither Rasha nor I have seen him since the Keep because, according to the knights and maids-in-waiting, "He's been busy."

Her girlish laugh is as oddly comforting as she is. "You should've just seen your eyes light up. Guess I'll take that to mean Eogan appeared." She pushes herself up and plants a quick pat on my hand. "While you enjoy that—alas, I have to trot off to get ready. See you at the banquet."

I nod and, with the door closing behind her, turn back to the court. The evening wind is rustling Eogan's sharp hair. He's finished bowing to our king and has turned to the Faelen people, soliciting another cheer as his eyes scan the assembly.

King Ezeoha.

The lost prince back from the dead.

The brave prince who shunned his own family rather than take Bron to war against Faelen.

The prince who is now king of Bron.

In less than a week's time, the minstrels have written fifty different songs extolling his noble virtues.

I smirk as Faelen's citizens tip their ridiculous puffed hats to both men. They explode in more applause when, together, the kings hold up the newly signed peace treaty that swears an end to the hundred-year war and ushers in an era of peace and rebuilding for all people of all nations and all abilities. Even Elementals. Breaking the old agreement signed with Draewulf.

Draewulf.

Five, ten, fifteen times I've mentioned his name since the fight at the fortress. But "Draewulf is gone," the knights keep telling me. As is his daughter, Isobel, with her betrayal and rumored Dark Army.

Then why, when you say it, does something whisper back that you're wrong? I want to ask them.

I haven't even brought up Lord Myles. *Did he survive the bolcranes? Do they know of his treachery?* They're all too busy questioning Adora in her prison cell and making good with Bron to ask.

I shift in my seat as the crowd quiets and King Sedric's voice rings out over the open court. "We are so thankful for this day. A day we've long sought and prayed for, a day we've fought hard for. A day of peace. Of new allies and united kingdoms, of conquered fears and forgotten wrongs. Of freeing all Uathúils. A day marking a turn in Faelen and Bron history, where we no longer see each other as enemies, but step into the future together as friends."

The erupting cheer shakes the jar of mugplant on the floor beside me. I reach out to steady it. *The future together as friends.*

I stare at one of the knives lined up, waiting to be used for new memorials. My skin itches for it. One for Colin. One for Breck.

When the people settle down, the speaking resumes. But this time it's Eogan.

"My friends, believe me when I assure you what an honor this day is, both for me and my people. For too long, our kingdoms have been on opposite sides of peace. Under my grandfather's, father's, and brother's dictatorships . . ." His voice lilts, and in it, I hear a hesitation, as if he is checking his notes. "Bron was forced to act as your enemy, when in all truth, the Bron people have longed for your camaraderie."

He steps back and the crowd erupts. Hollering. Whistling. Straining to make their agreement heard.

They're hungry for what Sedric and Eogan are offering.

I pick up one of the knives and balance its weight between my gimpy fingers. Unlike the rest of them, I don't know if I'm ready to move into the future just yet.

I nudge the window shut and glare at the blade, waiting for the grief that, without fail, has come every evening since the Keep. Emerging in that hollowed-out place that hides behind the right words and the dresses and the right answers to all the High Court questions about how, in fact, a female Elemental can exist.

This time when the grief comes, it's soft. Slow. Its salty, jeweled teardrops trickle down to fill my cupped fingers like tide pools, as my hurting heart swells and floods the room.

It lasts for too long, and yet not long enough.

Until, eventually, a shimmering glow extending out across my floor catches my blurred attention. As do the sounds of celebration replacing the kings' speeches—signaling that it's only a matter of time before I'm summoned to sit in the king's banquet hall.

I wipe my face with the clean memorial cloth and turn back to the window, only to lose my breath at the hundreds of globe lanterns filling the courtyard. They're ballooning up on the breeze to drift and dip as they make their escape into the sky.

Freedom.

He gave his life so that you could be free.

I grip the blade handle as a ripple runs down my spine. I stare at my memorial arm and imagine Colin's name carved in it. Then stall—noticing for the first time how much the markings there look like those on my owner-circle arm. Swirls. Coils.

I did it for you an' Breck, Nym. You deserved to be free . . .

I wipe my tears as slowly his words, his gift, settle over me. Reach into me where my soul still feels the etchings of his life. A life of worth, given for those he deemed worthy. Given free of guilt.

And for the first time I can ever recall, that twisted itching in my skin, in my chest, subsides on its own. My hands calm. My heart calms. I set the cloth down. A shamed memorial suddenly offensive. Degrading.

Unneeded.

I pick up the knife and slip it into my boot before placing a lid on the mugplant jar.

I straighten the wrinkles from my overly fancy, waste-of-a-good-fortune dress and walk over to the mirror. *Besides, there's a better way to honor him . . .*

With a few tugs at the clips, my Elemental hair slips from its bun to fall in long snow flurries down my back and around my bare arms. My eyes harden with the unease in the pit of my stomach. I shake the siren awake and the cold from my bones just as a soft knock hits my door.

He doesn't even wait for my "Enter." Just opens the door, steps in, and pushes it shut behind him with his foot. In one, two, three strides Eogan's in front of me exactly as I've been waiting for. As I've counted down the minutes for. A moment alone with *him*.

In one more stride he's got my chin in his rough hand while slipping his other around my arm. That unruly lock of black hair all but conceals the intensity in his emerald eyes as they search mine. Weary. Concerned.

"Are you all right?" His voice is ragged.

I nod. My heart dithers and thuds. Echoing with questions and uncertainty. About him. His future. About us.

I rest my hand on his chest, and then my head.

And for a moment, this is where I belong. None of the rest matters because my soul is at peace within me. My soul is at home.

It's been five weeks since Adora purchased me from Brea. Five weeks and fuller than any lifetime because I've spent them with him. I inhale his scent—which is no longer honey and pine but somehow musky—before lifting my head and sweeping my gaze over his neck, his face, searching out the healing bruises, the scratches and cuts I can see, and the internal ones I can't because they're hidden behind that annoyingly unfair tweak of a smile.

Until it ripples and widens. And suddenly his whole body is rippling beneath my fingers.

I step back. *What in hulls?*

He stretches his neck as if adjusting his shoulders, his back, then his grin broadens into a toothy smile, and he straightens to stare down at me. The firelight bounces off those teeth for a second. As if he is still Eogan. And yet he's not.

He touches my cheek and utters a soft growl.

I swallow.

No.

Very carefully, very purposefully, he sweeps his beautiful black bangs from his face and tucks them behind his ear in a characteristic trait that makes the storm in my veins stand still. He tips his head and the light glints off a long gash running down the back of his neck.

It can't be.

Suddenly my breath is reeling and my heart is choking out of my chest and my mind is screaming *no no no no no—this can't be.*

He leans in and tucks a swag of *my* hair behind my ear. And whispers, "I told you that you couldn't save them both."

NYM HAS SAVED FAELEN ONLY TO DISCOVER
THAT DRAEWULF STOLE EVERYTHING SHE
VALUED. NOW HE'S DESTROYED HER ELEMENTAL
STORM-SUMMONING ABILITY AS WELL.

To get the latest details as they release, visit
www.mchristineweber.com

THOMAS NELSON
Since 1798

9781401690342-A

MY POCKETFUL OF
THANK-YOUS

IN SOME WAYS I FEEL I'VE BEEN WRITING THIS PAGE my whole life. Gathering up my thank-yous like a pocketful of flower petals, reflecting on the journey and the generosity of those who've traveled with me. Who've allowed me to travel with them. Yet, when I actually sit down to type these letters, these names—to lay my thank-yous out in a daisy-chain mosaic so you'll each understand exactly what you mean to me—drat it all if the words don't fail, and instead tears fall. Thus this page comes stained with tear drips and blood spatters, markers showing just how deeply you've engraved your name on my world. *Thank you*, my fellowship of friends:

Allen Arnold, shepherd, big brother, tallest dwarf dude I know—for stepping into my Story and changing it forever. And for continuing to mentor me by living a Story of heart.

Amanda Bostic, treasured kindred spirit and Thomas Nelson editor, for inviting me to tea and then offering an adventure from which I'll never recover. And sweet Becky Monds, Thomas Nelson editor and friend, for bringing your literary magic and laughter to the journey.

My dear agent, Lee Hough, for quieting the room long enough to listen to the roar of this scared girl's heart. And then standing to roar with her. We did it. And to my agent, Andrea Heinecke, for picking up the mantle and adding your brilliance. And for being my friend.

Daisy Hutton, Laura Dickerson, Jodi Hughes, Ansley Boatman, Katie Bond, and my entire Thomas Nelson family, thank you for taking a chance and helping me fly. There aren't enough gratitude cupcakes in the world. Kristen Vasgaard, for creating a cover that made me cry. Julee Schwarzburg, editing genius—for making me laugh and my words make sense.

Jeanette Morris, cherished mentor, editor, precious friend. For always helping me find my voice—in my writing and, even more so, in my soul. And dear Nancy Rue—my Obi Wan, for holding my hand every time it shook and my heart when I cried. This book has your ladies' fingerprints all over it, as do my wings.

Word Divas, for the word shaping and courage. Sarah Kathleen, for capturing soul with your beautiful spirit and photo lens. Garth Jantzen, website genius, for believing in me from the first. Several Guys, for the video that rocked my world. SLO Nightwriters. Diane Ramirez. And my blogger friends who've laughed with me through the years—Danielle, Juju, Jade, Anne, Tania, Rob, Sara, Kristen, Brittney, Steph, Becca.

Jay and JM Asher, Lori and Will, Dani, the Morrells, and to

every one of my friends for making a place for me at your friendship table and sharing your strength and food and laughter.

My Father's House family and the RISE. You have my heart. You are my home.

Dad and Mom, for addicting me to books and adventure. You are the biggest heroes in my world. Mom, thank you for teaching me to write and dream. Dad, for believing in my dreams and for bringing *Storm Siren* to life through your beautiful maps and airship art. Also, my siblings David, Jon, James, Daniel, and your families, and to the entire Weber clan. I adore you.

My sister, Katherine Ayers, without whom this story (and my sanity) would not exist. Here's to you, dear Ariel-singing girl.

My three precious muses, Rilian, Avalon, and Korbin—the moments written in these pages are yours. Made up of your beauty and bravery. They are your "over the rainbow" songs.

Peter, my love, you truly have bewitched me body and soul, and anchored me in the storms. Thank you for risking the world with me and blazing a path to the moon. *I love you.*

Jesus. Because you are all this heart exists for.

READING GROUP GUIDE

1. Nym has a genuine desire to help others, especially the mistreated. However, fear that she will do more harm than good often holds her back. Can you relate to this dilemma? Do you ever duck away from helping others because you feel unqualified or worry that you won't be able to do it "perfectly"?

2. Both Nym and Breck have physical disabilities, but Nym doesn't view them as deficiencies like she does the Uathúil powers. In fact, when Nym finds out Breck and Colin are twins—supposedly "one gifted, one cursed"—she responds by asking which is cursed and which is gifted. What do you think about her question? What types of abilities does society often deem "gifted"? Cursed? What unique qualities did Breck's blindness and Colin's powers add to their world?

3. In Eogan's experience with training warriors, he discovered that focusing on the physical while neglecting the ethical

(what's right or wrong) resulted in an "end justifies the means" approach for many of the Uathúils. What do you think about that concept in relation to war and to our world today? Are there ever situations where not having a conscience seems necessary?

4. Nym sees her Elemental ability as a curse rather than a unique gift. What aspects of yourself or your environment do you view as "cursed" or negative? How might those aspects actually become a benefit or gift?

5. In the Valley of Origin, Eogan challenges Nym, suggesting that her inability to embrace the potential of her power is because she's afraid to accept and believe better of herself. How about you? What things could you overcome or accomplish if you believed more in yourself?

6. Just before they reach the Keep, Nym asks Colin, "What makes a person evil? If you believe a person was born to bring help, then were others born to bring destruction?" What are your thoughts on this? Are people born evil? Are they born good? Do you agree or disagree with Colin's response? Why?

7. Nym was torn between wanting to use her abilities to protect her people and knowing that in doing so she would harm the men in Bron's army. King Sedric encountered a similar dilemma when faced with Odion's treaty—signing it would protect some while requiring the sacrifice of others. How did the ultimate results of Sedric and Nym's choices affect Faelen and Bron? Were they right in their decisions?

8. Nym has a tough attitude toward the world but privately struggles with self-loathing, fear, and self-harm. Have you, or a friend, ever struggled with any of these feelings or behaviors? If so, have you talked to a safe person about it? Support and resources are available to you, including To Write Love on Her Arms (http://www.TWLOHA. com). Please reach out. I promise you are not alone.

SNAPSHOTS FROM *STORM SIREN*

QUESTION: Where did you get your idea for the world in *Storm Siren*?

MW: The world was definitely inspired by my love of history (I ADORE the Middle Ages) and a total obsession with all things steampunk and *Last Airbender*. Not to mention an old poem titled "Saint Patrick's Breastplate" in which St. Patrick is calling out to the elements to defend him (seriously, how awesome was HE?!).

Secrets of Storm Siren 1

QUESTION: If you could have dinner with any character in *Storm Siren*, who would it be?

MW: Ooh, can I have two? Because most definitely Eogan and Lord Myles. I would annoy the heck out of them. And then evil laugh.

Secrets of Storm Siren 2

QUESTION: Okay, can we talk about the meat-eating horses?

MW: *laughs* Aww, I love Haven & the others!! And who didn't want a meat-eating pony as a child?! (Or is that just my twisted brain?? Ahem.) It's also a bit of a rabid fan girl nod to Maggie Stiefvater & *The Scorpio Races*—which is one of the most perfect, atmospheric beauties I've ever read. (Seriously, if you haven't read it, go BUY IT, kiss it, then tweet at her about how brilliant she is. ;))

Secrets of Storm Siren 3

QUESTION: Why does Nym always refer to Colin as "the bald boy"?

MW: Prepare for me to cry. Halfway through writing *Storm Siren*, my agent, who was one of the kindest, most honorable individuals I've ever known (and a father figure to me in the publishing world) was given two months to live. I didn't write for two weeks—I just cried. On the third week I sat down and wrote chapters 34–35 (and wept the whole way through). To this day it is the only section that didn't really need an edit. Colin is "the bald boy" because my agent, Lee Hough, was bald. And Colin's goodness is my ode to him.

QUESTION: In the book, you address some tough subjects through Nym like insecurity and self-harm. What inspired you to add those struggles?

MW: I tend to refrain from purposefully putting "messages" in my writing unless they're authentic to the story (and even then I usually just trust they'll flow out if they're supposed to be there). However, I broke that rule with the issue of self-harm because it's one that's very important to me. I work a part-time job with teens, and self-harm is something that is so very real and tragic. Through Nym, I wanted to broach the struggle, but also show the power that true friendship, support, and embracing one's own internal strength can have to overcome it. I tried to do so in the most honest and caring way I could but also the most real. In the back of the book is a list of reader questions and the last one has to do with self-harm as well as offering a resource which those who are struggling can reach out to. I truly hope they do.

Secrets of Storm Siren 5

QUESTION: Did you listen to music while writing *Storm Siren*?

MW: Okay, I have to brag on my husband right here. He's kind of the best person ever!! He makes me these playlists for when I'm driving in the car (which is usually where I'm working out a scene or plot point), and they are FULL of music amazingness. For *Storm Siren* I had everything from Evanescence to Imagine Dragons to Weezer to my main girl, Taylor Swift.

Secrets of Storm Siren 6

QUESTION: Who do you picture Eogan as?!

MW: Oh, I love this question! Okay, imagine Idris Elba & Yuya Matsushita combined in a clone. You're welcome.

Secrets of Storm Siren 7

QUESTION: That last page . . . did Eogan really . . . Is he actually, you know . . . ?

MW: *hands you tissue and looks away* *sips coffee*

Secrets of Storm Siren 8

ABOUT THE AUTHOR

MARY WEBER IS A RIDICULOUSLY uncoordinated girl plotting to take over make-believe worlds through books, handstands, and imaginary throwing knives. In her spare time, she feeds unicorns, sings '80s hairband songs to her three muggle children, and ogles her husband who looks strikingly like Wolverine. They live in California, which is perfect for stalking LA bands, Joss Whedon, and the ocean.

Visit her website at mchristineweber.com
Facebook: marychristineweber
Twitter: @mchristineweber